NUDE WALKER

NUDE WALKER

BATHSHEBA MONK

SARAH CRICHTON BOOKS   FARRAR, STRAUS AND GIROUX NEW YORK

SARAH CRICHTON BOOKS
Farrar, Straus and Giroux
18 West 18th Street, New York 10011

Distributed in Canada by D&M Publishers, Inc.
Printed in the United States of America
First edition, 2011

Library of Congress Cataloging-in-Publication Data
Monk, Bathsheba.
    Nude walker : a novel / Bathsheba Monk. — 1st ed.
      p.   cm.
    ISBN 978-0-374-22344-1 (alk. paper)
    1. City and town life—Pennsylvania—Fiction.   2. Middle class
families—Pennsylvania—Fiction.   3. Immigrant families—Pennsylvania—
Fiction.   4. United States—National Guard—Fiction.   5. Arab Americans—
Fiction.   6. Interethnic dating—Fiction.   7. Culture conflict—Fiction.
8. Conflict of generations—Fiction.   9. Love stories.   I. Title.

PS3613.O529N83 2011
813'.6—dc22

                                                      2010033121

Designed by Abby Kagan

www.fsgbooks.com

10   9   8   7   6   5   4   3   2   1

TO PAUL

Sine qua non

PART ONE

ONE **KAT WARREN-BINEKI**

When I recall Afghanistan, I think of gray spiky plants with long taproots sinking into sand, shrouds of women kicking up dust as they move down the road, and skies the brittle blue of a prolonged drought. Arid. Ashy. Barren. So the sudden large cool drops made me laugh aloud as we trudged across the tarmac to board the C-128 at Bagram on the first leg of our trip home. I lifted my face to the sky to enjoy this farewell rain, which was like a kiss that would awaken the sleeping desert life.

"Bineki, did you lose this?"

I turned around. Max Asad, our unit translator, dangled a blue stone tied to a strip of black leather on the end of his index finger. "It was on the ground."

I was so startled to see him that I grabbed the amulet, but it slipped out of my hands and I bent to pick it up again. "Thanks. It keeps coming off." I fumbled as I tried to knot it around my neck.

"Here, let me." He took the two pieces of leather and tied them together, his hands brushing my neck and cheek, pulling out strands of hair that got caught in the knot. "Your hair is like silk, Bineki. It keeps getting caught."

I held my breath while he fussed over me, then I shoved the stray long hairs back into their knot under my cap. "Thanks. Again."

I hadn't noticed Max get in the queue and his unexpected appearance unnerved me. Actually, I hadn't seen him in almost a year: he'd been hijacked by the Special Ops almost as soon as we landed. After one month in Kandahar, he'd moved out of the tent he shared with my boyfriend, Duck Wolinsky, and into the Ops' barbed-wire enclave on the far end of the airfield so he could be ready to move out with them before dawn. The Ops paid native translators very well, but there was always the possibility that the enemy was paying *more*, so they wanted someone they could trust: that is, an American. Like all the best perks in Afghanistan, Max was theirs.

He turned me around and wiped some rain from my cheek with his thumb. "It's sweet, the rain."

"Yes. Sweet."

"Where did you find it?" he asked, touching the stone.

I clasped my hand around the lapis lazuli. It seemed hot. "It was a present. A friend found it outside the wire."

Duck had given me the stone, an intensely blue piece of lapis lazuli that he had found when he was repairing a satellite dish a couple of miles outside of Kandahar. The tie came undone easily and I'd lost it several times. Somehow, someone always managed to find it and return it to me, and it was starting to feel like a portent demanding my attention.

"You should be careful with stones. You never know what information they pick up."

"You think stones hear things?"

"Why are you surprised? We can't know everything. What I can't understand, I respect at least."

"I thought we invaded to get rid of superstition and give them good old American common sense. Et cetera." I was trying to make him laugh, but he was so damned serious. The only other time I had spoken to Max was a year ago, almost to the day, when the 501st was having a send-off party for itself. I had cracked a joke while we were sipping orange soda out of plastic cups, and neither he nor his father had laughed. I remember his dismissive look, because I wanted him to like me.

"Is that what you think? That Americans have no superstitions?" Max shook his head.

Everything he said was so unlike what other men said. I wanted him to explain what he meant by "It's sweet, the rain"; what he meant when he said stones picked up information; why he never seemed to laugh. I didn't understand him, and I wanted to. He wandered back to his place in line before I could answer.

After a year in Kandahar, I couldn't say I understood the East, either. Women weren't allowed off base without an armed male escort. So how could I claim to understand anything of a culture I never saw, a culture that measures time in generations and worth by the *size* of those generations, a culture whose people seem to grow out of the barren mountains, to float above the turbulence created by their many invaders—Alexander the Great, the British, the Soviets, and now *us*—waiting for an auspicious moment to touch down? Like everything in Afghanistan, my presence was just one more thing that would vanish in the desert, covered over with sand. Everything was ephemeral. Buildings were tents, laws were oral, and even the usual fortifications of civilization—

walls—were illusions swept away in the wind of the next sand-storm.

I didn't understand the East but I loved it, probably for that very reason. It was just out of my reach, and things you can't own, that keep surprising you with their *unknowableness*, if that's even a word, are a thousand times more exciting than things that jump in your lap.

The rain trickling down my face, the first we had the entire year we were in Afghanistan, was exciting because it was a surprise. But really, the weather was always a surprise at Bagram. The Taliban had destroyed the sophisticated weather-tracking equipment the Soviets had abandoned, claiming that only God could predict the weather, and now the base was dependent on decades-old weather balloons that the Czechs and the Canadians sent up and that Taliban raiding parties routinely shot down. The Afghanis trusted God to know the future, but their fortunes hadn't changed since Alexander, so even I could predict what tomorrow would bring to the average Afghani. Today would bring a rain of bullets and the death of a close friend who didn't agree with the politics of whoever was pumping the ammo. Tomorrow the Allies would rain herbicide on his poppy crop, saying it was immoral to grow a drug that the entire world wanted—a *lot*. Everything rained on Afghanistan, except the one thing they would have welcomed: water.

My unit, the 501st, was a supply and legal assistance company, consisting of supply personnel like me and lawyers who were helping the Afghanis write a constitution. Their highest authority was Muhammad, may he be blessed, as they say, and ours was the Constitution, may *it* be blessed too—why not? Right from the beginning, an idiot could see *that* wouldn't go anywhere. While our JAG officers were busy explaining to the Afghanis the importance of due process with its uncertain outcomes, their mullahs were yelling "Off with her head!" It was like watching two plays performed simultaneously on the same stage, critics wildly applauding, mistaking activity for progress, mistaking chaos for a script. It would have been funny if it weren't so screwed up.

As our queue moved slowly across the tarmac to board the plane, a muezzin's call to prayer echoed off the hills; then suddenly the sky got inky black and the gentle rain became a downpour and drowned out all other sounds. The muezzin's call had been part of the sound track for my year in Kandahar, along with the wailings of strange animals at night, exploding mortar shells, and the yelling that goes on in the military because everyone tries to be heard over the din of heavy machinery or is deaf from ordnance exploding near their heads. Sounds that you are forced to hear are *noise*. It wasn't until that ride home that the noise stopped and the music began.

The loudest noise of all, an insistent downbeat, had been the badgering of my tentmate, Jenna Magee, who never wavered in her mission to bag my soul for Jesus. I'm an atheist—probably more like an agnostic, because who knows? Like, Afghanistan shocked the hell out of me: that a place actually *exists* where a person couldn't even have a drink of water without carrying it on their head for a mile, and then the chances are pretty good that some jerk is going to shoot a hole in their bucket before they get home. I like the idea that there might be a spiritual heaven and hell, and it's fun to speculate on which laws are the *right* rules of the road, so to speak. But Jenna's brand of religion was as unambiguous as a car alarm at three in the morning. If she was right, then my indecision was wrong, and if I was wrong the consequence for me was hell—Jenna's syllogism of salvation. The *threat* of hell was weirdly exciting, I have to admit, and when she would talk about

Jesus taking over my life I'd answer, "Sounds good to me, *great* actually," and she even had me down on my knees in the sand one evening when I was feeling—and had the bad judgment to share with her—that life could seem kind of random.

"Doesn't it seem random to you sometimes, Jenna?" I asked her one night when I was particularly chatty from spiked Gatorade at a comrade's birthday party. "Why do we have all this stuff and the Afghanis keep getting their stuff taken away?"

"They haven't accepted Jesus into their lives," Jenna had said triumphantly. "They're like zombies, wandering aimlessly. They're dead. *You're* dead. If you ask Jesus into your life, He will take over *everything*. Explain *everything*. Nothing is left to chance. He has a plan for you. You'll see!"

Her passion ignited mine and I said, "Great, let's do it." We knelt in our tent. I was thinking it would be fabulous to have a get-out-of-hell card, although it did occur to me in the throes of my would-be salvation: What happens after this? You just go around the game board collecting points and demerits until you die?

Jenna grabbed my hand and closed her eyes. "Lord Jesus, Kat Warren-Bineki *knows* she's a sinner. She *knows* You died a *bloody and horrible* death to pay for her sins and she accepts Your *bloody and horrible* death on the cross as payment in full for her many sins. Kat Warren-Bineki knows that good works mean nothing to You, Lord, only belief. Right now, Lord, I ask You to save Kat Warren-Bineki and forgive her her many *many* sins and fill her heart with peace. Thank You, Lord, for saving Kat Warren-Bineki and help her live her life in a way that pleases You. In Jesus' name. Amen."

I was stunned that she lumped me in with all the other sinners, not mentioning my good qualities. Considering my lukewarm introduction to Jesus, as if I were just one of the hoi polloi, I wasn't surprised when, after two minutes of squeezing my eyes and waiting for the cosmic boink, nothing happened. "It didn't take," I said. "Jesus did *not* enter the building. Anyway, all that blood-and-gore stuff is disgusting."

"That's how you know it's real," she said. "No blood, no glory. You must have felt *something*. How can you *not* have felt something?" She demanded a redo, which I declined. By then I was feeling like I was on a blind date where I liked the guy more than he liked me.

"Besides," I said, "how can Jesus help me? He couldn't even help himself. His own father made him do that stuff. How creepy is that?" Although, if you look through the annals of parent-child relationships, what God asked Jesus to do is *typical*, really.

Jenna had a trove of pamphlets that supported her beliefs, and she flipped through them until she located the one that addressed my particular unbelief, thrusting it at me.

"You're missing the entire point. Yes, His Father asked Him to do it, but Jesus *wanted* to die for you. If you don't believe that He wanted to die for you," Jenna said, all snitty, "you're going to burn forever in hell. You have to believe the story of Jesus dying for you or you're *screwed*. Your life has no meaning. It's just random bullshit."

I was jealous of their passion—Jenna's and Jesus'—but I was delighted that after the 501st was deactivated I would never have to listen to Jenna again. I was twenty-five years old, still young enough to think that things happen once and then they're over; too young to know that human beings are, as my mother would say, a broken record.

We could sit wherever we wanted in the plane, and I found a window seat and moved into it, putting my backpack on the seat next to me, planning to move it when I saw Max coming. We were only one hundred and one people in the 501st, so there were plenty of empty seats. Jenna ambled down the aisle and stopped in front of me, picked up the backpack and handed it to me, then slipped into the seat. As there seemed to be no polite way to tell her I was hoping someone *else* would sit there, I bent my knees, put my feet on my seat, and hugged myself, trying to create a private space to be with my thoughts.

Reuber and Camacho, guys from downtown Warrenside, forged up the aisle. Reuber looked down and grinned at me. "Goin' back to *the world*, Bineki!"

"That's right," I said.

Soldiers call home "the world," as if everywhere else is just a bad dream you can hardly wait to wake from. After listening to soldiers from the 501st talking about "the world," an alien from outer space would think Warrenside, Pennsylvania, was El Dorado instead of a has-been industrial town that spat its families out a generation ago. If Warrenside was so great, why would its scions voluntarily join the army? It's the myth that keeps you going, that you have somewhere to go back to, a cool town whose residents can hardly wait for your return. In truth, you have lost your place in a cruel game of musical chairs. The world Reuber was returning to was light-years away from my world, but we would have the same reentry problem, because once you have gone to the bathroom in a fire latrine, you basically have nothing in common with anyone in suburbia; after you've convinced yourself with epithets and slander—hajji and rag head et cetera—that the people your army is trying to annihilate are subhuman, you have nothing in common with any thinking person. But unless you're a homicidal maniac, how else can you get it up to kill someone? Not that anyone in 501st Supply and Support killed anyone, but we were ready if we had to. Goddamn, we were ready. But here's the thing: the army may have given us night vision goggles, but they took away our ability to see gray. So what are you going to discuss over a Coffee Coolatta at Dunkin' Donuts back in the world? Your conversational repertoire is subverbal— loading up the revolver at four in the morning and staring at your mate in the dark until she wakes up and, petrified that you've gone berserk, shoves the kids in the pickup and leaves. Wait, honey, you want to say, I've *seen* things! You don't know what's out there. *I know!* And all Honey knows for sure is that *you're* the one with the gun and crazy ideas about how to fix things so they are black-and-white again.

"You are no longer on speaking terms with your world." That's what Duck used to say. "My dad was in Vietnam, so talk to him," he always said, "if you want to know about returning to the world you almost died defending." But you couldn't actually ask Duck's dad anything. He killed himself. Not in Vietnam, here. I mean, *there*. Home. The world.

It was pouring and our plane was still idling on the runway for what, I was beginning to suspect, would be hours. Jenna began chattering. "I am *so* glad to be out of here," she said, "and to be going home where people are God-fearing. Where they can talk about Jesus without getting their heads cut off."

"I guess they fear God here, too. That's why they're such fierce warriors."

"Fierce warriors. Ha." Jenna unzipped her Bible and turned to an underlined passage. "'A man can only come to the Father through Me,'" she read, then closed the book. "Without Jesus, they're just soulless bodies. They're killing machines. They are *not* fierce warriors."

"What about the part that says love thy neighbor as thyself?" I asked. "That part's in there too, isn't it?"

We'd had this same conversation for a year, but I was too polite to shut her off. The requirement to be polite had been drilled into me since I was a kid. It would make people feel bad, my mother said, to show up their ignorance. We had to worry about making people feel bad, because we were Warrens. According to the laws of a dominant male progenitor, I'm a Bineki, but you wouldn't know it to be around my mother, who insisted that we hyphenate our name. Warren-Bineki. The Bineki part could be lopped off if anyone important noticed it. My dad was like a stud the Warrens brought in to pep up the stagnant gene pool, then see-ya-later. Mother never talked about the Binekis, because they were ordinary. My mother was scared of ordinary people, a fear she learned from her grandfather, who was insane on the subjects of socialism, communism, and labor unions. He never stopped warning his family about the violence of the ordinary ignorant man. Ignorant people, my mother said, were unapologetically violent.

I disagreed with my mother regarding almost everything, but in this instance I had to admit she was right. In April, Jenna, who was *uncommonly* ignorant, had accused Barzai Marwat, the Pashtun who worked in the Admin tent, of inappropriately touching her while she was laying a Jesus trap for his Muslim soul. When she complained, our commander, Captain Whynnot, handed Barzai back to the Afghani warlord who owned him, and within twenty-four hours he was hanging on the town soccer field as an example. After I grilled her later, Jenna admitted the inappropriate touching consisted of the Pashtun's pulling a strand of her frizzy red hair through his fingers and laughing—he had never seen anything like it. That was it. He touched Jenna's spectacularly ugly orange hair. For that, Barzai died. After it happened, I asked Jenna if she felt remorse about Barzai's execution; she said if he accepted Jesus into his heart before he died, he could apologize to her in heaven for touching her.

I thought Jenna was lost in her holy thoughts when she said, "I was kind of open, sexually, like you, before I found Jesus. So I don't regret any of it. It was His way of finding me, I guess." She leaned in as if we were intimates. "He's looking for you, Kat."

"Sexually *open*? Are you insane? Duck's my boyfriend. Everyone knows that." I'm not bragging, but I am very sexy-looking and people—people who either want me or want to look like me—think I'm easy. I'm not. I'm one of those people other people use like a blank page for their fantasies.

Jenna opened her Bible angrily. She was jealous that I had a boyfriend and she didn't. After the Barzai incident most of the guys were overly polite to her, but that's it. They weren't taking any chances.

Anyway, it was ridiculous to think of Jenna as being sexually open. The entire time we were in Afghanistan, she never took off her long underwear. I don't think she got naked even to shower. I imagined she had three nipples or some other deformity. There was an otherwise perfectly normal girl in Basic Training who had an extra nipple underneath her left breast. She showed it off, as if it gave her extra sexual cachet. Of course, Jenna would see it as the mark of the Beast or something.

I got up from my seat, banged my head on the overhead, and wiggled over Jenna into the aisle.

"Hand me my backpack, will you?" I saw an empty seat farther up the plane. "I want to get some sleep."

Most of the soldiers were sleeping, their bodies contorted in positions any normal person would find crippling. I found out in Basic Training that if I wanted to sleep I couldn't always wait for a bed with sheets. Being able to fall asleep standing up was the most useful thing I learned on active duty.

I squeezed into an empty window seat a minute before we were cleared for takeoff, and in a while we were above the storm clouds, the snowy peaks of the Hindu Kush looming in the distance. I had to start thinking of Afghanistan as "there" instead of "here," and I willed my internal compass to shift as the plane climbed higher, separating me from Afghanistan. I tried to sleep, but the agitation of the soldier sitting across the aisle from me, obviously having a bad dream, kept me awake. When he let out a scream I got up, worked my way to the back of the plane, where Camacho, Reuber, and Duck were playing poker, and plopped into a seat behind them.

Camacho and Reuber lived on the same street in Warrenside. They were inseparable best friends the entire time they were in Kandahar until the last few weeks, when they were always fighting, as if to settle who owned that street before they returned. Talk about a booby prize.

They both had contracts in their duffels for three thousand dollars a month from the recruiter for Charon Corp, the private contractor that had a lock on independent enterprises in Kandahar, such as the laundry, food concessions, road construction, and private security guards. Three thousand dollars a month was an unheard-of amount of money in Warrenside. My family had seen to that. Three thousand dollars a month would solve all their problems, they *thought*. Poor people always think that money is going to solve their problems, that happiness rides into town on a pile of greenbacks.

Camacho and Reuber were smoking the Cuban cigars and drinking the twelve-year-old Jim Beam that the Charon recruiter had stuffed in their duffel bags for the ride home. They were drunk and seemed to be enjoying the sensation, for the first time in their lives, of having a high-rolling suitor validate their worth.

Duck came over and leaned against my seat. "You okay, babe?"

"I'm fine," I said. "I had to get away from Jenna."

"You think about what we discussed last night?" he asked.

What we'd discussed last night was that we should move out of our parents' homes and get married. We had known each other since we were six, Duck pointed out needlessly, as if knowing each other forever was a giant plus. Duck had always assumed we would get married, and I couldn't think of a good reason why we shouldn't, except for this irritable voice inside of me that kept whispering, *This is it? No more?* I pictured a vault door slamming shut while I practiced shallow breathing to ration the oxygen that had to last the rest of my life. Airtight safe.

A part of me wanted to risk my safe haven to see what else was out there, but I was afraid—of what, I couldn't say. And Duck assured me that rumors of an exciting life outside our bunker only meant that it was full of peril. People leave you, he said. People let you down. Sometimes I imagined that I could experience the world while safely married to Duck, but when I was with Duck, the only experience I had was . . . Duck. When I joined the Guard to escape my mother before I became infected with whatever infected her, Duck joined the next day, shuttering his thriving cabinet shop in Warrenside. He wanted to make sure I was all right. Protect his investment. I didn't speak to him for three weeks after that, because, after all, Duck was one of the things I wanted to get away from. But I couldn't stay mad. Duck is Duck.

He'd said last night we weren't going to find anyone better. We were only in our twenties and we weren't going to find anyone better? Maybe he was right. The men my mother found to distract me from Duck were like aliens. Once, I came home from high school and there was a boy, Jason, from Massachusetts with his mother in our living room. They were having drinks as if driving six hours to have a vodka martini in Pennsylvania was a normal thing to do. Our great-great-great-great-grandfathers came over on the same boat from England, which my mother thought gave us something in common but which would make them, I told her—after I drove Jason off with my boorish behavior—fellow religious misfits, and probably fourth cousins. Hadn't there been enough inbreeding? I asked her.

My mother told me they were the richest family in Marblehead, Massachusetts. They made their money in textiles, although the factories had been sold decades ago and they were now living on dividends from bank stocks, et cetera. When I asked Jason what he wanted to do after college, he looked at me like I was crazy. Part of me was being mean, but part of me really wanted to *know*, because I was going to have the same problem. I would never have to work. Thanks to my mother's indiscretion in marrying my father, we weren't *rich-rich*—like my second cousin Alix Warren, who once hired a mariachi band on the spur of the moment for a week-long party—but we were rich enough that, if I was prudent, I would never have to do an honest day's work. I would have just enough money to paralyze me. If you have a burning desire to do something—like if you know you just *have* to make movies or you *have* to draw apples or think about Aristotle—then not having to do anything *else* is probably a great thing. But most people aren't like that. Most people have to dream up ways to get money, and that ends up being their life, and then they claim it was what they wanted to do *all along* and they find ways to be happy about it. Which isn't a bad thing, it's just ordinary.

I always wanted to experience exotic cultures. I pictured myself a reincarnated Michael Rockefeller, going into unexplored territories like New Guinea—not getting eaten by the natives like he did, of course—but when I actually found myself in an exotic place, Afghanistan, aside from a few forays with armed male escorts to the local Saturday bazaar that was just outside the gate, I was required to stay within the barbed-wire perimeters of the post and go to parties at the mess hall for made-up events and drink the spiked Gatorade just like all the other soldiers. I had all this interest in the Afghani people, but I wasn't even allowed to talk to them. I would have very much liked to hear what they had to say about me, although I can see now that as far as they were concerned I was just one more thing that crashed uninvited into their lives, something that would eventually go away.

What I respected about Duck then was that he was unapologetically ordinary. He was a rock. He had a normal carpentry business and a normal guy's enthusiasm for hunting, fishing, and paying his bills on time, which was a big point of honor with him. Men liked him because he did things well. Women wanted to marry him, because they interpreted his reserve as self-possession, and they were jealous of me and thought I was a bitch because I was stringing him along. Did their jealousy arouse my passion? No. Of course I loved Duck, but I didn't feel passion, which I thought was like you had to be with that person or you would kill yourself, like Romeo and Juliet.

With Duck I never felt that desperation. But wasn't that a good thing? I had enough tumult in my life with my mother's instability that I thought one more tumultuous thing would probably unseat me. I tried, *stupidly*, to talk to her about Duck before I left for Afghanistan—should I marry him? et cetera—and she just said she'd read in an article in *Redbook* that what first attracted you to a person was the thing you would cite in divorce court as the reason you could no longer stand him. Look at me and your father, she said, our attraction was purely lust. And now she couldn't stand for him to touch her. That's when I lost it. Dad was great and she was lucky to have found someone to put up with her! I yelled and screamed and kicked her heirloom loveseat and knocked out one of the legs. The whole ugly sofa just kind of collapsed in slow motion with dust from about a thousand years ago rising up, making us both choke. You would have thought I kicked *her*, she got so hysterical. "That was to be yours!" she kept screaming, as if I had my eye on it, which I certainly did *not*. See, that's what you do when you have money and you don't have a job: you read magazines written for women who don't have a clue how to live their lives. And then she said, *I forbid you to marry Duck.*

Forbid! I stormed out of the house and got my bike, which I ride when I'm pissed off, out of the garage, and pedaled wildly across the Harlan Gardiner Bridge to the south side of town and got a flat tire on a piece of glass in front of the army recruiting station. The staff sergeant who came outside to see what all the swearing was about told me he'd fix the tire while I relaxed and watched a DVD about women in the army. In this film the women were fixing planes, flying planes, and shooting other people's planes out of the sky. "That looks *so cool*," I'd said to the staff sergeant, totally buying into the probability that I was a woman warrior, and he looked me right in the eye and said, "You have no idea how cool."

I reached out and squeezed Duck's hand. "Let's talk about it later, after we land."

"I don't know what we're waiting for."

"Duck, you in or out?" Reuber shouted over the seat.

"Fold. I'm out. I'm saving my money." Of course. He was saving his money for our future. That's exactly what he would do. He would make a list to facilitate our future together and check off each item until we achieved, relentlessly and inevitably, domestic bliss. He looked so happy with himself that I felt guilty for being the lone woman on the planet who couldn't seem to appreciate a man who wanted more than anything to take care of her. I was honest with Duck. I told him I didn't feel romantic about him, but Duck said romance was for children, that romantic love had a life as brief as a two-hour movie. *But don't you love me?* he'd asked. *I know you love me.* And I said, honestly, *I would be lost without you,* and he said, *Then we got lucky. What the hell else do you want?*

Now he touched the lapis lazuli that Max had retied around my neck. "Come on. Let's watch these guys play." And he dragged me into the seat opposite Reuber and Camacho.

"It's you and me, pard," Reuber said loudly to Camacho. "Mano a mano." He flicked his cigar like a gangsta and turned to me and laughed nervously. Reuber was a chronic gambler. He bet on sporting events, dogfights the Afghanis staged outside the wire, anything and everything that had an uncertain outcome. A couple of years ago he gambled and lost on Linda Pasko, a rerecovering coke addict he'd met when he'd wandered into a Narcotics Anonymous meeting in the church basement while waiting for his Gamblers Anonymous meeting to begin. He'd married Linda when the 501st was activated, and her picture, along with the picture of their kid (who he wasn't allowed to see) was now in another—luckier—soldier's duffel bag. No one in the 501st liked to be around him, because there is a superstition in the military that bad luck is contagious, but everyone loved to gamble with him because he could be relied on to lose all his money.

"You wanna go mano a mano, *pato?*" Camacho said. "Let's just cut cards."

"Temper, temper, Camacho." Reuber laughed.

"A thousand bucks a cut," Camacho said. "Cut the cards, *pato.*"

Reuber fanned the deck out in front of him. He studied the arc of cards. He looked at our faces: Duck had straightened up to watch; Camacho was staring at him coldly. He checked to make sure I was watching too, then laughed loudly, closed his eyes, and with his index finger pulled a card out of the line. He waved his hand over it like a magician and turned it over. A five of hearts. He groaned.

Camacho reached out quickly, picked up a card, and turned it over. A three of clubs.

Reuber jumped up and did a little dance, his hands clasped above his head. "Yip yip yip," he crowed. "Wanna go again, pard?" he said.

"Fuck!" Camacho screamed. He fanned in the cards and tossed them on the floor.

"Pick them up!" Reuber commanded.

"You pick them up, asshole." Camacho stepped up to Reuber, bumped him with his chest, and shoved him into the empty seat.

"Pay up!" Reuber shouted. He stood up and pulled a Nepalese kukri knife he'd bought as a souvenir out of an ankle holster.

"You gonna use that thing on me, *maricón*? You'd better be good," Camacho said.

Soldiers had spilled into the aisles and were jostling for positions to watch. Duck stepped between them.

"I don't think I've ever known two bigger assholes," he said. "Did either of you ignorant fucks even read your contracts? You don't see a penny of the money until your sorry asses deplane in Baghdad. Then the money gets deposited into your bank accounts, which I'm sure neither of you even have."

They looked stunned; then Camacho laughed. "Sorry, *pato*."

"You cheated me, you fucker. I'll kill you!" Reuber screamed.

"Hey," Duck said. "You guys want to get Article 15s when you're a couple days away from being done with this shit? What idiots." He pointed at the knife. "Give me that," he said.

"It's personal property. I paid for it myself."

"It's not yours anymore. Handle first," he said. Then he settled them down in separate seats like a father separating his squabbling children.

Watching Camacho and Reuber fight upset me, because it was a reminder of what was waiting for all of us back home. How could you be gone from your life for a year and not expect the seams to tear when you tried to squeeze back in? Personally, I would have been glad for the year I was able to defer my life, but really, my life—Duck Wolinsky—was right there, looking at me to see if I approved of how he'd handled those two delinquents.

I was walking back up the aisle, searching each row for my backpack, when I saw Max Asad's black head dip into the aisle to pick up something he'd dropped. It looked like a piece of paper fell from a book he was reading. I stopped, thinking of what to say. I wanted to erase the bad impression I'd made on the tarmac. I had met Max at the 501st's going-away party a year ago at the Armory, where he had stood awkwardly with his father, both with drinks in their hands, both clearly not knowing how to mingle in a crowd of enlisted men who were trying to control unruly children and chubby wives who couldn't stop crying. Wiry white hair swirled around his father's head like needles on a parched desert plant. He wore his trench coat draped over his shoulders, his elegance and grooming almost transforming his ugliness. Max, with his slender, graceful build and face—as smooth and tan as a ripe olive—right off a Persian frieze, wore his desert fatigues as if Armani designed them. He seemed like the only person in the room, besides me, who was truly alive. His brown eyes were slightly hooded as if something—no, everything—amused and disappointed him at the same time. It felt like a challenge, because I knew I wouldn't disappoint him. I wanted to make him smile. At me. Only. I watched him introduce his father to Captain Whynnot, and his father bowed his head slightly and shook Whynnot's hand, then casually turned away, uninterested. Max caught me staring at him, and he smiled and bowed slightly, that same amused look on his face, but he didn't make his way over to me as any other man would have. So I made my way over to him. I had to know who was inside that amused look.

"Your family isn't here?" he asked.

My mother had some imaginary—in my opinion—reaction to a new medication and couldn't leave the house, and my father had to work.

"My dad is coming later," I lied. "He couldn't get free."

He looked at me steadily. Just about the entire town was here to send off the 501st. "He must have an important job," he said.

While my father certainly thought his job was important, all his tales of office triumphs were of how he, once again, fended off the process engineers who were trying to consolidate, automate, and eliminate his position. "It's just a bad time."

I waited for him to introduce me to his father, but his father turned away from me.

"You have to excuse him," Max said. "He still isn't used to women doing men's jobs. He doesn't know how to treat you."

Then Max's father pulled Max away as if I were radioactive at the same time Duck thought of something urgent to tell me and was tugging me in the other direction, saying, "I'm surprised that *an Arab* would join up." It didn't matter. I thought we would have a year to clear up our unfinished business. But I never saw Max, much less had a chance to speak to him, the entire time I was in Kandahar. That first month I was busy setting up shop, and when I went to find him he was already gone, plucked by the Ops. I found out from Jenna, who kept the unit's personnel records, that he had graduated from Princeton and was fluent in Dari and Pashto, the languages of the tribes around the base. His father, as everyone in Warrenside knew, owned most of downtown, which included a strip club, a crime for which old Warrenside would never forgive him. My own dear mother had led the campaign to deny the Asads' application to the Lenape Country Club, saying they had no class because of that strip club. All you do at the country club is play golf and tennis and get drunk with people exactly like you, so who won that round? I knew some of the men from the country club went to the strip club after business dinners or when their wives were out of town. Anyway, if being rich was the criterion for class, and I could never discern another, the Asads had become the classiest family in Warrenside. So Max had even less financial reason than me to join the army, especially as an enlisted man, and I wanted to ask him why he did it. At least that was the excuse I gave myself for intruding on him. He unnerved me unlike any man had before, so I practiced what I was going to say before I approached his seat.

"Everyone's playing poker," I said. "Don't you want to play?"

"It's not sport to take advantage of children."

Duck had told me Max believed he was better than everyone. I sat down next to him, unnaturally unsure of myself, just as Melanie Martin, our embed from Channel 3, came up the aisle. She broke into a toothy smile. "Great," she said. "You're awake. You're the only one I don't have on tape." She pointed a small video camera at Max, who held up his hand.

"You think I am in a zoo?" he asked.

"I have to interview everyone in the unit. It's my job. It'll just take five minutes."

He closed his book and folded his hands over it.

"Come on," Melanie said. "Everyone else did it."

Melanie had done a video portrait of me and I hated it. I guess that's another thing I have to agree with my mother about: never allow other people to define you, especially the media. That's what an interviewer does: takes what you say and edits and rearranges and deletes until you look like one of those ransom notes with the words and letters cut out of different magazines. We talked for an hour with her damn camera on and I told her I wanted to travel and do some good. I was sincere, but she made me come off as a princess, and it really affected how everyone in the unit looked at me.

"So?" she asked sweetly, peering into the pop-out LED screen. "What did you do in Kandahar, Max?"

"You could have joined me on patrol anytime and found out," he answered. It was the joke in the unit that Melanie would never put her butt on the line. The only reason she'd taken the assignment was that covering a war zone was the only way for a reporter right out of college to get noticed by the bigger stations. Everyone wanted the same plum assignments. Television reporting was like anything else: your good fortune was someone else's bad.

"No, really," she said. "What did you do? I mean, what was your job?"

"I was in a *war*," he said. I could hear the violence in Max's voice. It made Melanie back away. The rest of the 501st were supply personnel, like me, or lawyers and legal aides who were, as I said, helping the Afghanis draft a constitution. Max was the only member of the 501st who actually saw action, and one of the things you learn early in the military is that the *only* people who brag about what they have seen or done in combat are folks who have actually seen and done *nothing*. If you've been there you'd rather forget it, if you can. I'd only heard snippets of what the Ops did on patrol, and it was dirty.

"Okay. *Great.* Weren't you like a *translator* or something?" She smiled encouragingly at him and swirled her free hand, palm up, as if to stir up his sluggish memories.

"Yes," Max said, smiling for the first time. He seemed to find the whole thing amusing all of a sudden. "Or *something*."

"So, what are you going to do when you get home?" she asked. It was the question everyone had been asking themselves and one another in the month since we got our orders. What are you going to do? It had only been a year, but already half the unit had been laid off from their jobs via e-mail.

"I will take over my father's businesses so he can go back to his scholarly work. Okay?" Max cut the air with his hand. "Enough."

In the month when Max was still bunking with him, Duck had told me that Max's father, Dr. Edward Asad, was a famous scholar and had in fact written nine books about Arabic literature, but that meant nothing to me. "Is that what you want?" I asked after Melanie had thanked him cheerily and moved away. "To take over your father's businesses?"

Max took his time examining my face, my hair, my neck, and then my hands, which were folded on my lap, and frowned.

He inhaled loudly and said, "You know what I thought of, the first time I saw you? I thought how much a girl like you would fetch in a harem." He seemed to be enjoying himself. "I think ten sheep and four camels. No, fifteen sheep."

I closed my eyes, imagining myself in harem pants and the payment arriving on my mother's front lawn. "That's actually not a very good price."

"The most famous concubine in Suleiman the Magnificent's harem was Roxelana. She was a Pole too, Bineki. It's a natural attraction, the North and the South. The North is the land of ice; the South, the land of fire and passion. If ice mates with ice, there is only more ice. And if fire mates with fire, there is a conflagration. But ice and fire make water and life."

I felt like he was drawing me under some kind of exotic veil and it was just us on the plane. I think I knew *at that moment* that I didn't belong under that veil, but the fact that it was forbidden made me want it. "Did you just make that up?"

He laughed. "Westerners know nothing of Arab culture, and they don't think they need to. That's why we'll be mired in the Middle East for decades. No, I didn't just make that up. It's Tayeb Salih, the most famous novelist writing in Arabic. You never heard of him, of course."

Why should I have? The winners write the history books, and the West was still the winning team. "I'll look him up in the library when I get home," I said.

"I'm sure you won't find his books in the Warrenside Public Library. The section on Arab literature is quite small."

I nodded, trying to place the Arab section in the library, which I actually frequented, then felt embarrassed again because there was no such section and he knew it.

"Roxelana was his slave. Suleiman conquered all of Eastern Europe, and Roxelana was one of many slaves. He freed her and married her eventually."

"I'm only half Polish," I said. "My mother is a Warren." He had made me say the one thing I'd spent my entire life disowning: that being a Warren meant anything whatsoever. Did he really think he could make me his *slave*? Who did he think he was? No wonder everyone hated him. I stood up.

"You are really nothing like Roxelana," he said hastily. "I can see it now."

"Believe me, you're not Suleiman the Magnificent," I said.

Duck, who had been watching from a couple of seats away, came over to us. "Hello, Asad," he said.

"Wolinsky," Max answered.

"What are you two talking about?" Duck asked.

I felt guilty, like I was betraying Duck for having what was a completely innocent conversation. If anyone was recording our conversation, they would find nothing whatsoever wrong with what we said. I told myself that. Yet I felt it was the most personal conversation I'd ever had, and Duck had caught us. *In flagrante converso.*

"Ready for the big day?" Duck asked him.

"What day?" I asked, looking from Duck to Max while Duck blathered about Max's intended, hand-picked for Max by his father from his mother's village in Lebanon. She was in Warrenside right that instant, selecting white tulle concoctions and ordering a five-tier cake held up with Doric columns. I could picture the little figurines on top of that cake: a plastic Arabian prince and a woman in a burka. Well, good luck to her. Duck was clearly waiting for me to congratulate Max.

"Fire and fire make a conflagration," I said. "Isn't that right, Suleiman?"

Max scowled.

"What? Hey, we're getting married too," Duck said, ignoring that I hadn't actually said I would. He patted my head—as if I was a dog—and my face burned red. "Come on with me, Kat," Duck said. "There's a couple of seats in the back."

I stood up meekly. Max grabbed my wrist and squeezed it until I looked at him. His eyes were alight. "And ice and ice is a frozen life, Roxelana."

I yanked my arm away and followed Duck.

BARBARA WARREN-BINEKI

Even before she gained a hundred pounds as a result of ingesting every new antidepressant and antipsychotic on the market, and even before her last birthday, her forty-third—middle age for a wealthy white woman with superb health insurance—with its attendant hormonal shifts and water pouches hanging like pink cherries from her cheeks and neck; even before all that, Barbara Warren-Bineki's eyes were slitted and suspicious, the eyes of the last soldier behind enemy lines waiting for reinforcements, hiding in daylight, maneuvering futilely against the enemy in darkness, because what Barbara couldn't see was that the war was over. Her side—status quo, old money, archaic standards of etiquette and social standing, specifically *her* family's social standing—had surrendered and left her for dead.

Barbara Warren-Bineki, heir to defunct Warren Steel, was fighting a one-person rearguard action for the retreating forces of Western Civilization. No one else in Warrenside cared that the

Puerto Ricans who inhabited the downtown row houses (deserted by unemployed steelworkers) painted them Virgin Mary blue. No one else cared that they used old living room sofas as porch furniture. Even the formerly reliable German Lutherans on the city council defeated an ordinance she had proposed to ban both practices. No one else cared that rich Middle Easterners were buying up downtown real estate, which had been devalued to fire sale prices. And certainly no one else in Warrenside cared that, by 2012, European-Americans would be the minority in Warrenside itself, because if they cared, they would do something about it. Was she the only one who saw that everything that mattered—their history, their language, even the way they alternated at four-way stop signs—was being overwritten with the story of strangers?

Kat had told her that Europeans had been colonizing the rest of the world since forever, and now they were seeing what it feels like: Warrenside had become a colony. Barbara thought it was a generational defect that Kat saw all sides of an issue. She marveled that Kat bragged about how it made her balanced. Maybe it did make her balanced, but it didn't move her forward. If you're busy weighing every situation, trying to see things through everybody's eyes, life moves on and happens without you. You have to see things through the one pair of eyes you're given, or you see nothing. At the ATM the other day, the computer screen asked her if she wanted to proceed in Spanish, Arabic, Vietnamese, Chinese, or English. She pounded on the screen, enraged, until the young man behind her in line told her, in a mellifluous Hindi accent, that he could assist, as he was a computer programmer. She stared at him, horrified; then she fled. If we don't speak with one voice, she thought—and said aloud whenever she detected a sympathetic audience, although she was increasingly wrong about people's sympathies—how can we be heard?

Barbara was trying to explain her fears, politely, to Liz Reville, the newscaster from Channel 3 who had come to the house with a film crew to interview her about Kat's homecoming, but there seemed to be no subtle way for Barbara to say that she thought her culture was better than that of those who were taking over the city. To even mention something like this was to be misunderstood, and soon it would be all over the Internet, and then her cousins would be asking her how in God's name she allowed their private family name to come under public scrutiny, which would mean that soon the public would criticize her family's investments; and didn't she realize that high-yielding investments were tricky things that some people might judge illegal or immoral, even though *somebody* had to make enormous amounts of money any way they could or the entire economy would collapse? It would do no good to protest that it wasn't her fault if every ignoramus with an electrical outlet could broadcast their poorly constructed, illogical, misspelled sentences into the stratosphere. *She* would be to blame for airing an opinion that, in this crazy mixed-up culture, made the Warrens look bad and made their retrograde laissez-faire investments look worse.

She waved an old newspaper clipping, which she'd had laminated before it disintegrated, and showed it to Liz. "Things are changing. When different groups take charge, things will not be as they once were."

"Different groups?" Liz asked. "What are you talking about?"

"Different groups respond to pain differently. It couldn't be plainer." The clipping was an old Mayo Clinic report that studied World War II veterans and their tolerance of pain.

Liz skimmed the article and widened her eyes at her cameraman before addressing Barbara. "Barbara, this is about Italians."

Barbara glared at her, willing her to see the connection: Italians, Spanish, Haitians, Africans, Jews, *Arabs*. They were all *warm-climate* people. Why couldn't this woman make the creative leap?

"Are you scared of *Italians*, Barbara?"

"Of course I'm not scared of Italians. I was just trying to make a point." She grabbed the clipping and slipped it back into a thick yellow cloth-covered book stuffed with other clippings. The book was called *The House Is Built!*, written by her father and published by Vantage Books in 1976. It was his magnum opus, one thousand and eleven pages, his obsession, his life's work. He began writing it when he was forty-five and unreasonably fit, and it had become clear that the only job left for him at the steel mill was to shut it down. He designed, built, and wrote about designing and building the house she was living in right now: a modernist marvel with the best materials—cypress wood, stone hand-picked from the Catawissa for the skin, ten thousand pounds of copper for the roof—and constructed by craftsmen he brought over from Italy. See? Her family loved Italians! She wasn't *scared* of them. She was around them all the time when the house was being built. She had a crush on the stonemason's sixteen-year-old son, Armando, who had a huge Adam's apple and a blue shadow beard and who spent one winter in her ninth-grade class trying to learn English while asking out all the girls until he found one who would go to the movies with him. It was all in the book! The book was about much more than building a house; it was about a way of life that he cherished, that of a steel industrialist, with all its privileges and sweet responsibilities and power—of course power was a big part of it—that was rusting over. When five copies of *The House Is Built!* were delivered to the house, he said, "Aha, ladies! Gather round!" and signed them in his flamboyant hand *Best wishes, Malcolm Warren*, even Barbara's copy. Then he and Barbara's mother flew to the Costa Brava, where he drove their Porsche into a tree, postponing for a few seconds their fiery descent to the ravine below.

She was left an orphan, but that didn't scare her. So why should Italians scare her? She wasn't scared of anything. She couldn't be scared of anything, because she didn't have the fear chemical, which is probably not a fact that most people knew about themselves, but which Barbara knew because she had a detailed report on precisely which chemicals were coursing through her bloodstream and in what amounts and proportions. The fear chemical, a little-known pheromone called "the alarm pheromone" that had just been discovered, was not a part of that train ride. She had a wonderful lack of pain chemical transmitters as well, which she attributed to her English background. That was the point of the Mayo Clinic Report on Pain, frayed, almost shredded, and now choking under a thick coating of plastic laminate: people of English heritage tolerated pain better than people of other European countries. An example of this was that British sport cars didn't have heaters. Imagine riding around in that cold, damp weather without a heater. Though her Lincoln Town Car had heated leather seats, she fancied she had pioneer spirit if not pioneer blood, for which she never apologized. Pioneers were descended from the Scotch-Irish side of the British Isles: definitely the wrong side of the islands in Barbara's social hierarchy.

She could talk for hours about chemicals and the differences between ethnic groups—it was almost a hobby—but Liz wanted to talk about Barbara's daughter, Kat. Channel 3 was trying to get some background interviews before the big day, when Channel 3 would have special all-day coverage of the homecoming.

"Well, Kat's coming home," Liz chirped, cueing the cameraman. "You must be so proud of her. I must say, too, that it's not usual for children of old established families to join the military anymore. So you must be doubly proud of your daughter for fighting the terrorists."

Barbara nodded. She wasn't proud of Kat for joining the army. Kat joined the army to spite her. She caught herself nodding for a very long time and realized it was probably because of a new chemical, Abilify, which had recently been added to her repertoire to counter the chemical imbalance caused by her schizophrenia. She imagined Abilify worked by weaving a protective shield from her own thoughts, which had a tendency to fly far afield, gathering spikes and innuendos, before coming back at her like a boomerang. Now she couldn't seem to break the bars of her chemical cage to form a thought about Kat that she could tell this woman.

"Barbara?"

She shook her head. "Sorry. I was just thinking about Kat."

"A year is a long time," Liz said. "What's the first thing you want to do together with Kat when she comes home?"

Barbara found she couldn't process the question very well because she didn't agree with the premise that a year is a long time. A year is no time at all! She kept getting stuck on that thought and was unable to move.

"What's the *first* thing?" she repeated, stalling, smiling. When the hell was the Abilify going to kick in? That drug was specifically made to help her move on. It said so right in the ads: "It will help you *move on*!"

"Her father will probably want to take her out to the range. They like to shoot." There, she said something. Barbara felt woozy. It said on the contraindications listings that nausea was a possible side effect of Abilify. "Would you excuse me for a moment?" she asked, and went to the bathroom, took a key from her pocket, and opened the cabinet that contained her drugs. She pulled out an Emend to fight the nausea. She poured a glass of water from the sink and looked in the mirror, a small eight-inch glass disk from an old makeup case hung at eye level. Her shrink had told her that if it stressed her to see her girth, she shouldn't look in any mirrors. It was so simple! She liked this psychiatrist the best of any so far. On her advice, Barbara had glued this tiny mirror on the wall and taken down the gigantic one that had been there for years, making her cry every time she looked into it and saw a beast looking back.

She walked down the stairs to find the film crew putting their equipment away. "May I get you something? Tea?" Barbara asked, but Liz was already out the door and shouting over her shoulder. "We have ten more families to visit. Thanks so much! *Love* your roses! They're so old-*fashioned*." And the door slammed and Barbara was alone, waiting for Mike to get home from his job at Titan Insurance.

Barbara knew from her research on chemicals that her attraction to her husband, Mike, twenty-five years ago had been purely chemical, as all love-at-first-sight affairs are. He touched her hand nonchalantly at a party after a high school football game—"Pass me a beer, babe, will ya?"—and her mouth started to water, her salivary glands pumping out phenylethylamine, which caused an addictive reaction in her; she wanted to touch him, which she did, brushing her hand over his, which caused neural transmitters in her pituitary gland to start chugging out oxytocin, which caused her palms to sweat, her knees to shake, and a general restlessness to overtake her, which could only be assuaged by kissing him fully on the mouth, which caused the substantia nigra and the ventral tegmental areas of her brain to produce dopamine receptors, which made Barbara feel just plain good and she wanted more, more, *more*, damn it—why hadn't anybody told her about this before?—until her adrenal glands kicked in with norepinephrine, which got her totally hooked on Mike Bineki, an

Adonis in a football jersey, even though you could tell by the way his hairline parted in two spikes halfway up the top of his head like a curtain rising at the theater that he was going to be cue-ball bald by the second act—a function of excessive testosterone, hoorah!—but still a guy with no money, no plan, no real talents except throwing a football down a field, and—before the night was through—a guy who was going to have a family to support.

Her uncles got him a job in Titan Insurance, a subsidiary of Warren Steel, as a middle manager, where he would think he was going to own the company one day, because . . . well, that's what men think when they're young, especially when they have excess testosterone, but the dopamine had worn off his aspirations long ago. The phenylethylamine of their attraction had been replaced by lactating hormones when Kat was born. The usual endorphins that fuel a successful marriage, the chemicals that make couples stay together, were nowhere in sight, and Barbara had had her pituitary gland tested several times, pinched, punctured, and slapped to see what the hell was wrong; where were the endorphins? But there was nothing wrong with her pituitary gland. Mike just didn't stimulate that particular organ any longer. That was Mike. That's who she was waiting for.

At five-thirty exactly—and that was the reason he was never going to own the company; he behaved like the blue-collar boy he was, coming and going to the sound of the dinner gong—he came through the door and, instead of saying, "Hey, babe, where's my drink?" like he usually did, he said, "You're never going to believe this. The sonsabitches fired me."

THREE

DR. EDWARD ASAD

Dr. Edward Asad slept well and woke up that morning with the hairs on the back of his neck tingling. This evening he would spend with his mistress, Anika Lee, who was also the head dancer at his strip club, Lucky Lady. Every man who came into the club desired her, and the knowledge of their lust fueled his own, making their semiweekly evenings together even more satisfying.

But even luckier than that, he had received word that his son, Max, was coming home with the rest of his company. Dr. Asad was afraid that the army would extend his tour of active duty because of the scarcity of skilled translators, but Max had called him yesterday to tell him they were outsourcing that function to the private contractor, Charon Corp. While he believed that paying contractors to perform such a vital function as translation was a terrible stroke of misfortune for the army, it was very lucky for Dr. Asad and his family.

Dr. Asad closed his eyes to make sure that the feeling—the soft breeze of Lady Luck blessing his good fortune—was there. Yes, there it was. He smiled. There could be no mistaking the feeling, because he had felt it before, many times.

Even the supposed misfortune for an Arab man of having only one son managed to right itself and prove beneficial to him. He had Max, who was worth twenty sons. And wasn't Max coming home to assume his place as heir, a place that Dr. Asad had so lovingly and single-mindedly prepared for him? Warrenside would support any bold moves that the Asads made, because Max had written him that he had been in combat with the Special Ops who patrolled the mountains hunting the Taliban, proving both his manhood and his American patriotism.

Dr. Asad's friends said that God smiled on him, and he pretended to agree. He went to church on Sunday, put a huge envelope stuffed with hundred-dollar bills in the collection basket, and publicly asked for God's mercy at the funerals of his friends. He did this out of respect for his community, which treated him, because of his education, intelligence, wealth, and success in America, as its leader.

But Dr. Asad didn't believe in God, certainly not the God of his Maronite Catholic church, who pitted men against each other like dogs in a deserted parking lot on a moonless night and gave back nothing but war and exile for Dr. Asad's people. His beloved Beirut was a ruin. His fellow expatriates owned failing clothing factories. Wasn't that this God's doing?

Perhaps such a God existed. But Dr. Asad didn't believe that God was responsible for his own enormous good fortune. Why would God favor a doubter above the other curs?

Dr. Asad gently lifted the covers off himself so as not to wake his wife, Bernice—who flip-flopped like a fish struggling for air all night until she finally collapsed at dawn—put his feet into leather slippers—which Bernice arranged every night in the same place for him long after he was asleep—and padded into the bathroom to dress.

Dr. Asad was born into a wealthy family in Beirut in 1944. He had added to the prestige of the family by becoming an authority on pre-Islamic Arabic and Persian literature—out of vogue now that Arabs were politicized and united under Wahhabi Islam—which consisted of poetry and fairy tales passed down orally. Still, he had written nine books on the subject, and when he emigrated, because he was already a financially secure and educated man, he had the choice of going either to Paris or America. According to Westerners, Beirut, before it was pulled into the maelstrom of religious madness, was the Paris of the Middle East, so Dr. Asad thought, why go to Paris, which he already knew? He came to America thinking he would find a position teaching Arab literature at a small American university, establish himself there, then jump to a larger venue. His colleagues in academia in Beirut advised him against going. The Jews, they said, had convinced Americans that Arabs were barbarians and had no culture worth passing on to the rest of the world. His Lebanese compatriots in Warrenside told him that Arabs were the new Indians. They got killed in American movies while the audience cheered, and ultimately Americans had no interest in Arab literature, Arab history, Arab language, or Arabs themselves, except as foils for the gun-toting liberators they fancied themselves.

And perhaps, Dr. Asad thought, all this was true. The Jews, who had made great fortunes in Warrenside in the garment trade, had sold their businesses to Lebanese immigrants who were ignorant of the fact that the bulk of the trade had already emigrated to Mexico and China, and the Lebanese—descendants of the Phoenician traders who'd once ruled the Mediterranean—felt great bitterness toward the Jews when they realized they'd been had. But to Dr. Asad, the cunning of a culture was a phenomenon to be noted and perhaps learned from, not judged. The nature of life is change—Fortuna's wheel turns relentlessly—and to be surprised by it shows ignorance. You are on top of the wheel one moment, then thrown off and plunged into the sea of misfortune the next.

He couldn't buy a garment factory. He was an intellectual; what did he know about making clothing? He bought a coffee shop, which became the first Dunkin' Donuts in the United States of America to sell baklava—strictly against the franchise's rules— thinking that educated American men would come and that they and Dr. Asad would engage in a dialogue on civilization over Coffee Coolattas and Lucky Strike cigarettes. He envisioned intellectual and political argument in his café, where his son Max would be initiated into the world of ideas and men. But the men who came to Dr. Asad's coffee shop didn't want to discuss the injustices of the world or the beauty of consciousness. They wanted to discuss the Eagles' inept coaching staff and lament the Phillies' place in the cellar.

The Maronite Church agency that invited him to Warrenside had enticed him by telling him it was an ancient university town. They didn't tell him that the university's sole function was to churn out engineers and football players, not aesthetes, and that there had never been a place in it for an Arab intellectual, certainly not an Arab intellectual whose area of expertise was focused on the irrelevant ancient world. Or that the industry that had fueled the town—steel—was dying. No, dead already. But Lady Luck came to his rescue, plucked him from the roiling waters of misfortune, and plunked him back on top. As Warrenside's industry crumbled so did its real estate, and Dr. Asad started to acquire properties in the downtown at, as he was fond of saying, bargain basement prices.

He bought Kelly's Emerald Isle, a huge Irish barroom and transient hotel on Neinmeister Boulevard across from the boarded-up train station, and turned it into an exotic dance club, Lucky Lady. At first he hired belly dancers, because that was what he knew, but when their relatively modest undulations failed to fill the house, he went completely Western, hiring strippers, to Bernice's dismay. She didn't like that her husband was spending so much time with these exotic American beauties—who could resist them?—but she was silenced by the huge profits their gyrations spat out, as if they were ATMs.

Then, with his profits, Dr. Asad renovated the old Warrenside Plaza Hotel into an assisted living facility where young Warren-siders could warehouse their parents when they grew enfeebled. With the money from these two enterprises, he bought blocks and blocks of row houses in the old downtown that were originally built to house steelworkers. In two years, he was the biggest landlord in Warrenside and was discussing, with the Oasis Casino Corporation, the idea of building a gambling emporium downtown, adjacent to the site of the old steel mill. The only thing that kept him from pulling the trigger on the casino deal was that people still rented his row houses downtown and—being more a humanist than a capitalist—he was reluctant to displace them.

Dr. Asad's daughter, Houda, to whom he had handed over the day-to-day management of Lucky Lady until Max returned, distrusted Anika Lee, whom she thought had jiggled her way into Dr. Asad's affections. At thirty-four, Anika was older than the other dancers by at least ten years but still the biggest draw in the club.

"She is like a daughter to me," Dr. Asad told Houda, trying to explain to her that it was not Anika's formidable physical beauty that appealed to him but the way she looked to him for protection. What man could resist that? Houda, who had inherited her father's intelligence as well as, unfortunately, his looks, said only, "You don't need another daughter, Papa."

And Dr. Asad knew she was right. Besides Houda and Anika's daughter, Allie, he'd had another daughter, who was killed with his first wife in a cross fire in Beirut in 1982. But it was the fact that he had been surrounded by doting women all his life—he was an only son among four sisters—that made him love them. He loved women. He was enchanted by all aspects of their souls and bodies, and the part that most American men found despicable—the melodrama of their small lives and petty concerns—he found fascinating, coming, as he did, from a culture of sheikhs who encouraged the jealousies of their harems in order to keep their wives from uniting against them. Dr. Asad could not understand why American men had allowed their women to band together to proscribe their peccadilloes. Was it any wonder that American women despised them?

At eleven that Thursday morning, when Dr. Asad arrived at his office in the club to look over the liquor order and the weekend dance lineup, Anika was waiting for him, her long legs crossed, the top one pumping impatiently. When Dr. Asad entered the office, she rose, her beautifully manicured hands tapering softly like bunny ears on her hips. One long stiletto-shod foot pointed at him from the bottom of her jeans. The short cobalt-blue peaks of her gelled hair flashed in the morning sun.

"There is a girl at the bar who wants to dance," Anika said. "Let's give her a try."

Dr. Asad removed his trench coat and hung it up. The bartender had left the mail on his desk in two tidy piles: bills, letters. No matter that Anika was the head dancer, as well as his mistress and the mother of his young daughter, Allie; he would not let her think that he assigned importance to her impatience. He picked up the bills and shuffled through them, then the letters. One was from Beirut. On the return address was a name it took him a minute to place: Fahad Abdallah. He immediately knew what Fahad had written. He wants to come to the United States and needs a place to work. Can Dr. Asad help him, please? A thousand blessings on Dr. Asad's family and so forth. He put the letter under a paperweight, unopened.

A second letter was from Max. He was proud that his son could do what European-Americans could not be bothered to do—learn to speak Arabic, Farsi, Dari, and Pashto, making him invaluable to the American mission, although what specifically that mission was he had tried not to question too closely. It would get into troubling matters of race and blood and where you put your loyalty, all of which eventually led to the discussion of whether Western Civilization was on the wane. He put that letter into the breast pocket of his suit to savor later.

"What were you saying, my dear?"

Anika put both hands on his desk and leaned toward him. "There's a girl at the bar now. Why don't you try her out?"

"Don't we have a full lineup of local girls?"

Most strippers work a circuit because regular clients get bored. Dr. Asad kept only a few local girls on the payroll to fill in when one of the circuit girls failed to show up or for special Friday matinees for the gentlemen from St. Maron's assisted living facility.

"Janelle is quitting. She's pregnant and wants to keep it."

"We were overstaffed anyway."

Anika hugged herself as if gathering her courage. "I want to try something else, Edward. I'm too old to dance, and I don't want Allie to think it's okay to do what I do."

Dr. Asad laughed. "You're only thirty-four! And you are the

reason most of the men come in." He took her hands. "You would bankrupt me?"

"Just look at her. I think she could fill in for me. She's smart and has some personality."

"What makes you think my clients want to see personality? For that, they have wives."

He brushed past her and walked into the barroom, dark despite the recessed lights in the black ceiling. He walked slowly toward the bar, where Fritz, the bartender, pointed his chin in the direction of a woman sitting there. The would-be stripper turned and smiled. He immediately sized her up. She was ordinary: a girl who knew nothing of life except that she was prey and the only way to keep her value was to stay uncaptured. Dr. Asad saw girls like this every day, and while they were charming, he easily forgot which smile belonged to which girl.

"Do you have any marks?" he asked brusquely.

"You mean what? Tattoos?"

"Or scars."

She laughed nervously. "You want me to take off my clothes?"

"Not now. I just want to know."

She shook her head.

"I see lots of girls who are normal weight, and then after a month they blow up like whales or shrink into toothpicks."

"I was her high school English teacher," Fritz said, as if that qualified him as an expert on eating disorders.

Dr. Asad had hired Fritz Toner a year ago when he was fired by the Warrenside School District for drinking Jameson from a flask at a class outing. Dr. Asad and Fritz had occasionally talked about literature, but Fritz made a point of pedantically correcting Dr. Asad's English until Dr. Asad finally ended their conversations. There was nothing wrong with his English. Fritz corrected him because he was embarrassed to be the hireling of an Arab man.

"He was my English teacher," the girl verified.

The problem with local girls was that the men in their lives assumed responsibility for them after they had a following in Lucky Lady, after they were profitable. Then these men would demand a cut of the profits or threaten to close the Lady down on morals charges. The usual economics of extortion.

Dr. Asad raised his hand to change the conversation. "Can you dance?"

"Anika says you let the girls keep all their tips."

"It is different with each dancer," he answered, annoyed that Anika would presume to tell a dancer what he would pay her.

"If you want me to take off my clothes right now, I will."

Dr. Asad could see the woman's breasts through her too-tight T-shirt. She had implants. He had made love to a pair of implants once, and it was like touching water balloons. His criterion for choosing dancers was simple: If he desired them, so would his clients. That's what kept them coming back.

"My girls are artists. They don't just strip. They have a theme, and they dance to that theme. Yes, certainly, at the end you've removed all your clothes, but in the middle is the art. You have to take me on a journey in my imagination. Like Salome."

"Salome?"

Dr. Asad took the letter from Max from his jacket pocket and read the return address: 501st Support and Supply Company, FPO New York. It had been mailed three weeks ago. He wanted to tear it open and read it right now. What did it mean that he found the prospect of reading a letter from his son more delicious than watching a woman remove her clothes?

"What do you mean, *Salome*, Dr. Asad?"

"Anika will help you," he said.

Houda was on the phone at his desk when Dr. Asad returned to his office. She looked out the window, not acknowledging her father, a trick she'd learned from him. Finally, she hung up.

"You have a new dancer?" she asked.

"Yes."

When she was angry, Houda made him feel like he was the child, and he was in awe of her air of authority.

"Can she dance?"

"I haven't seen her dance."

"You hire a dancer and you haven't seen her dance?"

"Anika said she will be good."

"Anika!" Houda stood up from behind the desk. "She knows nothing about business. She knows nothing about what puts meat in the seats."

"Houda! Don't talk like that! That's shameful."

"Where do you think you are, Father? This is not Beirut. Come down from your ivory tower. There is no such thing as shameful."

She put her hands over her face. She was ashamed of her Arab nose, which turned red when she was angry. Dr. Asad thought it was magnificent, as hooked and fierce as a hawk's. They argued constantly because she wanted to get an operation to change it. She had already painted blond streaks through her jet-black hair. She wore pants, like a man. She even carried a Beretta in her pocketbook when she went to the bank to make the Monday deposit. You are in limbo, her father argued, neither of the East nor of the West. She replied that it was he who didn't know who he was.

But if Dr. Asad was certain of one thing, it was *where* he was, the place in time he occupied. He tried to explain it to her, but she was a product of American schooling, which preached the fairy tale that all are equal.

"You and I are part of a people," he told her, "who have lost the time and place that we were given and have become pirates. Our gods and ancestors have deserted us, and we must trick lesser gods into protecting us."

Dr. Asad had a husband picked out for Houda from the old country, as he had a wife already chosen for Max, but when he surprised her one day after she came home from college on vacation—the young man and his people were drinking tea with the Asads—she ran out of the house and moved in with her college roommate, refusing to come back until he'd sent her betrothed and his family away.

"You will see her dance this afternoon," he told Houda now. "She is dancing in the matinee."

"What if I don't like her?"

"Then, my rose, you can fire her."

"Fine."

They talked about the preparations for Max's wedding, which was to happen next week. Joseph Aloub and his family were already here with their Nadira, who had been chosen for her great beauty. Dr. Asad was a practical man and saw that his family needed an infusion of beauty. Brains they had. Wealth they had. Beautiful grandchildren would be welcome.

"If it continues to rain, we'll have to put up a tent," Houda was saying, and Dr. Asad nodded assent. Houda would figure out what to do. It was her job to deal with picayune details.

Dr. Asad sat down at his desk and looked over an application for residency for a new couple: the Livingstons. A Jewish couple. That Jews came to him for a place to live convinced him that

America was ultimately a land of people who took advantage of the moment without apology. Pirates.

A young white man, Chris Schaeffer, slipped into the office and sat down softly on the settee by the office door, which he pushed shut with his foot. He was wearing an oversized Allen Iverson basketball jersey that hung to his knees. His hairless white arms were covered in tattooed Chinese cipher. Black baggy pants fell down his ass like a dimwitted child's, but he was not a child. He was a hard-nosed businessman, a white street samurai, a new breed doing the old business of protection.

"Any trouble at the club last night, Edward?" he asked.

"Of course not, Chris," Dr. Asad said, going to the safe and pulling out an envelope.

"We are keeping a lookout for terrorists," Chris said. "It would be a terrible thing for one of those suicide bombers to slip in."

Although Dr. Asad knew it was absurd to think that a suicide bomber would waste his juice on Warrenside, Pennsylvania, he knew better than to argue the fine points of protection with a professional who would shut Dr. Asad down if he declined to pay for his services. How would it look if the biggest Arab-American businessman in Warrenside refused to pay protection money? It would look as if he had nothing to fear and was in cahoots with terrorists. He took a hundred-dollar bill from his wallet and held it out to Chris, who nodded as Dr. Asad slipped it into the envelope.

Local businessmen had been spooked by Warrenside's turn of fortune. They could not see opportunities in the ruins. But to him, the collapse of an industry was inconsequential compared to the cataclysm he had suffered in Beirut. Attaching sentiment to that collapse was what paralyzed Warrenside and made its established wealth irrelevant. It was true that some of the old families thought he was a parvenu and resisted his increasing importance in the city, but that kind of acceptance took time. It would come, inevitably, if not in his lifetime then in Max and Nadira's, whose children would think they founded Warrenside. He knew the danger inherent in thinking yourself something other than what you are, but hadn't he come very far in this country and on its terms?

The phone rang. It was Anika.

"Houda says we can hire her," Anika said.

"Then hire her," Dr. Asad said.

"I'm going to train her to do the schedule," Anika said.

It was an act of defiance. Dr. Asad had seen her talking to an off-duty policeman when he came in early one day, and he could tell by their postures that their conversation was not about business. He was losing his hold on her. "Let's go out tonight instead of eating in," he said. Usually he had the kitchen staff bring food to Anika's apartment above the club. "There's a new restaurant in Whitehall that I've been very anxious to try."

"Really?"

"Yes. I'm ready for something a little different," Dr. Asad said.

There was a pause. "What do you mean, *different?*"

"Food. I'm ready for some new cuisine."

He heard her nervous laughter. Anika might think about leaving, but she would never go. She was, after all, thirty-four and too old to find the kind of support she was accustomed to from him. A policeman? What kind of life could he give her and her child? And even if Anika left, there was always another dancer to take her place. Things always worked out for him. Was he not a lucky man?

FOUR

WIND STORM

The young woman, small with straight blond hair, was early for her ten o'clock appointment but knocked loudly anyway. When Wind Storm sleepily answered the door, the blonde waved her gift certificate like an admission ticket.

"I'm early, I know," the young woman said. "I'm just so excited."

Wind motioned that she would be out, then checked her calendar to see who was scheduled. Wind always had a hard time telling one petite blonde from another. This one was named Krista. Or Kirstin. Or Kristin. Names that had nothing to do with physical life; names chosen from the shadow life on television. Silly names were a squandered opportunity. You are what you are called. If you are Singing Bird or Dancing Bear, the Spirits know what you are and send the animal guides to help you. Every time someone says your name, the Spirits hear and take notice. Who will help a Krista? That name goes into the air like a missile fired aimlessly.

These small-blondes-with-names-from-television made up her clientele. They gave one another presents of consultations at sixty dollars an hour with Wind, an Indian shaman, to improve their love lives. Women in Warrenside were free to find their own husbands, naturally, but without the mandates of family or strict social forms to bolster them, and—more important—without the help of the Spirits, these women were like huntresses without spears. They might spot the occasional buffalo, but they were powerless to bring it down. By the time they were twenty-six, these Kristas were exhausted from futile expeditions at overhunted watering holes, their wombs empty; then they paid Wind a visit.

The word in Warrenside was that Wind Storm was beautiful but weird, and when she came into town people laughed at her—mostly the young blondes who were her own age, the ones who eventually found their way to her.

"Clasp the stone like this," Wind said, closing Krista's hand around a piece of granite embedded with bits of garnet, the stone that attracts people to you and makes them see the best in you. "And chant with me."

Krista knelt on the ground, closed her eyes, and clenched her garnets. Wind had a low voice, and her chant sounded like the distant rumbling before a great storm. It was a gift, her father had told her. Proof of her shamanistic calling. Krista swooned and Wind held her up to keep her from falling. As she chanted, Wind sprinkled red rose petals on the small fire in a pot in front of them. Red roses for romantic love, petals from Wind's own bushes, which she had planted when she saw the romance that young women assigned to roses. She wasn't immune either. The intoxicatingly sweet smell circled the air, and Krista joined in the chanting and dancing in a trance. Wind drummed and looked at her watch. Fifty minutes. She wound down the drumming, and finally Krista heard the silence and opened her eyes.

"Oh!"

"How do you feel?" Wind asked.

Krista licked the sweat off her upper lip, considering. "I feel great!"

"Did you have a vision?"

"Yes! Yes, I did."

Wind nodded, a little bored, until Krista told her a bear was dancing in her dream.

"A *bear?*"

"Is that bad?" Krista asked.

"A bear in your dreams is your strong mother instinct. You will be a mama soon if you want," Wind said. It wasn't the first time a client had dreamed of a bear, of becoming a mother. Usually it turned out she was pregnant already, because dreams induced by a shaman don't predict, they tell what already is. But Wind didn't want to be the one to break the news.

"I do! I do want!" Krista said. She clapped her hands like a child.

"You have to think about that bear," Wind said. "You have to let the bear guide you to the man who will make you a mama. Let the bear tell you if he is the one."

"I will! Thank you, thank you, thank you!" She hopped on one foot, an impromptu jig, and turned around. She gave Wind the gift certificate that her friends had given her for her twenty-fifth birthday. She looked at Wind shyly, holding out the stone with the garnets. "Where can I get a stone like this?"

"Twenty-five dollars."

Krista pulled out a credit card, and Wind shook her head. "Cash." She should have charged fifty. She needed the money. But what the hell, twenty-five dollars wasn't going to make a difference. She needed twenty thousand.

Six feet tall, with astounding physical attributes—blond hair and finely etched features from her Swedish mother, skin the color of an autumn leaf from her Lenape father—Wind Storm was the locus of attention everywhere she went. It was embarrassing when she was a little girl, but somewhere after her twentieth birthday she began to see that possessing striking looks was an enormous advantage. She planned to use that advantage today when she picketed the party at the Armory celebrating the return of the local National Guard unit.

She carried three pieces of poster board out of one of the shacks that littered her property and dropped them on the ground next to a lineup of poster paints, then pulled a brush from a leg pocket in her carpenter pants, pursed her lips to lick the tip of the thick brush, and plunged it into the open jar of blue paint. She frowned for a minute as she thought how to succinctly phrase the idea she wanted to convey, which was that white people were doing the same thing in Afghanistan that they had done in the Americas: imposing a European way of life on a culture that clearly didn't want or need it. She laid the brush tip on the cardboard and wrote: COLUMBUS GOES BACK TO EUROPE AND CLAIMS THAT HE FOUND A NEW WORLD. THIS WORLD WAS NOT "LOST." *Pablo Abeita (Isleta)*. She bit her lip and tore up the piece of cardboard. No one ever heard of Pablo Abeita or knew what an Isleta was. She dunked her brush and began again: 3,000,000 AFGHANI REFUGEES. She smiled. Another one: THE GREAT SPIRIT SAYS YOU CANNOT SELL OR BUY LAND BECAUSE LAND BELONGS TO EV-ERYONE. Another one, in case someone wanted to join her: YAN-QUI GO HOME! She liked the foreign flavor of the spelling. She waved and blew on the posters until they dried; then she turned them over and stapled smooth wooden sticks to the back of each, examined them, and finally picked up 3,000,000 AFGHANI REFUGEES. Europeans couldn't argue with numbers and statistics. It was the only way to reach them. She had been picketing every federal event in Warrenside with her father since she was four. It seemed especially important to continue now that he was dead.

Jimmy Bird Storm had died three months ago and now—besides being stuck with his dream of being the Last of the Lenape, the marker on Lenape land so the ancestors could find their way home—she was stuck with all his junk. Jimmy had been a salvage man, demolishing old barns, cabins, farmhouses, inns, and factories in the surrounding countryside; taking them apart peg by peg, nail by nail, and reselling every antique peg, nail, floorboard, and beam to developers who bought them for the cachet, the "authenticity" they thought this stuff gave to their flakeboard mansions. But what is authentic? Wind always wondered. Is it authentic to try to disguise a flakeboard mansion? It's the opposite of authentic. The labor intensity of his work plus the cost of hauling and storage ensured that, despite the high prices vintage building materials commanded, he barely broke even in this venture. If he didn't get paid in advance, he sometimes didn't get paid at all.

After the structure was down, Jimmy Bird would offer the landowner his services under the auspices of Honest Injun Real Estate, of which he was sole proprietor, broker, and agent, and for which Wind constantly belittled him. "Real estate?" she had yelled at him. "You're an Indian! Where did you get such a stupid idea?" But her father said real estate was the only game an Indian could win. And he was determined to hold on to this piece of property that he had rented for years and then was finally able to buy with the U.S. government reparation settlement in 2002 for being Native American. "Hush money," Wind called it, "so you don't go on the warpath." Jimmy had told Wind that the property in Warrenside was the one thing he could bequeath to her and that the thirty riverfront acres behind their house made their property more valuable because it could be subdivided into building lots, but it wasn't until he died and she had the property appraised by a *real* real estate agent that she found out more than half of these acres were so crowded with unsold salvage it would probably cost at least twenty grand just to clean them up, an unfortunately large amount because she had a citation in her pocket from the city to do just that: clean it up. It was a safety hazard. When she asked to whom it was a hazard, seeing how she was the only one who lived there, the clerk told her it was a regulation that was enforced only when someone complained.

And someone *had* complained. You didn't have to be a genius to figure out who, she thought. Dr. Edward Asad had offered to buy the property as soon as her father died. He wanted to build houses for his children on it and had been polite when she declined, so she didn't think it was him. But the Lenape Country Club wanted to expand its golf course. She had already picked up more than one thousand golf balls that had found their way onto her property in the months since Jimmy died, getting stuck in pipes, winking out of mudholes after a rain. They looked like lost birds' eggs. Barbara Warren, the chairwoman of the country club building committee, had sent her a certified letter pleading the case for another nine holes, which Wind threw away. She was not going to allow those stupid white bitches from the country club to take her property. So they could *golf*? The enormity of the insult enraged her.

Plus, although she wanted to leave, she had promised Jimmy she wouldn't sell. She was the last of the Lenape in Warrenside, and it was her obligation, he told her on his deathbed, to stand strong and protect the earth, their mother. When the spirits of her people tried to find their way home, she would be their beacon. If she weren't there, they would become lost and confused amid people wearing plaid pants and carrying iron sticks to hit lost bird eggs. They would wander forever.

She tried not to think about the life she had imagined for herself and concentrated on where she was going to get twenty thousand dollars. Shamans measured wealth in spiritual currency. Her shaman business, though lively, was not enough to ever make her rich. To get twenty thousand United States of America dollars, she would have to sell the place. Well, that wasn't going to happen. She would find a way to get rid of the junk.

Part of the junk was a collection of ten outhouses, which reminded her of dollhouses. One had a roof like a Swiss Guard shack; another looked like a truncated corncrib. They were all rigged with stovepipes to ventilate her father's marijuana smoke. Jimmy Bird had been stoned every day for thirty-seven years, since the night he was on guard duty in Vietnam and a black sergeant gave him a bone of Thai. It was like the sky opened up, he said, and suddenly there were "angels and shit. I was just an innocent Indian," he said, "that got corrupted."

Her father's favorite was a 1920s outhouse lined with black-and-white photos of naked women: tame by current standards, terrifically outrageous in 1920, which was coincidentally the year the Lenape in Warrenside were officially relocated to Oklahoma. For a long time, her mother stored the chest of drawers that her family had brought over from Sweden in this outhouse, but now the chest was gone and Wind had no idea what had happened to it. Or to her mother, for that matter, who had taken off when Wind was ten.

Wind sat down in the grass, brown and grub-eaten, and unclipped the little drum attached to her waist by a leather thong. She had begun to thrum softly with her thumbs when an electric golf cart pulled up in the driveway. On the side of the cart was the Lenape Country Club logo—a silhouette of a Sioux, nothing whatsoever to do with the Lenape, proving the contempt that Europeans had for Natives.

Wind waited until the man had climbed out of the cart and was stepping over old shutters before she shouted, "You're trespassing!"

"Miss Storm?" he asked, then tripped on an old copper gutter as he came closer. "Ouch! Hey, you ought to move some of this junk."

"Trespass at your own risk," Wind said.

"I have this." He waved an envelope at her.

"Put it down. And get out of here."

He looked around the piles of junk. "Where?"

"Anywhere. I don't care. On the ground."

"It's important."

"I'm sure it is."

"I'm supposed to hand-deliver it."

"From your hand to my outhouse."

"I'm supposed to *hand* it to *you*."

"Tell them you did."

"I can't *lie*."

She snorted. He would be the first white person who couldn't. "Give it here." She watched him stumble some more and then stood up to accept the letter he handed her. She tucked the letter into a pocket and shooed him away. "What are you looking at?" she asked, when he didn't budge.

"You are the most beautiful woman I have ever seen. You're incredible! You look like that actress, Charlize Theron."

The green T-shirt that the young man wore had the hated Sioux logo over his heart and under it his name, CANTWELL. She smiled despite herself, then frowned. It was probably a trick to soften her up. "What are you, the Warrens' flunky?"

"I'm the golf pro."

"Get out of here."

"Can I see you again? No, wait, are you married? I hate it when guys ask married women out."

Wind pulled out the letter and began to read. Barbara Warren now wanted her to give back all the golf balls that had found their way onto her property or she was going to have her people come in and get them. She balled up the letter and threw it at Cantwell. "Is she insane? What's the matter with that woman?"

"Mrs. Warren says—"

"Well, you tell her she can have the golf balls back for twenty thousand dollars. And get out of here before I call the police," Wind said. "I'm going to close my eyes and count to ten, and when I open them you'd better not be here. One . . ."

When she opened her eyes, Cantwell was gone. Wind felt disappointed, but it was just as well. She couldn't consort with the enemy.

She pulled some fresh sage and sweet grass from her hip pocket and waved it in front of her nose to induce a trance.

She fell back on the ground and had a vision of herself laughing and embracing the land with a crowd behind her, including her ancestors, waving their support. Then it started to rain and the people in the crowd cheered even louder, because there had been a drought and the corn was stunted, but now the cornstalks began to grow so large that they were like ladders you could climb on, up into the sky, which was a good thing because soon the land was flooding and people were clambering up the cornstalks to escape the waters that raged below. But she couldn't get a grip on a stalk. She kept slipping into the swirling water until a giant blue heron, who had been visiting her dreams since her father died, flew toward her and swooped down.

"Get on!" he commanded.

Together they flew off, Wind clutching the sides of the bird. She lifted her head and let the rain sting her face. "What should I do?" Wind screamed into the wind. "I can't get that kind of money."

"You must figure out what to do," Big Blue answered.

"I *know* I must figure out what to do! I just don't know *what* to do," Wind said. "That's why I'm asking *you*."

"Land is very important to human beings. And this is your land."

Wind knew he was right, but in fact the land wasn't as important to her as it was to her father and her grandfather and all the people who came before her. She was the last of the Lenape and, according to her father, was obligated to stay to light the way home for her people. So where were they? When she stood on the land, she didn't feel a connection with her people. Her mother's Swedish blood running through her veins made her impervious to the land of her ancestors.

"And now it's flooding," Wind said, wailing, looking down from the bird's back to the rising waters. "It's worthless land."

"You wanted this flood," he said. "You made it happen. So find out why you wanted it."

"Hey, this isn't *my* flood," Wind said.

Big Blue dove toward the Catawissa. The fierce water jumping the banks roared like the traffic on the turnpike. She didn't know what she could do with a raging river. It didn't solve her problem, it compounded it.

"You dreamed it," Big Blue said. "It must be yours."

"Look, don't try to psychoanalyze me, just tell me what to do."

The rain was coming down in sheets, but the bird touched down on the water and shrugged Wind off his back. Surprisingly, she found she could walk in it without getting pulled under. Big Blue took off as if he were in a huge hurry, as usual. She wanted to cry after him to take her with him. She looked forward to his visits, even though his advice stank. She'd been unspeakably lonely since her father died.

"Hey, don't worry! I'm okay!" she shouted to Big Blue's retreating back.

She felt the rain pounding on her face, and her long braids were soaked. It was raining so hard now, she opened her eyes and shook herself out of her trance. She was lying in a pool of water and she had to sit up to see without the rain blinding her. She blinked. In front of her the creek had leaped over the bank, the water approaching her like a sheet of fluid pearly glass. It was a real flood. She got up and grabbed her placards. It was two o'clock. The 501st would be home at six.

Here's something I can do: In a fast-breaking situation, time slows down and it's as if I can predict what's going to happen next. I was a wide receiver in high school. I could see plays unfolding in slow motion, so I could just step into an empty spot and the ball would be there. When I'm fishing, it's most intense. I feel the fish nip at the line and jerk away, then I can literally feel vibrations up the line and down the rod telling me which way the fish is going to dart next and I can counter the move. Sometimes, you have to know when to let the fish run and tire itself out. People are impatient, though, and can't stand doing nothing. They don't realize that doing nothing is sometimes the most aggressive thing you can do. Most fish catch themselves in the end, if you let them. I had won ten fishing awards in Pennsylvania by the time I was eighteen; I stopped competing a couple of years ago when there was nothing else to win. The fish moves, I counter. It's actually easy, although I have found it's not something you can teach someone else to do. Either you feel the motion or you don't. Either you can act on what you're feeling or you can't.

I sat with Kat until we arrived in Ramstein, where we changed planes, and after we took off she said she wanted to stretch her legs, which she did dramatically, and walked down the aisle, and soon I saw her leaning over Max Asad, then sitting next to him, her head close to his. They weren't laughing but talking seriously. There should be no secrets between fiancés, so I figured I would find out later what the big discussion was about. My radar was out and probably I should have listened to it, but I didn't. I thought that now that Kat and I were getting married, things would settle down and we would be like any other married couple. I could hardly wait for the normalcy of that. I didn't know then that nobody is normal.

I fell asleep for a couple of hours, and when I woke up, Jenna Magee, that royal pain in the ass, was sitting next to me. "You look lonely," she said.

"Not," I said, forcing my eyes open. "I'm not." Jenna and I had gone to bed *once* in Afghanistan and now I couldn't shake her. I couldn't be out-and-out rude to her because I was worried she would tell Kat. Even though technically Kat and I were broken up at the time, women are jealous. "I'm okay," I said. "You got plans when you settle in?"

"I got plans," she said.

"My boss at Radio Shack is always looking for people," I said. "I could say something to him."

"I thought you were quitting Radio Shack."

"I did."

She sighed. "So then why would I want to work there?"

"I thought you needed a job."

"I can take care of myself, Duck."

Here's the thing about Jenna: everyone hates her because of Barzai Marwat getting hanged, and that was a bad situation, no question about it. But Jenna didn't know they were going to hang him. She couldn't have seen that coming. What was she going to do? Go around rending her garments and beating her breast? We didn't know what complete and utter freaks the Afghanis were. Killing someone for touching a woman? I can't believe it even now. But the truth is, no one really liked Jenna before she got Barzai hanged either, so it was just a big convenient excuse. She couldn't stop talking about Jesus, which was really annoying, no question about it. But I think she couldn't stop talking about Jesus because she was scared of *not* talking about Jesus, if you know what I mean. Well, here's what I mean: Jenna was an *animal* in the sack. Really, she was the best lay I ever had, and we did it as often as we could find a place to do it, not just once. I think she was scared of where unleashing all that passion would take her. All that Jesus talk reined her in. It shocked the hell out of me the first time she took her clothes off because she had the most unusual tattoo, which covered most of her body: a beautiful green snake winding up her back like a one-sided caduceus, its head creeping over her left shoulder, its forked tongue flicking her collarbone. It was gorgeous, emerald. A tree threaded around the snake with fairy-tale creatures living in its branches, who eventually started lives of their own on her rib cage, down her hips, and over her beautiful ass.

Fucking Jenna was like fucking the Garden of Eden. She had to have lived with whoever did that to her, but when I asked her about him she just laughed and said, "I'm really Persephone, didn't you know?" When I told her I didn't know who Persephone was, she just said, "Ask Kat Warren. I'm sure she knows. Didn't she go to college?" And when Kat and I got back together after one of our many breaks, I did ask her, trying to be nonchalant, but she narrowed her eyes, trying to figure out why I would ask such a weird off-the-wall question, assuming correctly that some woman had given me the name Persephone to pass around like a piece in a giant jigsaw puzzle that would lead to incriminating evidence that I had been unfaithful, even though, as I said, Kat and I had broken up. Local women were completely off-limits and there were only five military women in Kandahar at that time—three of whom were lesbians—so by process of elimination, Kat had to know it was Jenna. But she thought Jenna was so beneath her, she couldn't imagine in a million years that we had had sex. Women always think that men won't have sex with women who are beneath them. They are always wrong.

"In case I don't see you, good luck," I told Jenna.

"What do you mean, in case you don't see me?" Jenna asked. "Of course you'll see me."

I kept an eye on Kat and Max on the ride from Ramstein and by the time we landed at McGuire, Kat was touching Max for emphasis, having a good old time. Well, men like Kat and Kat likes men. That's part of her appeal.

At McGuire, we were loaded into buses and taken to Fort Dix, where all forward momentum stopped suddenly on the rumor that we weren't going to be able to out-process. They told us we were shipping out again, this time to Iraq.

They said we wouldn't even have a chance to go home. Everyone was *immediately* on their cell phones, calling to complain and asking their families to call our congressmen to see what was going on and wasn't it against the law to keep us on active duty? They couldn't activate our unit again, could they? Well, actually, it turns out they could. It seems as long as we were in uniform, we were prisoners or something.

Nobody was happy. The officers bunked in a hotel nearby and we enlisted just hunkered down and played cards to kill time. I was happy on one level, because once we left Fort Dix I would probably never see Max again and I felt like we had unfinished business. But it was pretty hard to finish our business with Duck plastered to my side.

The first two days, Max kept away from everyone, but on the third evening, when we were all in the mess hall after dinner— Camacho, Reuber, and Duck playing cards at one table, Jenna and

I at another, half reading books we had brought with us and half watching the game just in case something exciting happened— Max strolled in, poured himself a cup of coffee, sat down at an empty table, and then pulled a miniature backgammon set out of his fatigues' pants pocket.

"Anyone?" he asked, barely looking up while he set up the orange and green jade pieces.

The 501st was a poker crowd, but a few of the macho guys knew the rudiments of the game and came up to look at the board.

Camacho sat down first. "Whaddaya got?"

Max laughed at him. "I've seen you play, Camacho," he said. "You can't beat me. Keep your money."

After a lot of brow-furrowing and posturing, Camacho said he'd pass until he had time to practice. "Am I supposed to just give this *maricón* my money?" he said to the crowd of spectators. "Next time, buddy."

Max looked up at the soldiers crowding around the table. "Anyone want to play for five bucks a point?"

"We don't get paid till next week," someone said.

"I'll take your chits," Max said.

When no one stepped up, Max laughed. One by one, the watchers slipped out of the chow hall. He turned around to Duck, who'd been hovering at his shoulder. "You up for a game?" he asked.

"Nah, not tonight," Duck said.

I went over to Max's table and sat down across from him. "Why don't you show me what all the excitement is about?"

"Do you play?" Max asked, looking as if something was enormously entertaining.

"Not backgammon."

Max showed me the basics while Duck straddled a chair and, tapping his foot, looked on. We rolled the dice and moved the counters from point to point. Jenna had put her Bible down and come over to see what was going on.

"It's all just luck, really, isn't it?" I said, putting the dice in a cup and shaking them onto the board.

"If it were all just luck, it wouldn't be interesting," Max said. "What's interesting about chance? Even a moron wins the long straw now and then. The doubling cube speeds things up and adds another dimension of strategy." He put the rounded-off cube on the board and doubled the stakes.

I was losing easily, forging ahead on the board while Max picked off my pieces.

"You have to think strategically," he said. "In backgammon, when you're behind, the aggressive thing is to hold your position. But now is the moment in the game to make your move." He clamped his hand over mine and looked directly into my eyes. "Do you understand?"

"This is so boring," Duck said. He got up suddenly and knocked over the chair.

"I think it's *really* interesting," Jenna said.

"Come on, Kat," Duck said. "Let's take a walk or something."

I left with Duck, but the next evening, when Max opened his board and asked for takers, I was across from him immediately. So were Camacho and Reuber. Camacho waved a dog-eared copy of *Backgammon for Blood* at Max. He was wired. "I got this," he said to Max's impassive face. "Ever hear of it?"

Camacho had also brought along a fifth of bourbon and two glasses.

"I hope our drinking don't offend you," Camacho said to Max. He pushed a glass to Reuber and filled it with bourbon. "Because we ain't gonna stop. Are we, Reuber?"

"As I've told you before, Camacho, I am a Maronite Catholic, not a Muslim," Max said. "Drink up, kids."

Camacho lit a cigar and took a deep drink of bourbon, staring at Max. He probably thought it made him look tough, but it also bought him some time while he looked for the insult in Max's tone, because he felt it even if he couldn't identify it. "You're a Paki, ain't ya?"

"I'm an American," Max said.

"Not where I come from. Where I come from, you're a *Paki*."

"Shut the fuck up, Camacho," Reuber said, "and let's get this thing going." He was nervously counting a roll of bills under the table.

"I bet you don't have to go to Iraq with the rest of us," Camacho said. "I bet your old man will get you out of it."

Camacho was a hothead. He might have been a good artist if he had had a little training—he tattooed almost everyone in the unit and the results were pretty stunning. And he could fix anything with an engine. The only reason he wasn't running the motor pool was because he couldn't stop fighting the invisible unknowable asshole who'd dealt him such a lousy hand in life. And because he couldn't see his enemy, he fought everyone, figuring he would eventually nail the right guy. He particularly hated white people who were always trying to help him, the implication being that the life he had wasn't good enough—even though that's exactly what he thought, too.

Max beat Camacho pretty quickly, and when he laughed and told Camacho to keep his money, Camacho swept the backgammon pieces off the board. "Let's play a real man's game, *shall we?*" Camacho said. "Not this sissy shit."

Max smiled. "Name it."

"Old-fashioned. Five draw, three of a kind to win. Three raises. Buck ante." Camacho slammed a deck of cards on the table and threw a single into the center of the table. Reuber and a couple of others followed.

Max won five straight hands and swept in all their money. I'd given up my seat and was standing in the back of the group that had gathered to watch. Max winked at me. A few guys turned to see who the wink was meant for, and I felt what it was like to be the object of suspicion and hatred. Then I felt a tug on my sleeve.

"Let's get out of here before it gets ugly," Duck said.

I shook him off.

"Suit yourself."

Camacho stood up and swept Max's winnings off the table. "You want to fight?" he asked Max. "Let's fight now."

"I thought we were playing cards," Max said. "You called the game." He folded his backgammon board, picked up his money from the floor, and calmly walked toward me.

It's kind of dramatic to say I felt like this was the moment where everything changed, but I knew if I let Max lead me away there was no return. I would be turning my back on everything familiar, on everything I *was*. But what was so great about the old me? I yearned for the excitement of something new. And—it's a funny thing to remember—I thought then that if I went back to my old life with my mother in her mausoleum no one would ever see me. I would be buried alive trying to find meaning in old customs and memories whose physical touchstones had vanished before I was even born.

Max held out his hand for me, and I took it and we walked out of the mess hall with Camacho yelling in the background. "You think this is over? This isn't over, *maricón*. I tell you when it's over."

I never thought much about Max Asad before Fort Dix. I just didn't like him. He acted like everything was one big fucking joke: the army, Warrenside, things I took pretty fucking seriously. But when I saw that Kat was into him, I wanted to check him out. To be able to warn her about him, is what I told myself. After the backgammon game, where I asked her to leave with me and she refused, graffiti immediately appeared about him in red marker on the side of the chow hall: NO ARABS IN THE ARMY. ASAD = ENEMY. That should have been enough to wise her up, but apparently it wasn't. She was with him all the time, ready to throw away all we'd built together on this infatuation.

But I cornered him once, when he came into the barracks to shower and was changing into clean desert fatigues.

"How about teaching *me* backgammon," I asked him.

"Why the sudden interest?" He seemed both amused and annoyed.

"I always like to learn new things."

He checked his cell phone and I knew Kat was waiting for him, but he probably thought it was politic to keep me happy. He set up the board and explained the rules hurriedly. "Got it?"

"Yeah, I got it."

I was concentrating hard on the rules and trying to invent a strategy to get my counters around the board when Max said, "Lighten up, man. It's only a game."

My mom was always saying that to be responsible you had to consider the long-term effects of every action because "their consequences ripple through generations." She was referring, of course, to my dad's suicide, which we only discussed in code, though it sat like an improvised explosive device in the middle of our living room. But here's what I took from that disaster: Actions have consequences, and in real life you never get a chance to set up the board and start again. "Everything is a game to you," I said to Max. "Isn't it?"

"I guess it is. I never thought about it. But you're right."

"You think life is a game, too?"

He laughed. "Especially life."

"You can say that, you're rich," I said. "Of course it's a game to you. If things don't work out, you just reshuffle the deck and get out more chips."

"Okay. I started out with more chips. So what?"

I had switched from college prep to vo-tech my junior year in high school and worked nights at Radio Shack to help out my mom, who had struggled financially ever since Dad died. I was still helping her out. I could never seem to get a leg up. "I find that a little insulting."

"Look," Max said. "Why do you think I joined the army? I didn't have to. I have a degree from Princeton and my life has been laid out before me. Why do you think I volunteered for this crap?"

"Beats me," I said.

"I did it for my father." Max had graduated from Princeton right before 9/11, and afterward he'd made the case to his father that his going into the service when the country was at war in the Middle East would prove that although their family originated in Lebanon, "the Asads are as American"—he laughed— "as the Wolinskys," which made me cringe. He'd joined the Guard to placate his mother, who thought it would keep him at home. "No one accepts us in Warrenside," he said, "even though my father has given so much to the city."

"What do you mean, your father's given so much to Warrenside? Your father's gotten *rich* in Warrenside," I said.

"He was already rich. Are you saying that what's good for my family can't be good for Warrenside?"

I rolled a double four and moved four pieces around the board.

"Slow down," Max said. "When you're behind, hold your position in the inner board. What I don't understand is, what is a guy like you still doing in Warrenside? Why don't you take off and start somewhere else?"

My options in Warrenside were limited by holding on to my father's cabinet shop in Ringside, a neighborhood now known for its drug trade. I'd been losing money there for years because my customers were afraid to come downtown, but I couldn't bring myself to close the workshop where Dad had shot himself. I told Max that.

"In some ways, you're lucky," Max said.

"I'm lucky my father killed himself?"

"I don't mean that. I mean I'd like to be relieved of my obligation to my father, that's all. I feel imprisoned in the life he's built for me."

"I don't understand you. Family. That's all we got in the end."

Max offered me the doubling cube and I declined. "Your father's built a prison for you, Duck. If you don't break out, you lose."

"It seems like you're pretty entrenched with your family. You got a wife all picked out for you. You can run some of your dad's businesses, I assume. Are you saying you're a loser because you're doing what they want?" I wanted Max to admit that he was only playing with Kat; he would marry the woman his father picked for him rather than step out on his own.

Max frowned. "Families are jails. Even if they're comfortable jails."

"Yeah, well, maybe that's what families are for," I said, irritated that he didn't admit what I knew he felt: that Kat was just a diversion. "Everyone has a fucking jailer. At least, with your own family, it's a jailer you know."

When Max won a couple of games and left the barracks, I flipped through the piles of books that were strewn across his bed, trying to see where Max got his astonishing facts about life. They were big books, full of fairy tales, and they did nothing to dispel my idea that if life was a game it was played on a field laced with unexploded mines.

The barracks were hot and I went outside to get some air, get something to eat at the chow hall, maybe find Jenna—what the hell—and the first thing I saw was Kat's name, squeezed under Asad's, in some new graffiti: AMERICA FOR AMERICANS.

So, suddenly I had it: passion. By the time we arrived in Fort Dix, the only question I had was where Max and I could be alone. The real world—his fiancée, Duck, his father, and my mother—existed on another plane of reality where I could script their reaction to our passion, and I wrote that they would be happy for us. I even imagined that the army would be thrilled to be the catalyst for a pair of unlikely lovers finding each other. Because once Max touched my face to move a piece of hair from my eyes, my body sprang alive like a seed in the desert that had been waiting for rain. Blooms and lushness and fertility. This happened on the runway at McGuire. My sharp edges softened to mesh with his. On the plane we talked, yes, but I can hardly remember what we said aloud. He quoted a lot of poetry—"What is any of us but a straw in a storm, buffeted by an irresistible hurricane?"—and told me his favorite poet, Rumi, wrote that, which was *so funny* because that's exactly how I felt: a straw in a storm, buffeted by an irresist-ible hurricane. *Exactly* like that.

In any event, I couldn't stop the inevitable even if I willed it. The force of my feeling was so insistent it couldn't be stopped by regard for the expectations of others. "My father will be hurt," Max said. Yeah, but what about Duck? *My mother?* "Whoever claims to have made a pact with destiny reveals himself a liar and a fool." Max told me Rumi wrote that too, and now I loved Rumi intensely and wanted to read everything he had ever writ-ten. I wanted to read everything that Max had ever read to know what thoughts had gone into making him what he was. A pact with destiny! Of course you couldn't make plans when love so big and self-absorbed could come along at a moment's notice and knock down everything around it. Still, my expansive mood wanted to include even Max's betrothed. If she would be hurt I would be devastated, I told myself. What about Duck? He still imagined we were going to get married. I would be hurting my best friend, my protector since I was six years old, the only reason I turned out even halfway normal. But my need for Max came on so strong—explosively, suddenly—that I just didn't *care*. Love isn't only blind, it turns out to be cruel.

At Fort Dix, while everyone else was playing cards and going online, Max and I sneaked away into an empty old wooden bar-racks. On the third floor there were twelve bare cots in a long bay, gleaming green linoleum, metal springs, and freshly painted sills, and soon we had our clothes off, deciding which of the twelve beds would be the lucky one, arguing as only lovers do about who was more beautiful, he or I, and in the middle of our discus-sion, I gave in to a need that seemed almost chemical, like I was a junkie who needed a fix, and when we were finished with that, when I thought I had never been so made love to, he looked at me sleepily, his long lashes creating shadows on his cheeks that made his eyes look like enormous pools of longing and love, and said, "*Habibi*, we have eleven more beds."

Afterward, in the mess hall, the food was awful and I laughed, remembering all the expensive dinners at fancy restaurants that would-be swains had taken me to; it seemed silly. I was relieved that Duck, usually right around the corner, was somewhere else. Jenna was in the chow hall, Bible open, chewing her nails, a cup of cold coffee in front of her as though she were in a real coffee shop and needed the cup as proof that she bought something and so could remain just a little while longer before they asked her to move on.

"They were looking for you," she said as I nodded and kept walking. She got up and followed me and whispered loudly, "I didn't tell them where you were."

Max was right behind me, so I didn't have to answer. She glared at Max and slunk back to her cold cup.

Somebody was writing ugly graffiti in red marker about Max and me on the outside of the barracks, the mess hall, the infirmary, and other buildings. In typical army logic, the base commander decided that since we were *named* in the graffiti, clearly Max and I were responsible for it and should clean it up. For the next ten days, while everyone else was playing computer games or gambling, we went to the supply shack and packed a dolly with paint remover, lacquer thinner, drop cloths, and rubber gloves. New Jersey is hot and humid in July, and we took our time, setting up shop beneath each damning assertion declaring Max a traitor. In a show of chivalry, Max quickly eradicated the ones that proclaimed me a slut; then we took our time stripping away his alleged sins. In retrospect, it seems like an odd way to get to know someone—under signs that judged us unpatriotic and illicit. In sadder moments—now—I see it was a portent. At the time, though, Max said he was glad to have something to do besides raking in everyone's poker losses, and I was happy to have a chance to be alone with him, seeing how that's all I wanted.

Max laughed at each piece of graffiti before he took a brush to it.

I asked him, "This doesn't scare you? That they hate you so much?"

"This isn't new, Kat. At least they've turned in their weapons."

He told me that sometimes before they went out on patrol, the Ops would draw straws—jokingly—to see who would off him in the mountains. They couldn't accept that a man with an Arab name who was fluent in Pashto, the language of their enemy, could be a real American. It would look like an accident if he turned up with a bullet between the eyes.

"I can't really blame them for that," Max told me. "They thought I would sell them out because I'm not like them, because I wouldn't join in their macho games." He said he knew he was playing a dangerous game when he joined a unit with orders to go to Afghanistan, because the war on terrorism was going badly.

At the start of Operation Enduring Freedom in the fall of 2001, a strike force of Special Ops, marines, and native militia had boxed Osama Bin Laden into caves in the Hindu Kush—in a nice touch of irony, the same caves that the CIA had built for him in the 1980s to hide from the Russians. But as they'd closed their fists on Bin Laden, our politicians and generals—incomprehensibly to the men in the field—had ordered the marines to pull out. No hearts-and-minds theatrics afterward could alter the fact that they'd allowed Bin Laden to slip away. The marines were ferried via helicopter back to the offshore battle fleet. The Ops returned to their barbed-wire compound and seethed. They were transferred to Kandahar to chill out, but the damage was done.

The Ops were an all-white boys' club, and their sense of betrayal brought to the surface their innate disdain for anyone darker than themselves. What simmered for two years as keep-to-yourselves racism found its focus with the arrival of the 501st in spring 2003. Max was Arab-American, but scratch the suffix and he was just an Arab. The perfect scapegoat.

Even though they didn't trust Max or his loyalties, they distrusted the leader of the fifteen-man Pashtun militia they were forced to patrol with—Batoor Khan—even more. Batoor Khan was twenty-four, the same age as Max at the time. Max described his trim black beard, calm jet eyes. All his front teeth were gold. Unlike the other Pashtuns in his militia, a mixed bag of poorly armed old and young who were ill at ease with Americans, he was taller than the tallest of the Ops and had an air of self-possession that infuriated them.

Batoor Khan was the son of a Pashtun warlord on the take who, like other chieftains supposedly allied with the Americans, got paid huge bucks to put fighters at their disposal. At fourteen, he'd run away to fight with Ahmad Shah Masood, the Lion of Panjshir, first against the Russians, then against his own people—bandit warlords vying to turn the homeland into their personal fiefdom—and now against the Taliban, whom he considered benighted. He yearned to see his country free of all foreigners and Luddites. He'd worshipped Shah Masood, who'd been assassinated by a pair of Bin Laden's human bombs on the eve of the American invasion. When he'd returned home, his father had put him in charge of his tribal militia to fight on the side of this latest army of occupation. Batoor Khan found it humiliating to be fighting for money, but his father claimed it was beneficial, and loyalty to family and tribe was foremost in his culture.

"I liked him, I respected him," Max told me, "and I sympathized with him and his compromised loyalty, more than I would admit to anyone but you. It's not that I feel loyalty to Lebanon. I don't, at all. I'm American. But I do feel loyalty to my family, and sometimes it's difficult to decide if loyalty to my family means disloyalty to my family's new country. I understand how the Japanese-Americans must have felt during World War II. If you hate the country where your family came from, you hate yourself. Unquestioned loyalty is the biggest offense, in my opinion."

"We locked them up," I said.

"Who?"

"The Japanese-Americans."

"So you did," he said. We had dragged our dolly to the mess hall, on the side of which was an indecipherable message. "At least this message you can't read."

"I don't think it's about us," I said.

We stripped it off anyway.

Naturally, Melanie Martin found us. "Omigod, somebody's actually doing something I can record. It doesn't look good if all the folks back home see is guys playing poker." She aimed her camera at us, clearly oblivious to the story behind our mission.

"Since when are you concerned about our image?" I asked her.

"Since I won the poker tournament this morning!" She pulled out a roll of bills. "I have a reputation as a hardworking journalist to maintain."

I had to admit my respect for her increased. Even Max smiled.

Before Melanie Martin became our embed, a petite middle-aged woman named Claire Pyc was assigned to us. She bunked with me and Jenna briefly, before demanding to be closer to the action. She was determined to learn Pashto and report from the trenches—her antique phrase—and she insisted on going on patrol with the Ops. I had forgotten about her until Max brought her up.

"She was a disaster," Max told me. "She knew nothing of the customs or history of Afghanistan. She thought she was there to bring civilization to the barbarians."

Viking, the Special Ops squadron leader—all the Ops had taken names from Norse mythology—let her tag along once, thinking, Max said, that she would get his unit some good PR back home that might bring some of the updated equipment they needed.

At five one morning, the eight Ops and Max, with Claire in tow, joined the Pashtun militia in the foothills outside base.

Batoor Khan raised his arm in greeting as usual. *"Wekickazz-today,"* he said, grinning. He spoke run-on pidgin slang in imitation of one of the Ops.

Viking nodded.

Batoor Khan frowned when he saw Claire standing next to Viking.

"Inshallah," she said, eager to establish her bona fides.

He didn't answer "God willing" as was customary, but said to Viking, "A woman?"

"A reporter," Viking said.

"She speaks Pashto?" Batoor asked Viking.

"I've been studying it," Claire said. She pulled a phrase book out of her backpack.

Batoor Khan inspected her face, considering what it meant, this intrusion of a woman into their war party; then he bowed slightly and said, *"Ustaa moor kay mandam."*

"Which means 'Fuck your mother,'" Max explained to me.

When Batoor Khan saw the blank expression on Claire's face, he continued. *"Daga me ra wazbaisha"*—"Suck my dick"—and folded his arms. His bodyguard, incredulous, stepped away and unshouldered his rifle.

Viking looked at Claire to answer.

"Khuday pa amaan"—"May God protect you"—Claire answered, using one of the phrases she'd mastered. Batoor Khan turned away and hacked as if dust were caught in his throat. His bodyguard reshouldered his rifle and laughed.

"Leave her alone," Max ordered in Pashto.

"What did the *hajji* say?" Thor demanded of Max. Thor was the Ops behind the pre-patrol straw drawing. He trailed Max like a pilot fish.

"He's making a stupid joke."

"Aren't you supposed to tell us what they're saying?" Thor asked.

"He said you have a particularly tiny dick," Max said.

Viking laughed.

Thor took a step toward Max and lowered his M-4.

Viking stepped between them. "Cut the shit, both of you," he said.

Batoor Khan asked Max in Pashto what was being said. Max told him, and he turned away laughing and ordered his men to move out.

"I was almost killed that day," Max told me. No one in the 501st knew about it and I felt cold, even in the New Jersey heat, when he told me how close I'd come to losing him.

The Ops and the Pashtuns were walking into the mountains to surprise a village where an informant claimed there were underground tunnels full of rocket launchers and Russian Kalashnikov rifles. For two hours they climbed silently in the darkness, single file on a narrow rocky trail, the Pashtuns in the lead. At seven, a white-hot sun exploded above the drought-stunted peaks, and the sky turned a startling blue.

Max had walked partway up beside Claire, taking her arm when she stumbled, listening to her whisper into her cassette: "A tableau worthy of Remington! The juxtaposition of our twenty-first-century techno-warriors with a war party of nineteenth-century Mongol hybrids. Kipling should be here."

Max said he'd laughed to himself. Wanting to put things in a literary perspective reminded him of his father.

By ten, Claire's high had given out—she was a middle-aged out-of-shape woman. She was near collapse when they reached a plateau studded with boulders and bordered by yellow cliffs. Suddenly, someone shot into a pile of rocks.

One of the Ops laughed—"It's a fucking rabbit"—and they climbed on.

The ping had echoed through the hills, giving their position away, and everyone was unnaturally tense. Max said he could feel his hairs stiffen. All of a sudden an angry bee buzzed him, then another. Max tried to swat them away. They were all over everyone.

"Jesus, you hit a beehive," someone said.

An itinerant native beekeeper, moving through the mountains with his beehive on his back, must have seen them coming and, after the shot hit his hive, run off, deserting his bees.

One of the Ops took out a candy bar, unwrapped it, and threw it away from the war party, and the bees finally followed.

Viking walked to the back of the queue where Claire was kneeling on the ground, struggling to rearrange her head scarf. "You all right?" he asked.

"I'm fine." She was shaking. Viking put out a hand and yanked her up. "Stay behind me," he said, striding to the front of the queue, pulling her behind him. When he got to the lead, Max and Batoor Khan were talking in Pashto.

Thor was right behind them, angrily bobbing his head. "What's he saying?" Thor demanded of Max.

"He says he has to take a piss," Max said.

"I think you're cooking something up, asshole. That's what I think." Thor bumped Max with his chest. "You're a *hajji*, ain't you? Just like them."

"Look, Thor," Max said. "While we're up here, why don't you just do your job and let me do mine? We can arm-wrestle back at base."

Viking pushed Thor out in front of the war party. "What's the matter with you?" Viking asked.

"There's nothing wrong with me," Thor said. "What the fuck's wrong with you? He's probably plotting to get us whacked. How do we know? He was talking on the radio back there. What if he was giving away our position?"

"He was giving them a fake position," Viking said.

"Well, I don't trust that arrogant motherfucker. You watch. I don't care what kind of uniform he's wearing, he's not one of us."

Suddenly, Viking raised his M-4 and swung it toward a ravine, fifty yards ahead. The other Ops and the Pashtuns raised their rifles as well, as fire began coming in. Claire threw herself to the ground and got tangled up in her headpiece, which had come unwrapped, and her head struck a rock. A Pashtun militiaman straddled her body, firing next to Viking.

Max crawled to Claire and dragged her behind a boulder. She looked up at him and said, "Pashtun fight standing erect. Just like redcoats!"

Max said he was smiling at this reference when a couple of pings chipped the rock right above his head and he looked up to see Thor looking down his sight at him from twenty yards away. Thor laughed before he casually swung his rifle toward the enemy. Claire rallied for a few seconds, saying into her recorder: "Everything's so confusing in combat. Were our guys firing at us?" she asked Max. Then she passed out.

Scuttlebutt said she'd told the unit commander what she thought she saw. She was gone the next day.

It seemed almost like summer camp that day. When we were done with our detail, we headed out into the sandy pine barrens. Max had purloined a thermos from the officers' mess and filled it with lemonade. It was easy enough to get sandwiches from the enlisted mess. For a while we sat with our backs against a dwarf pine, not talking.

"Are you okay, *habibi*?" Max asked.

What he'd told me had gotten lodged in my throat. I finally swallowed it and began to cry.

"No more," I said. "Don't tell me any more."

He took my face in his hands and kissed me. "I told you that story, *habibi*," he said, "so you'll know who I am and what you're in for if you love me. It's not just the army. This doesn't end."

I think our time together was sweeter because we believed it would end. If the 501st got orders to Iraq, it was unclear whether Max would come with us. So we picnicked and made love and, while I deliberately tried to avoid making plans for our uncertain future, I couldn't help it; I demanded that Max say something. He couldn't just pretend we didn't exist.

"So what about Nadira?" I asked him, after we had come in from an afternoon of unreality of the woods. "Are you going to tell her?"

"There's no need. I've never spoken a word to her in my life. It's not like we were in love. Like us." He pulled me close to him, and I believed I could pick out a silver pattern, I guess, because I felt almost giddy by the time we made it to the mess hall for dinner. The idea that my future was Max was frightening—look at what he'd told me, and there was new graffiti on the mess hall wall—and exhilarating. Look how I felt!

"It's possible to live in both worlds, mine and your father's," I told him. "We can have Sunday dinner with your family every week. That's fine with me."

Max laughed. "What a funny idea. You see my father as a place we go for Sunday dinner. To me, he is the largest person in the world, and you see him as a host. That's why I need you."

"See?" I said. "We can be a normal couple."

"We are in the wrong time in history for that."

Finally, after almost two weeks of waiting, we got our orders. We were going back to Warrenside to be discharged. And then reality started to settle in.

That night at dinner, I gorged myself on spaghetti and meatballs and garlic bread and Coke, as if it would somehow muffle the question I hadn't yet asked: What was I going to do now? Because obviously I was going to hurt people left and right, and I was so happy it fired up all the electrons in my body. I wanted to cry out, *Live! You only get one chance!* That's how I felt. Other people's expectations clamp you in a box. This is what I kept telling myself on the ride home from Dix to Warrenside: You can't make other people happy if you are miserable. That's what I said. Our love was going to make everyone so damned happy.

I saw a beautiful blue heron, a sign of good luck I was sure, on the last leg of our trip home, before it started raining hard, and Duck tapped me on the shoulder. "We'll meet up later after we have a chance to say hi to our folks, what do you say?"

I nodded, unused to any other response to Duck. Did Duck think this was just another fling to get out of my system before I got down to the real business of living with him? How could he not see the new thing that consumed me? This new me was so huge it was taking up another seat.

Max squeezed my hand. I was Eve in the Garden of Eden. The apple was delicious, and yes, thank you, I'll take another bite. Like Eve, I understood the consequences of my appetite, and I didn't care.

After rotting for two weeks in limbo, waiting for orders either to go to Iraq or out-process, the word came down that we were being released and going home. Then, in typical army hurry-up-and-wait fashion, they bussed us around as if they couldn't wait to get rid of us: to the finance building and the personnel building, where we filled out financial paperwork, redesignated life insurance beneficiaries, updated our personnel files, and got debriefed; then on to the medical building, where our blood was drawn for an ongoing army study in field hygiene. A Pentagon report based on Soviet army medical records hypothesized that the Soviets had lost Afghanistan because at any given time during their occupation a third of their troops were sick with hepatitis, typhus, malaria, amebic dysentery, or meningitis because they didn't wash their hands, and we didn't want to make the same mistake. Our last stop was an auditorium, where we watched a DVD with General Hodges talking about the importance of freedom and what a giant privilege it was to die for it, and since we'd survived we were being given a second chance to die for it; recruiters were standing by in the auditorium lobby with high reenlistment bonus offers and dismal Warrenside employment statistics.

Then we waited again for the seemingly endless process of army orders to play themselves out. We drank, sobered up, drank, sobered up, argued, made plans, played cards, and finally, after a week, we got our orders and boarded three buses—one red, one white, one blue. I made sure that Kat and I were on the same bus, the red one. Naturally, Max got on it too.

After exiting Dix onto Jersey 68, we were joined by a motorcycle escort, an honor guard of thirty Harleys, all ridden by Vietnam vets who shepherded us across New Jersey into Pennsylvania, gray ponytails flying, stars-and-stripes T-shirts hugging beer bellies, their old ladies riding shotgun, waving black POW/MIA pennants and flashing Vs to oncoming motorists. I thought of my dad then. I couldn't help it.

"I haven't seen a woman in thirteen months!" Reuber shouted at a tattooed Amazon on the back of a bike, giving the full monty to the soldiers hanging out the bus windows. "How about a mercy fuck?"

When we turned north onto Pennsylvania 611, our escort peeled away because it was starting to rain. Hard.

"Feels like we just left a Grateful Dead concert," Reuber said.

The landscape changed from the sandy pine barrens of New Jersey to fields and groves of trees, and Camacho yelled out suddenly, "Look! What's that weird bird?" and we all pushed to the windows to get a good look at a prehistoric-shaped avian with a slender neck like a rubber hose gliding low over a small lake, its head down, looking for fish.

"That's a blue heron!" Kat shouted. She was right behind the driver, and she turned around to give the news flash to everyone, then turned to Max. "There's a family of them in the creek by the country club. I'll show them to you tomorrow." And Max, that prickly bastard, who had never cracked anything but an ironic smile the entire time I knew him in Kandahar, grinned like a fool.

"Don't you know a blue heron when you see one, Camacho, you ignorant fuck?" I said, and everyone laughed and the guys punched one another because we were home, where we could hunt deer in the fall; and home, where we could take a walk without inhaling burning sewage; and home, where we could speak to people without translators; and home, where we could tell friends from enemies because everyone has the courtesy to wear the right fucking uniform; and home, where most of us would have to figure out how to reinsert ourselves into lives that had managed to get along without us—quite well, actually—for the past thirteen months.

Kat had stopped looking at the heron and was looking at Max Asad. She had been with other men before—it was my idea that she sow her wild oats before we settled down—so I knew this infatuation with Max was just a reaction to our serious talk of marriage. This was her way of saying, Yes, we're getting married, but can I just see who this person is before we dive into our cocoon? This is the thing about Kat and me: we were made for each other. We're family. I held her up when her mom stopped taking her meds and walked downtown naked. She held me up when my dad blew his brains out. My dad had some drawings he brought back from 'Nam, and one was of a dragon eating its own tail, an ouroboros: a perfect circle of life renewing and feeding on itself, not needing anything besides its own body. As soon as I found out what the ouroboros meant, I had one tattooed on my left shoulder. That's how Kat and I felt about each other. You can't break a ring like that. It's stronger than steel.

Anyway, as long as there was one Warren alive in Warrenside, she would never take up with an immigrant. Hell, even if she convinced herself that she was in love, she'd tire herself out fighting her own mixed feelings about being a Warren. She didn't know it yet, but a Warren was all she knew how to be. You eventually become all the stuff your parents pour into your ears, like it or not. When we used to talk about getting married, she would say it would be difficult with me being a Polack, conveniently forgetting her Bineki part. She was more like her mother than she wanted to admit. She needed me just like her ma needed her Polack. She wasn't going anywhere. I would loosen the line and let her run.

The rain started coming down really hard and we pulled down the windows on the old school bus. Jenna called out, pointing to the Bluetooth in her ear, "They say the Catawissa is probably going to flood!" and everyone moaned, because if there was a flood, the National Guard would be called in for detail.

"You know," she said to me, "if you trust in Jesus, things always happen for a reason. You just don't know His plan for you."

I got the distinct impression she thought Jesus' plan for *her* somehow included me. "Shut up," I said.

And we rode the rest of the way in silence.

Dr. Asad and Bernice sat in their black Lincoln SUV in the parking lot of the National Guard Armory on Fifteenth Street, where several hundred relatives and friends of the 501st had been waiting since midmorning under colorful umbrellas.

Despite the rain, Dr. Asad rolled down his window and amused himself by watching ancient Legionnaires lecturing Boy Scouts; divorced parents making polite conversation for the sake of their returning child; wives with fresh hairdos trying to control children who were getting soaked in the rain, chasing each other in uncomfortable new—and now wet—clothing; eager girlfriends; and not-so-eager girlfriends, with the stress of their breakup— bad news written on their faces—who just wanted to get it over with and didn't know what was taking so long for a couple of buses to make it in from New Jersey.

The local pizzeria, Dough Boy's, had donated one hundred pies in return for permission to hang a ten-foot Dough Boy's banner on the outside of the Armory's chain-link fence, and empty pizza boxes and plastic soda bottles littered the parking lot. Dr. Asad didn't want Max to see this litter and called Chris Schaeffer to get down with some industrial-sized garbage bags to clean up the mess. Chris pulled up in his own black SUV, powered down the windows, saluted Dr. Asad, and then three clones of Chris ran out of the vehicle and started to police the grounds.

"Take it to the club," Dr. Asad said of the garbage, and, to his wife, "We should have brought the Aloubs."

"They will have him long enough," Bernice answered. "Let's have him a couple of hours to ourselves."

They had argued last night over whether to ask the Aloubs to come, Bernice finally persuading her husband that it was enough for Max to see his own family first. It annoyed Dr. Asad that Bernice resisted his mandate that Max's life resume as if he had never left. If he hadn't enlisted, he would have married Nadira a year ago. And so, Dr. Asad claimed, Nadira and her people should be here—thirty Aloubs, including two uncles and their sons who had flown in from Beirut. It bothered him that Max's welcoming committee was so paltry.

A woman close to their SUV crouched down under her umbrella and smoothed her three-year-old daughter's hair. "Do you want Daddy to see you like this?" she asked the little girl, pushing tendrils of blond hair back into a cloth-covered elastic while the child tried to remember who Daddy was. "Do you think Daddy loves messy little girls? No, he doesn't."

A woman who had stationed herself at the parking lot gate with a Bluetooth in her ear yelled, "The buses made a pit stop at a diner in Shimertown on Route 202. They're back on Route 202!" she shouted. "It's Duck! My son!" She pointed at the contrivance in her ear and people nodded politely.

Two little boys dressed in K-Mart camouflage chased one another, playing war.

"Get some of that," Liz Reville from Channel 3 commanded her cameraman, who dutifully pointed his camera at the boys.

"I just killed you!" one boy screamed. "You can't get up."

"You missed!" the alleged victim retorted.

"I didn't miss. I shot you right here." The shooter pointed between his eyes.

"I'm not dead," the other boy said. "I get to say when I'm dead." He wandered back to his mother, who tousled his hair absently and used a tissue to daub her running mascara. She saw Dr. Asad staring at her, smiled, and said, "It's so hot, my God! This rain isn't helping a bit."

A very tall woman with blond braids down to her waist, wearing a short white cotton dress over her jeans and holding a placard—the only person not holding an umbrella—tried to get the cameraman from Channel 3 to film her sign, but the reporter pushed her away. "Don't pay attention to her," the reporter said, when the cameraman started to film her. She put herself between the woman and the cameraman. "This is their day. Whose side are you on? Aren't you a real American?"

"I'm more American than you," the woman shouted.

The reporter pinched her lapel with a small enameled American flag pinned to it. "Are you ashamed of the flag?"

The tall woman turned and Dr. Asad recognized her; then he read the placard: 3,000,000 AFGHANI REFUGEES. He felt a stab of apprehension. These were not things you were allowed to say aloud.

The day had started out muggy and sunny. Soon, storm clouds had rolled in from the east and with the sudden torrents of rain there were flash floods reported from small creeks in the area. There were rumors circulating that the soldiers wouldn't be released from duty; they would be assigned to flood cleanup. It had been thirty years since the Catawissa had breached its banks, just enough time for people to believe it could never happen again. But the intensity and insistency of the rain made Dr. Asad think that a major flood was likely. He owned the low-lying blocks of row houses downtown near the river. The sewer system would be overtaxed quickly. As soon as Max arrived, they would have to attend to the possibility of a disaster.

People were looking up at the sky from under their umbrellas, chatting inattentively with one another, focusing mostly on a group of teenage boys who had clambered up as lookouts on the overgrown Fifteenth Street railroad trestle.

"They're here! They're here!" the boys yelled when two yellow buses crested Fogel Hill. Everyone rushed toward the Fogel Hill Road side of the Armory parking lot—false alarm; just county prison buses. Deflated, people went back to talking, not really listening. Having been deprived of their loved ones for over a year, no one wanted to be left out of the first wave of screaming.

A white Chevy Blazer marked SHERIFF's DEPARTMENT pulled in at a fire hydrant behind Dr. Asad's SUV. It disgorged Alvin Barbour, the county sheriff, who nodded imperiously to the folks straining to see if his passengers were soldiers. "Hey, Dr. Asad," he said. He was a regular at Lucky Lady. A butter blonde, Linda Pasko, whose short hair showed an inch of black roots, got out of the Blazer on the street side, came around to the pavement, said something to the sheriff, then leaned against the car hood, a bored look on her salon-tanned face as she accepted an umbrella from Alvin. She wore tight jeans and a skimpy halter top. Her fingernails were painted electric blue; a rhinestone was pinned in her navel. Sheriff Barbour adjusted his trousers, pleased that folks might think Linda was with him for some more flattering reason than to ID her ex-husband, Reuber, when he got off the bus. Reuber had apparently gambled away all his child support money, because he hadn't sent any home in a year.

Duck's mother, who was holding a hand over her right ear as she listened to the Bluetooth in her left, cried out, "Oh! Everybody! They're almost here." And then the boys on the railroad trestle let out another shout and the crowds lining Fogel Hill Road began to cheer. A red bus lumbered into the Armory lot, a blue one and a white one right behind it. A crush of people closed in around the buses. Soldiers hung out the windows, touching outstretched hands. The door of the blue bus opened and Captain Whynnot stepped out to a burst of applause. He shielded his face against the rain.

"Inside, folks, please," he shouted. He pointed to the Armory, where a reception was waiting, climbed back in the bus, and the door closed behind him. But the crowd didn't move, and after two minutes, the drivers stopped trying to inch their vehicles forward, put on their brakes, and the doors of the three buses opened, spilling soldiers out.

Sheriff Barbour had forced his way to the middle of the mob, Linda Pasko in tow. She was wearing a yellow poncho the sheriff had given her and stood on tiptoe. When Reuber stepped out of the red bus she nodded—"That's him"—and ran back to the Blazer. The sheriff stationed himself behind a knot of people by the gate, oblivious to the rain, and focused on his prey. Reuber approached the gate at a trot, his duffel over his shoulder, and stopped to look around. Sheriff Barbour reached between two women and grabbed Reuber in his hammy hand. Reuber tried to squirm away, but the sheriff pinned him to the fence with his stomach and cuffed him. A couple of the soldiers noticed what was happening but didn't intercede. Everyone knew Reuber was unlucky; as soon as he got out of this mess, he would just get into another. As the sheriff led Reuber to the back of the Blazer, which was fenced off from the front like a dog's cage, Linda rolled down the window on the passenger's side. "Welcome home, prick," she said.

Amid the screams of joy and tears of recognition and umbrel-las, which were blocking his view, Dr. Asad strained to see Max. "Stay here," he commanded Bernice, and got out of the car and made his way through the throng to the buses. When it seemed like no one else was coming out, his beautiful boy appeared on the steps of the red bus. He looked around, saw his father, bowed his head slightly, and smiled. And just when Dr. Asad thought his chest would explode with happiness, he saw Max turn and take the hand of a female soldier, leading her down the stairs and through the crowd toward him.

ELEVEN **WIND**

Wind's tussle with the reporter, whom she would've clocked but didn't because she didn't want that kind of publicity, made her decide to move her protest outside the chain-link fence. Holding up her sign decrying the 3,000,000 Afghani refugees, she walked ten steps to the left, turned around, and walked ten steps to the right in front of the Armory gate, so that every soldier and every family member leaving the Armory would have to pass her. The rain was pouring down her face, and she doubted that anyone actually saw her, but she felt she had to do it. The soldiers and their families were already in the auditorium at the party, but then she saw a straggler. A red Ford Focus pulled up; the driver rolled down his window and said, "Hey, when are they coming?"

"They're here already," Wind said. She leaned into the car and dripped water onto the driver, whom she recognized as that monster Barbara Warren's husband, Mike Bineki. "They're in-side."

Wind stuck her protest sign in the window so he couldn't close it. "Hey," she said.

"What? Could you please move away, you're dripping all over me."

"It's only water," Wind said.

"What do you want? I got to find my daughter."

"Tell your wife to lay off my property."

Mike squinted at her. "Hey, you're that Indian. Oops, Native American."

"No. Indian is actually better," Wind said.

"I can never keep up with that stuff," Mike said.

"Shut the fuck up," Wind said, "and tell her I have her in my crosshairs. Got that? Indians have powers, and I intend to use them. *Secret* powers."

"Well, use those powers to stop this rain, babe," he said, rolling up his window, "or we'll all be taking the boat home."

A sergeant in a dress raincoat, who had been loitering near the gate, approached her. "A big strong girl like you should be at work. I bet you need a job."

"I know what kind of jobs you have," Wind said. "Stick it."

"If you're smart enough, you can do anything you want. We'll train you. Can't beat the benefits."

"Look, I know you have quotas and all that stuff, but I don't need to join the army. I make a good living right here in Warrenside."

"And may I ask what you do?"

"I'm a shaman. Got anything like that in your army?"

The sergeant laughed. "Maybe you're *not* smart enough."

Wind wanted to punch the smirk off his face. "Listen, I just don't have a problem with the Afghanis. Got that?" She poked her sign at his chest. "And I don't fight white men's wars. Got *that*? Find some other chump."

"You mean you don't have a problem with terrorists? Is that what you're saying?" He was looking up at her sign. "Because that's what I'm hearing." The sergeant pretended to be concerned. "But if you sign up, I'd know that you didn't mean it." He chuckled. "Got you there."

"Leave me alone." Wind lowered her sign and walked toward her car.

"Listen," he said. "I bet being a shaman doesn't pay much, does it? What is that like, a psychic? I bet I could get you into Officer Candidate School and you could be a chaplain. Or a counselor. The pay is a lot better than what you're making now. And you could probably qualify for a signing bonus. Or flight school. Bet you do a lot of flying up here." He circled his finger in the air around his ear.

Wind heard herself asking softly, "Bonus? How much?"

The sergeant leaned in and whispered in her ear as if people were listening. When she looked surprised at the amount, he said, "I'm not promising. But I've seen them go that high."

"I'm not interested," Wind said.

"Suit yourself."

He made a big deal of writing down her license plate number and then gave her his card. "For later, after Homeland Security visits you and you change your mind."

The second I stepped off the bus, I was overtaken by my mom, who knocked me in the eye with her umbrella. "Sorry, sorry, sorry, honey," she said, and, with a free arm, locked me under the umbrella and dragged me away. "You can get your stuff later," she said, "it's only army stuff," which a couple of guys were moving out of the buses to the Armory where Captain Whynnot's mother was trying to put on a party, which I don't think anyone really wanted to attend. We were home, damn it; we didn't want to stand around sipping punch and eating Pecan Sandies or some such shit. I didn't want to see these people anymore.

"I gotta find Kat," I said, and wrenched myself away from Mom. I looked around to see Max leading Kat toward his father. "Wait, Mom, I see her."

"Don't worry, she'll find her way home," she said.

"Yeah, but I want to make sure." I was blocked by the crowd, and something about the way Kat was holding Max's arm made me stop. Mom never liked Kat. She thought the Warrens were snobs who had nothing to be snobby about, and when I tried to tell her Kat was nothing like that, she would say, "Here's what I know about being in love, Duck: it makes you stupid."

A reporter from Channel 3 was in her element, unstopped by the torrential rain, and I did everything I could to evade her microphone, but she seemed to be keying in on me because I was the only one not moving briskly toward transportation out of there. "Let's run, Mom," I said, and soon we were in my old Barracuda.

"You're awfully quiet, Duck," Mom said, getting the car in line to drive out of the parking lot.

All I could do was nod. "I want to see the shop," I said, meaning my shop—formerly my dad's shop—and my mom said she wanted to get home, she had a surprise she had to prepare for me, so I dropped her off and drove back into town, to the old neighborhood called Ringside—so called because the Irish who worked in the Hammacher brewery on Front Street two generations ago would beat each other senseless on payday nights outside its barrooms.

I said it was my Barracuda, but it was my dad's too. My mom had driven all of Dad's belongings to the dump in his black 1973 Barracuda the first week after his suicide. Then she'd parked the car in our tiny one-car garage and hung up the keys in Dad's toolshed. On my sixteenth birthday, she'd handed me the keys and said, "Don't kill yourself," and realized it was the wrong thing to say, so she backtracked and said, "Just be careful." I'd detailed the Barracuda and driven it to school every day of my senior year, experiencing newfound popularity. I'd asked Mom to start it every day for me while we were in Afghanistan, and she must have, because it was running like a champ, and soon I was parked in front of the shop.

Before I left for Afghanistan, Latinos were selling crystal meth on the shop's front stoop as soon as I locked up and went home. Sometimes they didn't even wait until I was gone. But I couldn't sell the place. It was as if I would lose a piece of myself, my past, if I sold it. And it would be a betrayal of Dad. Was there a statute of limitations on keeping someone's memory alive? If Kat and I were to get married, though, I had to look at everything through her eyes. And what I saw when I looked at the old wooden structure like *that* was pretty dismal: a two-story clapboard building with all the windows in the second floor bricked over. I never washed the windows on the first floor, thinking, I guess, that part of my dad was still on them. My dad used to sleep over on the filthy futon on the second floor when he had too much drink or some asshole had sold him coke. Mom and I used to be afraid when he didn't come home; then we became increasingly relieved not to have to deal with the drama.

I headed home and Mom had a celebratory steak dinner all ready for me with Gus Czernak, one of Dad's old Vietnam buddies. Gus and his wife, Cyndi, had brought casseroles over to the house long after everyone had stopped being sad about my dad's suicide, but there was no sign of Cyndi tonight. Gus helped Mom with the dishes in such a way that I knew it wasn't the first time he had done so, and while they were all chummy, cleaning up the kitchen, I noticed that Mom was dyeing her hair. After dinner we went into the living room to have coffee and dessert, and Gus and I exchanged war stories, leaving out stuff for Mom's benefit, and we agreed it was the same old stuff all over again, "redux," I think I said, or something equally assholey, trying to even the score, because as the communications sergeant for a supply company I didn't really see any action and Gus *did* in 'Nam. Just when I got sick of waiting for him to leave, I realized they were waiting for *me* to go to bed so they could be alone, which I did with as much grace as I could at that point.

And I called Kat.

"What's it like?" I asked her. "Being home?"

She sounded worried. "Duck, you're my best friend, right?"

I felt a familiar end-of-the-world sensation and I said, "Okay," but I already knew what she was going to say, of *course* I knew, so I stopped listening.

It had been fourteen years since my father locked the wood-shop door, put the barrel of his shotgun in his mouth, and by stepping backward pulled the trigger with a piece of wire he'd tied to the handle of a vise. I had been sitting on the stoop, talking to a friend, when I heard the police lock jerk into its housing, and when I stood up to look through the shop window, I heard the shot and knew instantly what Dad had done. The three of us— Dad, Mom, and me—had been living, forever it seemed, in a movie running at the wrong speed, and when that shot went off the movie finally ended. I had run to the building's backyard. The back door was locked, so I squirmed in through the small cellar window and ran up the stairs. Dad was lying headless by the work-table. The neighbors and my friends were looking in the shop window, and I ran in and closed the blinds. "Why didn't you go down to the river?" I yelled at the corpse. "Who's going to clean up this mess?" Of course, *I* did. Then I called the police and called Mom, who'd been working as a customer service representative at Titan Insurance since my father quit his job. It was so clearly the only way it could end for my dad that Mom and me never discussed the whys of it. Some things are just too broke to be fixed.

I was saying "Un-uh, un-uh, un-uh" as Kat told me of this overwhelming fucking love that had come into her life in the person of Max Asad. I sounded horrible—I could hear the despair in my own voice—but Kat didn't notice.

I thought about the conversation I had had with Max, that my father was my jailer. But Max was wrong. My dad wasn't my jailer. When I closed my eyes to picture my life and what was keeping me working at a dead-end job in a dead-end town, it wasn't my dad. It was Kat.

PART TWO

THIRTEEN **BARBARA**

Barbara had had enough psycho-talk therapy over the years—
before they determined her problem was innate, chemical, *who
she was*—to understand that one shift in her daily reality would
cause a corresponding seismic alteration of the chemical equation,
which would bring the whole house tumbling down, at which
time she would need an emergency team of chemists analyzing
the shifting balance, prescribing countermeasures and antidotes.
At times of frantic tectonic activity—and Kat's return after a year
away was definitely such a time—Barbara had instructions to
concentrate on *who she was* so her little vessel of selfhood would
not be tossed in the stormy waters of other people's expectations.
It was emergency first aid until her team of chemists could be
assembled.

Who she was was delightfully intricate.

For one, Barbara was a woman with a driver, albeit a driver
who wore a scratchy navy-blue wool double-breasted, brass-

buttons uniform with a matching cap who would have looked more natural mounting a running board than her Lincoln Town Car. The job required the ability to fit into the "perfectly good uniform, there's no reason to change it." Mike thought a guy might be a little uncomfortable in that getup in the choking July humidity of the Catawissa River Valley, and he suggested changing the uniform to a black T-shirt with DRIVER in white blocky letters across the back, like the FBI or the police. That was quickly vetoed. Barbara was surprised when Mike told her the driver spoke better Spanish than English—"What's his name, babe? You don't know his name, do you?"—but she decided if he didn't object to ten dollars and fifty cents an hour, he was complicit in their agreement. She was thrifty and she wasn't a big conversationalist and she didn't have anything to say to her driver. She certainly didn't care how uncomfortable the driver was, though she noticed that he couldn't close his pants; the top button was open, so he wore suspenders—a nice touch in her opinion—to keep the pants up. Seeing that ancient uniform in the front seat of a car she wasn't driving: that's who she was.

Also important was the furniture in her modernist mansion. "We don't *buy* furniture," she told Mike twenty years ago when he wanted to update the living room, get a comfortable sofa that he could actually lie down on to watch a football game. "We already *have* furniture." Had her father lived, he would have surely replaced the ungainly furniture that Jeb Warren judged suitable for his eighteenth-century Puritanism. But he hadn't lived, and Barbara was religiously devoted to the way the founders did things, to the way things had always been, like the Amish eschewing buttons or Hasidic Jews wearing the beaver hats of the Polish ghetto.

For a couple of years Mike struggled to get comfortable on the Louis XV—"Say *looey cans*, Mike"—settee, which someone in Barbara's family tree had dragged home from a year abroad and which still wore its original upholstery of creamy brocade. People who tried to sit on it would immediately jump up as if they had sat on a hot piece of metal, the seat was so narrow and hard. It had been bought in a French bric-a-brac shop whose owner couldn't verify its authenticity, so it and its tainted reputation had chugged through several Warren families before groaning to a halt in theirs. Mike eventually bought himself a white leather monstrosity to put in the partially finished basement where he'd initially put his office and, soon afterward, a big color television, and finally the rest of his life, while Barbara happily did her living on the looey cans alone. Every time she perched her own increasingly large loony cans on that uncommonly hard seat, she remembered that other Warrens had set their own bony behinds on this very spot and it made her smile, the continuity of it, the idea that she was part of something bigger than herself.

Kat—always Kat!—scolded her that it was materialistic to define yourself by things. But how else can you define yourself—by your ideas? In a police lineup, what do people see? "That's him! I'd know him anywhere, officer! He's the one with the profound love of Ayn Rand!" It's as if, Barbara thought, your mind has nothing to do with the body that carries it around. Nothing is more materialistic than your body, nothing is more your own property, more *you*, and she knew all about that from the relentless testing her doctors did on her when they discovered a part of her even more interesting than her desire to shed her clothes and walk "naked into the night"—her words, which put a poetic spin on an otherwise embarrassing urge—and that was her superb Chubb health insurance, which practically begged the doctors to find out as much as they could about Barbara Warren-Bineki. *Who she was.* Besides the usual oxygen, carbon, hydrogen, nitrogen, calcium, phosphorus, sulfur, potassium, sodium, magnesium, chlorine, silicon, iron, fluorine, zinc, rubidium, strontium, bromine, lead, copper, aluminum, cadmium, boron, barium, tin, iodine, manganese, nickel, gold, molybdenum, chromium, caesium, cobalt, uranium, beryllium, and radium, the normal ingredients that managed to coalesce into the soup called personality, doctors were interested in a mysterious brain substance called cryoglobulin, or Cg—which name Barbara preferred, as she was impatient with vowels and their ability to change sound relative to the company they were in. The doctors wondered if, with a slight increase in temperature, Cg would bind with complement components and produce antibodies to autoimmune suppressors and, well, did they therefore have a role in her schizophrenia? Unfortunately, the only way to study Cg was on cadavers, and the studies coming out of Romania and Armenia were painfully slow and had to be translated, "both literally and figuratively," her doctors told her, meanwhile giving her samples, as well as generous prescriptions, for other chemicals that might possibly rebalance what was surely a misreading by her DNA of the chemical requirements for Barbara Warren-Bineki.

See, Barbara thought, *that* was her. All those chemicals and substances in ratios peculiar to her, *those* were her. The beautiful clear skin that rich people always have, *that* was her. The luxurious red-brown hair that curled just enough to have some body, but not too much to be vulgar, *that* was her. Even the human appurtenances of her life—Mike and Kat—*they* were her. Luckily they were beautiful and presentable, and when Mike went to his job every day and was too tired to socialize with the type of people she thought they really ought to be socializing with—even though you never knew when Mike would say something outrageous as if he hadn't thought for one minute about where he had come from and how grateful he should be even to be allowed in the same country club with these people, not to mention their living rooms—she was glad not to have people confirm their original opinion of Mike, which was that he was a buffoon. Mike hadn't been to the country club in so long, Barbara concluded hopefully that people had forgotten what they thought of him. Kat, too. When Kat joined the army, Barbara practically went into mourning so as not to have to answer the inevitable questions and accept the inevitable judgment: if she hadn't married so poorly she wouldn't have birthed a daughter who joined the military, a thing that, after the extreme manpower shortages of World War II, her uncles assured her only sluts and lesbians did.

And now, suddenly, both those appurtenances—ordinarily displayed only on show occasions—were in the living room, taking up a lot of physical and psychic room, and the Abilify that she used to swing the balance in her favor had lost its oomph, its ability to make her move on, move away. The balance was swinging like a giant pendulum and was going to knock her over.

"That's just so fucking unfair," Kat told Mike, who had lost his job, the one thing that kept him out of the house during the day and sitting on his leather monstrosity in the basement in the evening, like a giant id, his manliness and uncouthness tucked safely out of sight but still throbbing down there ready to be unleashed. The Telltale Id.

She could feel it sometimes, when she had forgotten her medication and was lying on the looey cans reading, and he was doing whatever it was he did in the basement—she would feel a pulsation and it would make her hormones wash over her like a bath of lava and suddenly she was soaking wet and taking off her clothes.

"I think you have a lawsuit, Dad, I really do. It's so obvious. You're over forty and then suddenly, poof, you're out?"

"That would be like suing yourself," Barbara said. "What would Uncle Peter say? I'm sure he would forbid it."

"Uncle Peter is so far out of the loop, he's irrelevant," Kat said. "He is, in fact, loopy."

Kat was home from—somewhere—after a blessed year away, drinking Coke out of the can and commiserating with Mike about the unfairness of being fired for cresting the actuarial hill of forty-three. "They are ageist bastards. I'm sorry, Mom, they're your family, but they're assholes."

"Uncle Peter is older than Dad," Barbara said, "so he can't be an ageist."

Kat got up off the floor, where she had been sitting. "There is no logic in that sentence *anywhere*, Mom. You can be a racist African-American. You can be a self-hating Jew. Plenty of old people hate other old people."

What Barbara hated was that Kat thought she was stupid because of her schizophrenia, when schizophrenics are actually smarter than the rest of the population. There were all kinds of studies about that, which she couldn't bring up because it would draw attention to her imbalance and then everything would be filtered through that sieve and suddenly her schizophrenia would be all they could talk about and then they would be suggesting rest, as though a good long rest would make her chemical imbalance go away, when Barbara knew it would just energize it. Resting was the worst possible thing she could do.

Then, abruptly, Mike was leading Kat away to the basement— "You won't believe what I got going"—and she was sitting prettily on the looey cans, relieved that Kat didn't say anything about that Wolinsky kid—hopefully that had finally run out of steam— and holding another letter that she was going to send to Wind Storm, owner of the property next to the country club. It was the fourth letter in three months, and Barbara didn't know why the foolish woman just wouldn't take the money and run. It had been bothering her, giving her pounding headaches that started on the top of her head—that was unusual, wasn't it? She would ask her doctor about them, a new symptom to investigate—because this *thing* she knew about was going to explode, and her family's name would be part of the detritus.

This *thing* she knew was this: The Lenape Country Club, which her family had built in 1940 to soothe the tired brows of steel executives who were working day and night on the war effort, was sitting on fifty acres of sludge from the mills, sludge resting comfortably in covered trenches but nonetheless sludge that contained some of the most interesting—from a chemical point of view—stuff to come out of the iron- and steel-making process. It included benzene, butane, butylene, ethane, ethylene, hydrogen cyanide, methane, propane, propylene, toluene, and xylene. Barbara had nothing against these chemicals per se, knowing from personal experience that there was no such thing as a bad chemical, only unfortunate situations where specific chemicals didn't belong. And these particular chemicals didn't belong in covered trenches under places where people played golf and next to properties that could be subdivided and houses put on top of them.

Even though Warren Steel had shipped the sludge to the landfill years before reprocessing it in a sintering operation to recycle the offending chemicals had been an option, and years before anyone started monitoring things like unfortunate chemical situations, back when people thought chemicals leached down and so couldn't contaminate anything on top of them, Warren Steel was technically responsible for cleaning it up or at least containing it. But Warren Steel no longer existed, and its corporate records were stored in an unmarked corporate grave, and nobody but her really remembered that it was landfill anyway because her grandfather had hastily covered it with sod, thrown some white balls around, and cried "Fore!" with his fellow execs before anybody remembered.

Her father, in *The House Is Built!*, was the one who cried foul. Dumping toxic waste before the 1970s wasn't illegal, except that now, in 2004, she knew where the body was buried, so to speak. If she didn't say anything and allowed people to build homes on it, it was a sin of omission, her Catholic husband would say. Her own Presbyterian background told her she wasn't responsible for—well, for anything, actually. Her faith told her that she was part of the Elect just by being born rich, so no worries there. Dr. Edward Asad's offer to buy the property as a compound for his family made her think, though, that subdivision meant perking the soil and God knew, really, what they would find in that soil. She woke at 3 a.m. from nightmares of goopy red sludge spewing out of the eighteenth hole and charging like a locomotive through the Storm property and down to the Catawissa while the people of Warrenside cursed her name. Her name! In the end that's all she had. She needed to make a preemptive strike.

This letter to Ms. Storm offered to pay her fines for not cleaning up the junk on the property, as well as a very handsome sum for the property itself, "acknowledging the permit for subdivision and the land's subsequent value." Could this letter be an acknowledgment of guilt? She didn't know. Hastily she folded it, stuffed it in the envelope, and licked it closed just as Kat and Mike were coming up the stairs from the basement. Mike was shaking his head, saying, "There's no accounting for love, babe. It just can't be helped," and Kat was saying, "Hey, Mom, we're having company for dinner."

At the Armory, after Dad opened the car door for me and kissed my cheek, the first thing he said was, "Wanna go to the range before we go home?" and I did, to postpone seeing Mom.

My dad comes from a family that stops *everything* for three days at the start of deer season, and I got a Daisy air rifle when I was twelve, which might seem like an odd present for a twelve-year-old girl in other parts of the country—parts of the country that are not Pennsylvania. My friends at Boston University thought I was a homicidal maniac when I suggested one boring November Saturday that we go shoot clay pigeons. Guns and the firing range seem normal to me. Everyone in Warrenside owns a hunting rifle. Even my mom would probably hunt—all her uncles did—if she wasn't certifiable and unable to get a license. Part of our myth about ourselves is that we're close to nature; that if you haven't killed or caught your dinner at least once in your life, you don't know the price of a meal. Part of me believes that, but part of me knows it's like the cracked logic alcoholics use to rationalize their drinking. Most people who shoot do it for the thrill, the adrenal rush of power, not because they want a piece of meat.

Since it was raining, we went to an indoor range in Whitehall, the town next to Warrenside. The man behind the handgun counter, Chester, an old Vietnam vet, saluted me when I came in. "Yer back," he said, and went about the business of getting out targets and practice ammo for the handguns Dad had brought with him. The rest of the place was empty. We put on our ear protectors, the same kind that construction workers wear to jackhammer, and took two lanes next to each other. Dad opened his gun case and I picked up a .357 magnum and began loading it. Dad seemed unnaturally quiet. But then, I was too. I was waiting for a chance to tell him about Max.

"Aren't you going to ask me about Afghanistan? If I'm okay?"

"I assume you're okay, because you're here. I don't think you had much fun."

"It was boring, actually."

He grunted.

"You okay, Dad?" I asked finally. "Everything okay?"

"Mmm."

"You're so quiet."

"I was fired."

"What?"

He attached his target to the clips, then turned on the pulley, and the target went twenty-five feet down the lane. He emptied his semiautomatic's magazine into the target and brought it back. He'd shot a nice twelve-shot cluster to the right of the bull's-eye.

"Getting fired hasn't ruined your aim," I said.

"I'm focused. More focused than ever."

"What are you going to do?"

He reloaded his magazine, jammed it in the gun, and sent the target back down the lane fifty feet. "I'll tell you later."

I got my own target in place, loaded my revolver, and began firing. My aim was completely off because I was focused on Max, not shooting.

While I was bringing back my target, a young man with a shaved head had come into the lane next to me and was firing his Glock at a target at point-blank range. It gave me chills, but not as much as the three punk teenagers who came in with their own targets, which were full-size blowups of a smiling family.

"That's the kind of shit that's going on in Warrenside," Dad told me. "The whole place is going to hell."

"You sound like Mom."

"Your mother isn't totally wrong about everything. Jesus, everybody has a gun. Every thug, every drug dealer."

"You have a gun," I pointed out.

"I'd be a damned fool not to have one. Let's get out of here. I don't like the vibe."

At the Armory, Max's father had dismissed me as if I were a pal, and I was pissed that Max didn't jump in to set him straight. Of course, I would have my whole life with Max. I would have given anything to have seen Nadira, though. When Max talked about her—and we talked about her and Duck and everyone else quite a bit during those weeks at Fort Dix—he always said her name in the same breath as "great beauty," as if she were the most beautiful woman to walk the earth. But I'm sorry; all beautiful women look alike. Check out any magazine. Some people think *I* look like a model. I'm not bragging, just saying. Still, I was curious. And perhaps a little jealous, because Max was, after all, still engaged to her, and he hadn't asked me to marry him yet. I wasn't worried about it, but that was the fact of the matter.

And so when Dad and I were sitting in the car, I finally told him about Max. Dad gave me the third degree, asking what the hell I was doing with Max Asad. I was defensive and touchy, and somehow the planets didn't seem aligned as they had when our passion ignited.

"I thought you didn't *like* rich. What the hell do you see in him?"

I tried to tell him that you can't *dissect* why you love somebody. It would be like dissecting a peacock to see what made it beautiful. The very act transforms a magical creature into a dead bird. And Dad said, Yeah, he knew what I meant.

"But what about Wolinsky? I thought you and him had a thing going," and I said, "He's okay, Dad, but I know him *too well*, do you know what I mean?"

And, to his credit, Dad *did* know what I meant and said that once you know somebody really well, things change. He didn't say, "Like your mother," but that's what he was thinking. He said he was happy for me, but frankly he didn't seem interested in what was probably the most important thing to have ever happened to me, because he kept saying, "But wait till you see what *I* got going."

I said, "Why don't you just tell me now?" so we could get that part of the conversation over with and get back to me, but he showed unusual restraint and I finally suggested we leave so he could show me what he was up to and be done with it.

I could hear Mom upstairs when we got back, but she didn't come to greet me, which was kind of a relief. Dad threw my duffel bags in the dining room, led me down to his office in the basement, and booted up his computer.

"So what's going on, Dad?"

"Look at this, Kat," he told me, pointing at a form on the computer, "This is so cool. If you want to bill the professional component only for the diagnostic CT colonography, which is what I want to do, I key in 0067T on a single claim line with a 26 modifier in the first modifier position. So it would be"—and he keyed 0067T-26 into a blank field—"but to bill the technical component only for the diagnostic CT colonography, report 0067T on a single claim line with a TC modifier in the first modifier position, so TC would be where the 26 was. To bill the professional *and* technical components for the diagnostic CT colonography in the office setting (POS 11), report 0067T on a single claim with no modifiers."

He keyed away, yakking the whole time, and finally hit the enter key and said, "Voilà. Case closed. Another four grand in the bank." He looked triumphant.

"I thought you were fired."

"I was."

"Then *what?*" The truth kind of washed over me. "You're *embezzling from Titan?*"

"Before they go down. And, baby, are they going down!" he said, punching in the procedure code for an endoscopy for a dead subscriber and billing it for a fictional physician's group. "Anyway, 'embezzling' has a pejorative sound that makes me think you don't approve."

I thought this thing would end with him in jail, which I told him, and he said, "I am taking money from a bunch of thieves. That's what it's come down to in this country. Insurance companies are a band of pirates. If I steal from a thief, who is going to press charges? Thieves don't tell on other thieves. Ha!"

What Dad was doing was obviously illegal. He was stealing from Medicare, billing procedures for providers who didn't exist on behalf of subscribers who didn't exist because they were dead, and I should have been mad, but I was secretly glad he had finally found a way to come out from under the umbrella of the Warrens. He had jumped ship.

"I don't know what to say," I said. That the alarm that says *Embezzling is just wrong!* didn't go off in my head is some indication of how far up in the clouds my head was.

"You didn't think your old man had it in him, did you? I always told you I would get those fuckers before they got me."

"Does Mom know?"

He snorted. "What do you think?"

I nodded, annoyed that he dropped this bomb on me when I had something earth-shattering going on in my own life. It seemed as if my parents would never get out of the way so I could live my own life, have my own drama.

"So, Dad, he's coming here tonight and I want you to be really nice to him, because *this is it.*"

He looked confused for a moment. "Oh, yeah, the Asad kid. Great! I'd like to meet his old man, actually. There's a crafty sonofabitch! Old man Asad riding around town in his goddamned Cadillac SUV, plundering all the loot. I'd like to hear *his* version of how he came to own half of Warrenside."

"What are you talking about?" I asked. "Everybody *hates* them. Max almost got killed because he's Arab-American."

"What do you mean?"

"Nothing. I mean, it's nothing you can do anything about."

"All I know is, he's not even an American and he practically owns the joint, and the company I work for is being outsourced to Indonesia; some Muslim asshole in Indonesia is going to be doing my job, the job I've been doing for twenty-five years. You saw me put that code in. No one at my level knows that kind of detail in Indo-*fucking*-nesia. At least they didn't ask me to move there. They asked some of the guys to move there."

That's when I found out that Dad wasn't actually fired for being Dad but that the entire operation was moving to Asia— bought out in an insurance-bundling move by some bigger insurance firm. "It's to everyone's advantage," Uncle Peter explained to Dad, saying how the actuarial pool was now larger so premiums would be down and claim payments up. I really doubted that. The only part I believed was that Warren Steel was now completely out of Warrenside, Pennsylvania. Warren Steel had been a feudal duchy in its heyday. It had owned the electric company; the gas company; farms and dairies south of the city, which supplied the food for the company's executive dining room; the grocery stores in town—it took care of everyone's needs like a giant tit—and on and on all the way to Titan Insurance Company; which supplied the life, health, and disability insurance for everyone associated with Warren Steel, which is to say, everyone in Warrenside. With Titan gone, there was nothing left of Warren Steel, and I could see what my mother was talking about when she mourned the death of our family's history.

"So now what?" I asked him.

He said he would just take a small amount—"Three million, tops. No need to get greedy, that's when you get caught"—and relocate to Argentina. "That's where it's happening, Kat. You're too young to be hanging around here. This place is dead. Over! You should come with me."

I was sure that Max's father would have something for him to do. He was making plans, Max told me, to put in a casino downtown. He would hire trusted family members, and now we were family, I said. Or would be soon.

"You're going to marry this guy?" he asked. "Did he *ask* you to marry him?"

"He's coming for dinner tonight, so why don't you ask him his *intentions*. See if they're honorable."

Dad patted my hand and we went upstairs to tell Mom the good news: I was in love with this great guy. "Not one of those *Asads*!" Mom screeched, and disappeared to her bedroom for the rest of the evening while Dad and I waited until nine o'clock, when it became obvious that Max wasn't going to come. Dad smiled encouragingly at me when my cell finally rang. I yelled "Hello?" over laughter and whiny music in the background, and Max said he would come as soon as his engagement party was over.

The great pleasure in being sixty years old, Dr. Asad thought, was that he had already experienced everything at least once in his life, so he did not have to cope with surprises. He earned his cool façade by repelling decades of life's ambushes, squashing mutinies in his family and his businesses as well as conquering his new country. Smooth sailing for his last twenty years had lulled him into thinking that his life was on a very agreeable autopilot. And yet when Max walked up to him, after more than a year away, with a tall, pretty soldier clinging to his arm, he felt his boat buck and in the distance saw a giant wave forming, swelling with irresistible force, and he knew he had to take control of the craft immediately or it would be pulled under the water, they all would be drowned, and the vessel—which he had steered successfully through two civilizations—smashed.

Dr. Asad bowed to Kat, reminded Max that a party was waiting at Aladdin's, and suggested that his friend would want to see her own family before she socialized with *comrades*—he chose the word knowing the deadening effect it would have on the girl. Max had pulled her aside under an umbrella and kissed her forehead as well as her mouth, whispered something in her ear, and kissed her again—before he was persuaded to come into their car and say hello to Bernice and be whisked away to Aladdin's, where thirty members of the Aloub family and sixty of the most prominent Lebanese-Americans in the city were drinking tea, Selena the belly dancer was warming her substantial hips to the steady throbbing of Alfred Younis's *durbakeh*, and the food was simmering atop Sterno burners. Dr. Asad shook the trench coat off his shoulders and allowed the hostess to take it. Alfred ran up to him and took Dr. Asad's hand in his and thanked him for having the party at Aladdin's, pouting a little because, he, Alfred, had five daughters—and no sons, a complete disaster—and Dr. Asad could have chosen one of them for the honor of marrying into the Asad family. What was the difference between women, after all? And it would have made the monthly checks that Alfred accepted from Dr. Asad easier to bear. Alfred was a gifted musician, on call at the Presidential Palace in Beirut, where he was more famous than Dr. Asad, but no one cared for Middle Eastern music in Warrenside. Dr. Asad subsidized both his restaurant and his music to keep their homeland alive, and Alfred met his other expenses with his winnings from the high-stakes poker game he hosted weekly at the restaurant.

The beautiful Nadira sat with her family, knitting her fingers beneath the tablecloth, pretending to be bored. It was up to Max to come to her.

"Nadira is there." Dr. Asad nudged Max forward. "She has been anxious to discuss certain household matters with you." He had designs for three houses that he intended to build on the thirty acres that abutted the country club, one of the only tracts of land remaining in Warrenside that could still be subdivided. The blond woman had refused his offer, but she would accede when he came back with a sweetened deal. Everyone has a price. "There is a certain matter of the family room in the design. Do you want to use it as an office instead? You can speak to her as soon as you thank everyone for coming."

The restaurant looked very good, Dr. Asad thought. The perimeter was lined with sofas and plump pillows to recline on. Tables were set for the feast. In the arched nooks, covered with thick fabrics in rich blues and reds, were ceramic camels that made him long for home, unaccountably, because camels were really the stupidest of animals, but a camel was exactly the thing you wanted to be atop when you were crossing the desert. Little lights poked through the tin ceiling, creating the look of a star-filled night. It was not the real thing, of course, but it conjured up the home he left behind, the best of which he had brought with him.

"Father, I must speak to you *immediately*," Max said. "I know this is probably not the best time, but actually there is no good time for this conversation."

Dr. Asad feigned concern as he simultaneously motioned for the food to be served, put his arm around his son, and walked him to the kitchen. "What's this?" he demanded.

Houda came in to find out what the holdup was. "What's going on in here?" she demanded. "Max, everyone is waiting for you to say something. Get out there. Now."

Max seemed relieved to see Houda and said to his sister what he was unwilling to say to his father. "I can't go through with this."

"You can't eat? Don't you feel well?" Dr. Asad said, purposefully misunderstanding his son. "What's the matter?" He put his hand to Max's forehead, and Max batted it away.

"No," Max said. "I am in love with someone."

Houda snorted, then laughed loudly. "That's very funny, Max. I don't know how you're going to tell Nadira. She already has your house decorated and it's not even built. Her entire family is here. What are you going to say to them? Have you thought about that?"

"Stop it," Dr. Asad commanded her. "Go make sure the food is being served, and take care of your mother. And you," he said to Max. "Have you gone mad? Is it the war? What's going on?" He thought he knew his son too well to take anything he said at face value. "Are you on drugs?" Of all the vices Max could be susceptible to, drugs were a worry.

"I can't go through with this wedding. I'm in love with someone. It's very simple, really." He looked as if he did believe it was simple, and for that Dr. Asad wanted to slap him.

"Love? What does a boy like you know about love? Is it that girl you introduced to me at the Armory? It *is* her, isn't it? You can keep her on the side until the flame goes out, and believe me, it will. Passion dies, my boy, if that is indeed what you're feeling. But you must bow to experience—come on, you must admit that I am more experienced than you—and I am telling you that what you are feeling is passion. It is nothing to build a life on. You build a life on duty and responsibility and a love of where you came from."

Max laughed. "Love, passion, what's the difference? This is the first emotion that has been completely my own, an emotion that hasn't been prompted by something I owed the family, or owed this country, or owed your country. Owed *somebody*. This is like a gift."

Dr. Asad was saddened by his son's joy. "You are tired from the journey home. From your year abroad. From the war."

"I don't feel tired, Father. I feel energized. Alive."

Dr. Asad felt a breeze on his neck and thought, This can't be Lady Luck. There is nothing lucky in what is happening here. I have a son who does not respect his father. Who does not respect what has been built for him and who thinks that life can be lived successfully in one generation. It takes many generations to build a successful life.

The kitchen smelled of garlic and spices, and Dr. Asad allowed himself a moment where he existed in neither East nor West. All this uprooting. For what? To build a home for his family, to build a fortress for his son, so Max could enjoy the pleasure of existence. Look at the beautiful wife he had picked for him. There was no one more beautiful than Nadira. That female soldier was a novelty Max would soon tire of. And look: Dr. Asad had many businesses and Max could take over any or all that he wished. The casino he planned to build in downtown Warrenside was Max's if he wanted it.

Dr. Asad knew about love and passion. He had had passion with his beloved first wife, Mariam. He had loved her in the way that young people love each other, chemically aflame and tabula rasa. After she was killed, he had accepted that he would never find that kind of passion again. Not because there were no women as good as Mariam but because that portion of his heart had already been written on and there was no room for more. And his love for her was played out against the backdrop of a burning city, his beloved Beirut. The dangerous part of his life was over, for which he thanked his lucky stars. How long, he often asked himself after Mariam was killed, can you sustain yourself on passion? He loved Bernice in the way a left shoe loves a right shoe. He loved his daughter Houda, of course. Luckily, she was not beautiful, so he did not have to push aside silken tresses to see into her manipulative soul. Lucky the man who has plain daughters, he thought. He will know their motives as well as the motives of the men who profess to love them.

But more than his wives and daughters, he loved Max. The women in his life accepted this as normal. Wasn't it natural for a man to reserve his best love for his son, the man who would remember him after he was dead and give continuity to the short space of time he was on this planet? The man who would forgive his weaknesses and measure himself against his strengths and, if he was lucky, surpass them, to the delight of them both?

Dr. Asad *wanted* his son to be a man. It was unthinkable that Max wouldn't want to claim the place his father had so lovingly prepared for him.

"You will assume your place in this family," he told Max. "There is nothing to discuss. If you want this girl, you will have her in some other way, I can't stop you from doing that, but you cannot marry her. And I will tell you this as well. It is bad luck to have a mistress on your wedding day. Your wife will know and your mistress will be angry and find a way to sabotage you."

Before Max could answer, Dr. Asad raised his hand to silence him, and then Chris Schaeffer came through the kitchen door, saying, "Edward, the police have issued a flood warning for the downtown and are recommending that people voluntarily evacuate from Front Street to the three hundred block."

Houda was right behind him, her raincoat already on. "I'll deal with this, Father. But please, both of you come in an hour."

Then she was gone and Chris was gone and Max was back in the dining room where Selena the belly dancer was entertaining the Aloubs, who were shooting angry, questioning looks at

Dr. Asad—this was no way to treat your in-laws!—and Max was on his cell phone, undoubtedly calling that girl, and Dr. Asad was thinking that in his country, in Beirut, a flood was a sign of renewal, of life refreshing itself. But here, like all transplants, it would turn into something else.

I waited in bed, listening to my mother and Gus Czernak down-stairs. Cabinet doors closing, coffee-bean grinder whirring, the low hum of conversation. Once, they both laughed, then quickly lowered their voices, as if remembering that I was upstairs. A chair scraped the kitchen floor; then the back door closed and I knew they had both left for work.

My mother didn't announce that Gus had moved into our house, but that was the fact. Our old house had only one bath-room, and the evidence of the living arrangements was a Gillette Mach II razor neatly resting in its original plastic packaging and a can of Barbasol shaving cream, neither of which were mine; a bar of Fels Naptha soap; and an orange—orange!—toothbrush, all tucked on their own shelf in the bathroom cabinet.

I jumped out of bed and went to the window, pushing aside the curtain. Both their cars were gone. Then I went into their bedroom and opened the closet again to convince myself that Gus lived there. Mom had thrown out Dad's clothing, but men's clothes lined half the rod: plaid flannel shirts and work pants, hunting clothes. His hunting rifles were stacked in the corner, just like Dad's used to be. A navy blue sport coat hung over khaki pants. Shoes, size 13—Gus was a big guy—were arranged on the floor. They were polished and had shoe trees in them.

So what was I supposed to do, kill Gus? I wasn't happy about Gus, but I wanted to be for my mother's sake. Gus was there for Mom after Dad killed himself. Gus's then wife—what the hell happened to her?—made macaroni casseroles for us long after everyone else got sick of our grieving and moved on. Apparently, *she* had moved on. Mom was moving on. Now it was my turn—I had to move out before they asked me to.

That day's flood detail had been called off. We were to report tomorrow, so I had the day to myself. I'd finished all my cabinet-work before the 501st was activated for Afghanistan and now had to wait while word got around that I was back. My boss at Radio Shack had told me via e-mail that he would hire Jenna, so I figured my account was even on that score. With any luck I wouldn't have to see her again, although a big part of me was really sorry about that. More than that, I had to physically restrain myself from dialing Kat's number.

I repacked my duffel and put the rest of my things in a couple of boxes to move into Dad's hunting cabin in the woods. I owned mostly electronic junk from Radio Shack, and I wouldn't need that now. Mom liked to play with electronic toys, so I figured she could keep them. The rest was fishing and hunting gear, which was all I needed. A couple of pots, a few dishes.

Downstairs by the coffeepot was an envelope with my name on it; inside was the lapis lazuli I had given to Kat. No note. She must have dropped it off when I was asleep. Did she think she could just walk away like that? I tied it around my own neck and yelled, like a madman, "We're not over, Kat!"

Mom came home from work just as I had finished packing and was leaving.

"I was going to come back tomorrow and tell you," I said.

"Tell me what?"

"I'm going to Dad's cabin."

"I was going to go up there and clean it out for you," she said.

"Well, now you don't have to."

Gus came in the door right behind her. He saw what was going on and nodded. He understood that the house wasn't big enough for two bucks. "If you need anything," Gus said.

"Yeah."

"Anything at all," Mom reiterated.

"I just have to figure out what I'm going to do next."

She looked pointedly at my hunting rifle, which I balanced over the two boxes I was holding.

Once, in a fight with Kat, I had told her that all women eventually turn into their mothers. Did all men eventually turn into their fathers? "I'm fine, Mom."

I drove out of town along the river, happy to see it hadn't breached its banks yet, and into the woods, and finally found the overgrown road leading to the hunting cabin, an ongoing family project started by my grandfather. The land had belonged to the Lenape and before them, legend had it, the First People. My grandfather told me it was one of those ineluctable places that fit a template in man's brain: this is what home should look like. Men would fight over a place like this for generations. Spirits of broken dreams inhabited places like this, he said. Not because the men who came here were inferior, but it made them dream big, and not all dreams bloom.

I parked the Barracuda under a tulip poplar behind the hunting cabin and carried my duffel, boxes of belongings, fishing gear, and hunting rifle inside. The air in the cabin was musty and thick. I'd missed deer season last fall because I was in Afghanistan and the fall before too, now that I thought about it. I'd been busy helping Kat out of some mess.

I went outside, turned a valve on the side of the house, went to the well, and pushed the handle on the water pump, up and down, up and down, until the tension eased and I could feel that the water was flowing. Dad had done some fancy plumbing upgrades, and instead of the pumped water coming up to a pail, it was pushed into pipes and flowed into two spigots in the house, one in the kitchen and one in the bathroom. It would keep flowing until you turned off the valve outside the house. Then I switched on the circuit breaker. My grandfather had installed knob-and-tube wiring in the 1940s and I would have to replace it eventually, especially if I stayed up here full-time, but for now it was okay. I thought maybe I could get a couple of solar panels. I wasn't planning on getting any big appliances. A couple of lights were all I needed, and a gun to keep away the building inspector. That was the joke in my family: a gun could keep away the code enforcers.

"Maybe in the old days, Grandpa!" I said aloud.

I moved the old maple couch and pried up some floorboards. My grandfather's lever-action Winchester, with its silver filigreed walnut stock, was there in its hiding place, its old leather case wrapped in a bedsheet. My grandfather loved that gun, and I felt a surge of happiness, knowing it was mine. I laughed aloud at the image of myself as a crazy man in the woods shooting at code enforcers and tax collectors. I was already talking to myself. Why not? I thought. I *was* a crazy man! My past was being stolen; things and places I had loved were being overwritten with a new story, a story in which I would have no say in how things turned out or how I would be remembered.

In the army we were trained in disaster evacuation. It was important, the major giving the training said, to include mementos of your past, photos and whatnot, in your evacuation pack, so when you have to start over you are a whole, integrated person with links to where you've been. It causes psychosis to segregate portions of your life. Cutting off the past, no matter how painful, is never a good idea, because you become an automaton with no history to build on. But what's the point if your history was obliterated? Things were always changing. That didn't mean I had to like it, but neither did it mean I could just take my gun, confront people and make them behave like they used to, like I wanted them to. Isn't that what happened to Dad? He couldn't accept that life had changed while he was in Vietnam. More than that, he couldn't accept that *he* had changed while he was in Vietnam. When he came back from 'Nam he'd lost his place and lost himself. His new self didn't know where to go.

My head started to hurt and I willed myself to stop thinking about Kat and Dad and Mom and Gus and everyone changing and becoming people I no longer recognized. I didn't want to become the madman of the mountain after being up here for one hour.

I made myself a pot of coffee. Then, despite the rain, I went for a walk in the woods down to the river. Sometimes the rain will abate at sunset. I never understood why, but now the sun was turning into a fiery red ball and splinters of it sparkled on the water as it fell below the treetops. The Lenape had a legend about the First People. The legend said that right before the First People became extinct, the Catawissa caught on fire, burning for a month. Eventually the braver of the First People took pieces of the fire into their own longhouses, which proved to be their downfall—trying to own something that was meant for everyone. Is this what the First People saw when they thought the river was on fire? My heart felt lighter than it had in years. For the last hour I hadn't thought about Kat's desertion or Dad's suicide. The space they'd preempted in my brain was superseded by the breadth of creation all around me.

The sun disappeared and it began to rain heavily again. I started back up the trail to the cabin. As I walked, I untied the leather cord around my neck and felt the heavy weight of the lapis lazuli in my hand. My whole life I had tried to keep Kat tied to me with amulets of our oneness: the ouroboros I had tattooed on my shoulder and the identical silver bracelet I had given her and jealously made her wear, the high school ring I bestowed on her in a solemn ceremony and the anguish I felt when she carelessly mentioned that it had slipped off her finger because it was too big. It is childish to think you can tether someone's heart to yours with metal or stone. The heart is a slippery fellow and can wiggle out of any of those prisons. I couldn't capture Kat's love acting like a child. It was time I acted like a man.

I tossed the lapis lazuli in the air lightly, caught it, clutched it, then stopped and pitched it deep into the woods.

"There's some bread and stuff over there in the bag. Get it out."
Wind carefully removed two burnt hot dogs from sticks, put them
on a piece of tinfoil, skewered two more, and handed them to
Cantwell, who had come by to see how she was managing with
all the rain, if her property had started to flood yet. It hadn't. She
was glad she was still dressed from a consultation earlier: short
white linen dress over her jeans, chest full of silver and cabochon
jewelry, clean blond hair that she hadn't bothered to braid. It
flowed loosely over her shoulders and down her back.

"Here, you do this. Hold them over the fire," she commanded
him; by fire, she meant the blue gas flame of the old range in her
kitchen. "There ya go. You're a natural."

Wind pulled out a stack of paper plates from a brown shopping bag on the table—ketchup, mustard, plastic knives and
forks—while Cantwell toasted the dogs. She had bought all this

stuff for the memorial service she never had for her dad, recognizing at the last minute that there was no one to invite.

"I'm kind of surprised you eat like this," Cantwell said. "I thought you would be more—I don't know, authentic or something."

"Everybody thinks they know what an authentic Indian is. What do *you* think authentic is? Are you authentic? Let me bring it home for you: What does it mean to be an authentic ass-kisser in the employ of the Warrens?"

"I know what you mean," Cantwell said. He smiled broadly. "You're right."

Wind was dumbfounded. Cantwell just wouldn't get mad. Whenever she had a good blast of hot air going, puffing into her sails so forcefully that she could feel her vessel move, he smiled and the air would calm.

He said, "When I was a kid we lived in this old house, it was like a historic house? And every time we wanted to paint the shutters or something, we had to go through the Historic Commission to make sure the color was just the right shade of dark, dark green, instead of black—which isn't authentic, by the way—and to make sure it wasn't too glossy, but not too matte either. They had paint samples so we could see what people on the *Mayflower* would approve of. We couldn't even get aluminum replacement windows, you know? No such thing as aluminum replacement windows in 1632."

Wind frowned. The Historic District was on the north side of town, and it was expensive as hell to live there. It dawned on her that Cantwell was one of *the* Cantwells, who were just as bad as the Warrens in their own way, if not worse. The Cantwells built a museum to house a collection of Lenape artifacts after they had expelled the Lenape themselves to a reservation in Oklahoma, thinking that preserving Lenape artifacts made them more human. "See, that's what I mean. Where do they stop the authenticity clock? If you want to be really authentic, you would knock the whole thing down and let it revert back to nature. Colonial isn't my idea of authentic."

"So what's authentic, Wind?"

Wind made all the Kristins, Kristas, and Kirstins address her as Ms. Storm. Cantwell was the first person to say her name aloud since her father died. It was important to have your name shouted into the universe so the appropriate guiding spirits heard you and sent help, and when Cantwell said "Wind" it was as if a gust came rushing through the trees and caressed her. "Well, this is an *authentic* Oscar Mayer wiener," she said. "Authentic pig lips and snouts and lots of salt. It doesn't claim to be anything else. I think that's what authentic is."

Cantwell had showed up at five o'clock, unannounced and uninvited. He was driving his own Jeep this time, and although she had tried to insult him to drive him off, he stayed and said she must be starving; wasn't she starving? And as if to prove she *wasn't* starving, she pulled out the hot dogs and began to cook. Hot dogs over the gas flame were one of the two meals in her repertoire, the other being turkey, which she cooked every year at Thanksgiving, tossing it into a fire afterward as a protest against the holiday. Jimmy would catch and kill the bird; she would cook it, thanking its spirit for its pointless sacrifice, then throw it on the bonfire they built for the occasion. Now that Jimmy was dead, she would have to get her turkeys at Food Giant and figure out how to defrost a twenty-three-pound bird with an unnaturally large breast. Jimmy had told her that these monstrous birds, which were raised in coops, had to be slaughtered each year. They couldn't mate because of their super-large breasts: nothing fit where it was supposed to. They were impregnated, continuing the insult to their spirit, with turkey basters.

"You know what I always wanted to do?" Cantwell said. "I always wanted to hunt turkeys. Eat a real turkey. I see them sometimes on the golf course, walking in a line from the ninth hole down through the trees to your property. They look like a bunch of monks with their heads bobbing and their tails swaying. They look like they're begging to be eaten."

Cantwell's legs were crossed, ankle over knee, the hated Sioux logo from the country club embroidered on his green sock. He was branded, she thought, and the brand didn't even reveal his real owner. Typical white trickery. She said, "They look easy to catch, but they're not."

"How do you know?"

"I hunt them all the time," Wind lied so fast she couldn't take it back. "Hey, you know why the turkeys are here? Lenape used to live on the golf course."

"On the golf course? You mean on the *golf course?*"

"It was the most beautiful bend in the river. It still is, don't you think? Who wouldn't want to live here? We lost it in a walking purchase in 1762, which turned out to be fake; the whites cheated. We rioted and massacred the farmer living over the fourteenth hole, probably."

"Am I supposed to say I'm sorry?"

"Am I? Nothing is ever black-and-white. Our own people, the Iroquois, refused to back us up. The Iroquois representative, Canasatego, told us, 'They conquered you. You are women, they made *women* of you. Give up your claim to your old lands and move west. Never attempt to sell land again. Now get out.'"

"That's harsh."

"They were pissed off because we didn't ask their permission to sell the land in the first place. Politics is just about power. I never understood why a person would want power over another human being. Do you?"

Cantwell examined his hot-dog roll. "Well, now you're here," he said, finally.

Now I'm here, Wind thought. The last of the Lenape on land that was bought with her father's blood money, and she would like nothing better than to get the hell out and move somewhere else and stop being a professional Indian. Except she promised her father she'd keep the flame alive. Now she was keeping the flame alive in her own kitchen with a descendant of the people who tricked the Lenape out of their land in the first place.

"Well, I'd really like to learn how to hunt turkeys," Cantwell said. He put down his plastic dinnerware and looked at her as if she were the most magnificent person in the world. "Hunting your own food is authentic by any standards."

All of Wind's instincts told her that she should chase Cantwell out of the house, off of her property, but this was the first conversation with anyone who wasn't paying her since her father died and it felt good just to say "Pass the mustard." Plus, he had said she was the most beautiful woman he had ever seen and she was good-looking enough to believe that it might be true, and while she was savvy enough to know that women always fell for men who complimented them as a way to seduce them (isn't that what all the Kristas complained about?), Wind found herself enjoying the wait to see if he would say it again.

"Why don't you show me right now!" Cantwell asked, jumping up from the table.

"It's raining," Wind said.

"It's only water."

"And I still have to clean this up."

"Leave it, I'll clean up later. Grab your boots."

"I don't have boots," Wind said.

"What? It's not authentic to stay dry?" He laughed. "Here, put this on." He threw her his slicker and was out the door.

must have dropped it off when I was asleep. Did she think she could just walk away like that? I tied it around my own neck and yelled, like a madman, "We're not over, Kat!"

Mom came home from work just as I had finished packing and was leaving.

"I was going to come back tomorrow and tell you," I said.

"Tell me what?"

"I'm going to Dad's cabin."

"I was going to go up there and clean it out for you," she said.

"Well, now you don't have to."

Gus came in the door right behind her. He saw what was going on and nodded. He understood that the house wasn't big enough for two bucks. "If you need anything," Gus said.

"Yeah."

"Anything at all," Mom reiterated.

"I just have to figure out what I'm going to do next."

She looked pointedly at my hunting rifle, which I balanced over the two boxes I was holding.

Once, in a fight with Kat, I had told her that all women eventually turn into their mothers. Did all men eventually turn into their fathers? "I'm fine, Mom."

I drove out of town along the river, happy to see it hadn't breached its banks yet, and into the woods, and finally found the overgrown road leading to the hunting cabin, an ongoing family project started by my grandfather. The land had belonged to the Lenape and before them, legend had it, the First People. My grandfather told me it was one of those ineluctable places that fit a template in man's brain: this is what home should look like. Men would fight over a place like this for generations. Spirits of bro-

ry. You shouldn't try to kill something if
gh to eat it."

immy's outhouses looked like they were
ing water, about to go downstream to
n to go. It would solve her problem of
nk.

k over here from the ninth hole this
id. "They'll probably be by again to-
l on the Internet about animal habits.
hem." Cantwell looked up into the
er the rain. See, it's not so bad."
from her father that an Indian
dn't. "See this tree?" Wind said. "It
n the fall to make jellies and ton-
of a hawthorn. "But you got to

n't poisonous?"
h the birds. They know."
ight."

she pictured as a jigsaw house
would trap her inside forever.
hat possessed her. She would
t was Jimmy as long as she
'It's easier to go out and just

tensified the smell of new
ed to bury her face in the
et about hunting a stupid
of prickly stalks. "Look,
uple of weeks, when the
big and plump, and the
go crazy." She immedi-

ately felt embarrassed for talking about aphrodisiac berries and rammy bucks.

"This is where the turkeys cross over," Cantwell said. He pointed and moved his finger across the field. "Every day at six-twenty, exactly."

Wind tapped her watch, a geeky black rubber contraption with lots of knobs. "It's past that now," she said, relieved.

"I'm surprised you don't use a sundial," Cantwell said.

"What are you doing on my property anyway, spying on me? That's trespassing. I could have you arrested."

"We're friends, so no one would believe you."

Well, *now* we're friends, she wanted to say. We weren't when you were spying on me. "Let's sit under the pines and wait for them. Put this over your head." She handed him a green army blanket. "So they don't see us. Turkeys can see red and yellow."

They covered themselves and squatted under a couple of bayberry bushes, which had just started to bloom with tiny reddish flowers, their exquisite cup-shaped blossoms catching the rain before it overflowed onto them. Wind grabbed a branch and pulled it to her face, inhaling the new aroma. This is what she thought of when she thought of the land: bayberry bushes. She didn't have to stay here to have bayberry bushes. She could plant them anywhere. They were perennials in twenty zones. "The ground is cold," she said, releasing the branch. Snapping back, it shook the bush, splattering water all over them.

"There are usually twelve of them. They walk really slowly, with a kind of rhythm." He swayed his shoulders slowly back and forth, moving his neck in an exaggerated motion.

"We need some stones," Wind said. "The idea is to stun a turkey with a stone from a slingshot, which we don't have, and pounce on it and either cut its throat or snap its neck before it recovers."

the closet again to convince myself that
[h]ad thrown out Dad's clothing, but men's
[go]od: plaid flannel shirts and work pants,
[hu]nting rifles were stacked in the corner,
A navy blue sport coat hung over khaki
[hi]s was a big guy—were arranged on the
[a]nd had shoe trees in them.
[wanted] to do, kill Gus? I wasn't happy about
[for] my mother's sake. Gus was there for
[hers]elf. Gus's then wife—what the hell
[m]acaroni casseroles for us long after
grieving and moved on. Apparently,
[m]oving on. Now it was my turn—I
[a]sked me to.
[had] been called off. We were to report
[m]yself. I'd finished all my cabinet-
[depar]ted for Afghanistan and now had
[th]at I was back. My boss at Radio
[tha]t he would hire Jenna, so I fig-
[a] score. With any luck I wouldn't
[b]ig part of me was really sorry
[had] to physically restrain myself

[the] rest of my things in a couple
[a] cabin in the woods. I owned
[S]hack, and I wouldn't need
[elec]tronic toys, so I figured she
[ng] and hunting gear, which
[few] dishes.
[an] envelope with my name
[giv]en to Kat. No note. She

Jimmy had shown Wind how to snap a bird's neck in the chicken coop, which Wind had emptied out as soon as Jimmy died.

"Look, there they are!" Cantwell shouted. "Let's get them!"

Wind's heart beat fast as she ran toward the hens, amazed and laughing at how fast the huge, ungainly birds could move when pursued. The ground was soggy and slippery, and when Wind caught up with them she tripped and fell on the slowest hen, screaming for Cantwell to come quick. The hen's body felt like an oversized football clamped under her arm. She wrestled with it as it pecked her and tried to get to its feet.

"I can't kill it. You do it," she said. She was crying.

Cantwell finished the hen with a deft twist of his wrists while the other turkeys ran, gobbling, into the woods.

"My dad taught me how," he said, and Wind thought, How kind of him not to say anything about authenticity. Because right now she felt like an authentic jerk. It was only later that she remembered he told her he didn't know how to hunt.

"I got the rest," he said, and cut around the perineum of the bird with a pocket knife, yanking out its guts, which he left in a pile on the ground. "Let's get out of the rain; what do you say? We're completely soaked." He held the bird by its legs and ran ahead, Wind sprinting to catch up.

Wind felt her foot skid on a stone and exclaimed lightly when she saw it was blue, unusual for the area, and, when she picked it up, saw that it was looped with a strip of leather. She held it up and let the rain wash the mud off it. "It must be a present," she said, when she caught up with him.

"From your gods?" Cantwell asked.

Wind clutched the stone. Back at the house, she stomped off the rain and put the turkey in the sink, where she would pluck it and clean it and maybe even cook it—she could manage to do that much—but not before she said a prayer to the spirit of the turkey who had died only so she could show off in front of a man who proclaimed her the most beautiful woman he had ever seen; then she put the lapis lazuli around Cantwell's neck.

"No, I think it's a present from *your* gods," she said. The stone was hot and almost lit up the room with its glow.

"Now, why would the gods give me a present?" he asked.

Wind, whose shaman business was to monitor the progress of love, the absence of love, the totems and harbingers of love, recognized that this was a love stone. As soon as the lapis lazuli nestled into the U of his collarbone, Cantwell's eyes danced with a twitch of hope, a fog of blindness, and an eagerness to believe the best of everyone—a state of mind that is reserved for that subset of madness called love. "Maybe it's a present for me," she said, holding out her palm to show him the little blister the stone had left. She shooed him out the door, promising him he could come by tomorrow for a cooked turkey, then collapsed on the floor, inhaling the sage and sweetgrass she waved in front of her face.

Immediately, Big Blue swooped down and carried her away. She closed her eyes against the rain and held on tightly to the heron's thin back, feeling the beating of tiny wings around her head and shoulders. Dozens of hummingbirds struggled against the wind, trying to keep up. She tried to swat them away with her hand, but they were persistent. "Stop it! Stop it!" she cried. "What are these hummingbirds doing here?" she shouted.

"We are in a race," Big Blue answered. "We have been for a week. I'm exhausted."

"When is the race over?" she asked.

"When we get there, of course! I am very busy. Did you need something specific?"

He flapped steadily while the hummingbirds darted off to suck nectar out of flowers and then raced back to catch up.

"You're never going to beat these little birds," she said, batting at them. "You might as well concede. They're, like, doubling around you."

"It would be a lot easier if you didn't call for all this rain," Big Blue said.

"Look, I don't think this rain is all me."

"Whatever. I'm getting tired."

"Okay, okay. One thing. I need to know if Cantwell is in love with me," she said.

"Why do you need to know that?"

"Because if he is, then I can be in love with him."

"Why can't you be in love with someone who isn't in love with you?"

Wind wondered how this animal guide could be so dense. "Because it's a giant waste of time to be in love with someone who isn't in love with you."

"What a funny idea. Someone has to start the ball rolling. Someone has to be first."

"Just yes or no."

"It's not that easy."

Wind wanted to cry. "Please."

"I really think you should just ask him. That's the easiest way."

"But I don't know if he's using me for that bitch Warren to get me to sell the property, or if he really likes me."

Wind rested her head on Big Blue's neck and acknowledged her loneliness. If Jimmy were alive she could talk to him, even if she had to admit that her father, especially after he smoked a bowl, was just as unfathomable as Big Blue.

"Enjoy it! This is the best part," Big Blue said, veering toward the ground.

"What, saying goodbye to me?"

"It's the part of love where nothing bad has happened. Where you think only of good things when you think of your beloved. Isn't it sweet?"

For pain, yes, Wind had to admit, it was pleasurable. "Good luck with your race!" she shouted as Big Blue flapped off into the rainy night, followed by his escort of jewel-colored hummingbirds.

EIGHTEEN

BARBARA

Barbara tried the basement door, gently, so as not to alert Mike. It was locked. She *tsk*ed and went back upstairs to lie down on her Louis XV to feel the vibrations coming up through the floor and was annoyed when the doorbell rang, and opened the door to see a Hispanic man in army desert fatigues who asked if Kat was home. "I'm supposed to call her when we're activated. She has to call the next person on the list," he explained to Barbara's blank face.

"I seem to remember that Kat has already left," Barbara said, wondering if Kat knew even one normal person. She was sending exotic friends around to anger her, Barbara knew. The man who picked Kat up earlier was swarthy too; they left practically stapled to each other and Barbara felt the old throbbing and went to find Mike, who was in the basement, the door to which was locked, and then this other man showed up.

The man introduced himself as Camacho. "Are you her mother?" he asked. "I can see the resemblance."

Barbara, who was charmed by social lubricants in any form, especially social lies, wanted to believe that Mr. Camacho could see her resemblance to Kat under the hundred pounds that camouflaged her beauty, so she invited him in. "It's so wet out there. Come in and I'll fix you some coffee," and Camacho, who seemed glad for the postponement of duty and the chance to look around the house, trailed her into the kitchen.

"You don't have to help," Barbara told him, alarmed that he had followed her and had already taken a seat at the counter.

"My dad built houses like this all the time in Puerto Rico," he said.

"Who is your father?" Barbara asked him. She started to prepare a sandwich too, saying, "You can't count on the army to feed you," with which Camacho enthusiastically agreed.

"My father told Asad he would fix up all his houses downtown, but Asad doesn't want to do it. He said it's not worth pouring money into *rentals*. We live down there, and with just some new glass and some paint it would look like new. He's a cheap bastard."

"You live in an Asad property?" Barbara asked, pushing potato chips on him.

"Where do foreigners get off owning us? Aren't we at war with them? My father planted a *noni* tree in the backyard and Asad made us rip it out. He said it was in the lease that we couldn't plant trees. I heard he doesn't want the expense of tearing the trees up when he plows up the whole downtown."

Barbara forgot for a minute that she disliked Puerto Ricans like Camacho almost as much as she disliked Arabs. "My great-great-great-great-grandfather founded this town," she said. It was something she had to get in every conversation she had with strangers, to make sure they understood where she perched on the pecking order—at the top. "I'm sure you don't even know who your great-great-great-great grandfather *was*."

"Are you kidding?" Camacho said. "I have sixteen middle names! We Puerto Ricans can tell you how we're related to *Adam and Eve*," which Barbara sincerely doubted, but she offered him a cookie and milk to prolong their conversation, which had actually run its course, and then he left.

The conversation about the Asads knocked Barbara off balance, and she went downstairs and pounded on the basement door. "Mike? Mike, I know you're down there. I need some help up here." She heard some mumbling or grumbling and then quiet. He'd been here every day since he was fired. He said he was starting a new business, but starting a new business scared her, even though it was always what she said she loved about her great-great-great-great grandfather—he actually started something, didn't just live on the residuals of someone else's initiative—and here Mike was starting something, and now the idea of all that responsibility overwhelmed her and the picture of the gurgling landfill under the golf course kept appearing in front of her eyes. She hoped he wasn't doing something that involved chemicals. Today she *hated* chemicals. They were supposed to act in certain ways under certain conditions, certain prescribed ways. That was their beauty, the miracle of them. And yet the chemicals—Abilify specifically—that she had been taking for the past month were acting any way they pleased, without consultation as to where she wanted to go. They didn't let her respond fast enough this morning to Kat's new boyfriend, and Kat's presenting him here as if it were a normal thing to do, without any warning or—and this irked her most of all—without any apology, was unforgivable, but Abilify was supposed to free her to think of a withering response to his brazen appearance, and it hadn't. Then she remembered she hadn't taken Abilify today.

The doorbell rang again and this time it was Cantwell from the club, with the bad news that Wind Storm wasn't selling, and now she was left with the uncertainty of not knowing whether the uncooperative woman was not selling to *her* or not selling at all.

"That's such a pretty stone," Barbara said, admiring the lapis lazuli around his neck. "There's something mesmerizing about it."

"Look, Barbara, I'm the golf pro. My job doesn't include snooping around for you. Neither does it include hitting golf balls onto her property so you can harass her. I'm off the case."

Barbara reached out to feel the lapis but it gave off heat, like a warning.

"She's a nice person. Why don't you deal with her directly, woman to woman?"

Barbara wondered where he got such a stupid idea that *directly* was the way to deal with anyone. The less someone knew of your motives, the better off everyone would be.

"The club is starting to flood," Cantwell said as he left. "It's a mess. I sent everyone home. If I were you, I wouldn't check in today, either."

Meanwhile, the vibrations from the basement continued. Barbara knew she had to get out of the house or she would explode. She wasn't hot a moment ago, but now taking off her blouse seemed like the only solution to the oppressive heat that was emanating from her own being. Then she took off her bra, because the sweat was sliding down between her breasts, which she wiped with her blouse. Then she removed her skirt and her knee-high stockings. She was just so *hot*. She thought it must be the Abilify, but she actually hadn't taken Abilify today. Or yesterday, either. She couldn't remember. She hadn't taken any of the chemicals she was supposed to take. This heat was *her*. This is what she felt like. It had been so long, she didn't remember.

She pounded on the basement door and was met with his stupid, arrogant, working-class silence. "Mike," she whined. "Mikey, *please*!"

She thought she would fix herself up and force him to see her. She went into her bathroom to comb her hair, but she couldn't see her entire self—just her left eye, then her right eye—in the little mirror glued to the wall. Breathing hard, she ran into Kat's bathroom, which not had only a full-length mirror on the back of the door but white tiles and fixtures so Barbara could get a really good look at herself.

"Ah!" She covered her mouth with the back of her hand. No wonder. She opened the drawers on the vanity until she found a red lipstick, brilliant red! She was so pale. When did she get so pale? She ran the lipstick round and round her mouth until she was happy with the lips, but then her cheeks looked like landing fields, large expanses of unblemished white, so she drew circles on her cheeks and colored them in with the red stick. Her nipples, too, were pink and tiny on her colossal breasts. She could hardly see them, they were lost in waves of flesh, so she started to color her nipples with the lipstick, which broke off, she was pressing it so hard, so she picked it up and mushed it around her breasts, getting the red all over her fingers, which she wiped on the front of her belly, panting. It was better, better. But her hair! She was only forty-three, and yet gray hair had sprung up at her temples. She foraged around the vanity drawer, found a pair of grooming scissors, and cut off the tip of one long lock, then shorter and shorter and then all around her head except the back, which she couldn't reach. Her eyes were burning, and she couldn't see the clumps of fine auburn hair that stuck to her body where she applied the lipstick.

She ran downstairs and kicked the basement door. "I hate you!" she screamed. Then she ran to the dining room and grabbed the cheap red alligator tote—Delmonico, fine imitation leather—that Mike had given her for her forty-third birthday, which contained her wallet and keys and her father's wonderful book *The House Is Built!*, stuffed with clippings and pertinent articles, and opened the front door. A cool breeze drifted over her face. The raindrops felt wonderful. She tucked the red alligator under her arm, pulled the door shut, and felt a satisfying draft on her bare behind. Then she charged down the street.

The flooding downtown was three feet at the deepest parts, but Captain Whynnot, our company commander, told us that people have drowned in a foot of water. The block that I was to work in was less than a foot deep, but it surged in a strong current and I had to walk in rhythm with the waves so I wouldn't lose my balance.

Worse than that, though, the water stank, and Captain Whynnot said there was just as much danger of dying of disease as drowning, because the old downtown cast-iron sewer pipes couldn't take the sudden influx of water and the sewers were backing up. The water was green and gunky; I had to stop thinking about it or I couldn't wade in. I was in charge of a very elite group—me and Jenna Magee—giving out bottled water to people, then ushering them out of their row homes on Front and Second streets and onto Humvees and pickups that a local dealership had loaned for the evacuation. Most of the people rented their houses, and it showed. Broken windows were covered with plastic sheets or plywood, boards were torn out of steps and porches, front doors were weighed down with police locks, brass key escutcheons and doorknobs were ripped off, and stained-glass transoms were cut out of vestibules, probably by junkies who resold them. If I lived here, I would be glad for a vacation, even if it were just to the high school gym on Mountain Avenue, which is where the evacuees were going. But I don't think I ever saw people move so slowly. It was as if they thought they weren't going to come back. Which, it turned out, was exactly what happened.

"He wants the downtown," an old lady on Front Street shouted from her porch. She was holding her white lapdog in a metallic tote bag like she was Paris Hilton, and it made me laugh because while the old lady was technically a platinum blonde like Paris, the rest of her was *strictly* a cautionary tale of what happens if you don't floss your teeth and eat your vegetables. "Bring all your medicines and your glasses," I told her as we'd been instructed. "False teeth. Do you have everything?"

"I got everything I need," the old lady said, hugging her dog closer.

We were supposed to discourage them from bringing their pets, which could turn feral in groups. In Kandahar, a safety officer gave us a presentation on how to evacuate civilians and someone asked the question: What do we do with their dogs? The captain, kidding, said you put all the dogs and a bag of food in the back of a deuce-and-a-half and see what's left at the end of the ride. We all laughed, but the real answer isn't much better: you shoot them. Marauding dogs are dangerous. "We don't know when you can come back, so make sure you have the essentials," I said. I let Paris Hilton keep her dog. I was pretty sure that if I looked in her tote, I would find the dog's medicine, not hers. I moved on to the next family while Jenna tied plastic bags over the woman's feet and escorted her through the stygian sludge into a Hummer.

"*He* wants the downtown." I had heard it three times already before the old lady and her dog, and I finally realized they were talking about Max's father. Everybody downtown thought in some weird magical-thinking loop that Dr. Asad had *caused* the flood so he could expropriate their houses, demolish them, and build something more lucrative than subsidized housing. How paranoid can you get?

Max had been sent to the high school to translate for the recent wave of Middle Eastern immigrants. Most of the Lebanese and Syrians lived in brand-new developments in the suburbs, which I thought were just nicer-looking ghettos, shtetls, whatever. The burbs were so high up they didn't have to be evacuated, and I was jealous that I was working so hard and Max was probably doing nothing.

We had talked that morning. He said his father was adamant that he go through with his marriage to Nadira. "And what?" I had asked, feeling frantic. "You can't marry her! How can you marry her if you love me?" And Max said that of course he would not marry her but, in his culture, love actually had nothing to do with marriage, he was just *saying*, and I said, "Well, in mine too, but who cares?" He agreed, but the look on his face said he wasn't happy about it.

"Where will we go, *habibi*?" he asked. "We'll have to run away like criminals." Which he promised we would do as soon as the flood subsided; we would run away like criminals. We just had to figure out where that would be. His father had postponed the wedding until the flood detail was over, and *then* he would straighten it out.

When I insisted he straighten it out *right now*, he looked miserable and said he would. "It's what you want, isn't it?" I said. "I

mean, I'm not asking you to do something you don't want to do."
I had the sickening thought that maybe I felt more than he did
about us. It couldn't be!

He took my hand and stroked it while he thought, turning it to
kiss my palm. "Whatever you want is what I want," he had said.

"I'll take care of this person." Jenna stepped through the flood
gunk to a porch where a lone woman was waiting. The woman
was wearing cheap fake survival gear from Walmart: poncho and
carpenter pants. Her hair was tucked into a dark blue working-
man's handkerchief. Her feet were already wrapped in plastic
bags. She was blandly pretty, slender. It was almost impossible to
tell how old she was, her face was so serene. She was sitting on
top of an army duffel on her porch steps. She smoothed her hair
self-consciously when she saw me looking at her. Jenna reached
out her hand to help the woman off the porch and grabbed the
duffel herself.

"Hey," I said. "We're not supposed to carry their stuff if they're
able. That's the rule."

Jenna ignored me, escorted the woman to a vehicle, and came
back with water to give to the people—a whole family—waiting
on the next porch. She picked up a little boy about three years
old and hiked him up on her shoulder while the mother and father put plastic bags over their feet, grabbed their gear, and used
it to nudge the other children ahead of them.

I knocked loudly on the next door, which swung open to
reveal an old man sitting motionless and staring at a dark television as if waiting for the electricity to come back on. "Sir? *Sir!*" I
said. "We're evacuating you."

The man shook his head. "I'm not going anywhere."

"It's not safe here," I said.

He laughed loudly. "You're just finding that out now? I'm not
going anywhere; now go away."

I called the detail sergeant on my cell phone and left it up to him to figure out what to do.

"Hey, you're not supposed to carry their stuff," I told Jenna again.

"What am I supposed to do? Their stuff is all they have."

"I'm just telling you the rule." I was losing it. Just being downtown was creeping me out. On the porch of one of the houses, where no one responded to my insistent pounding, were empty brown crack vials. In the living room window was a doll collection arranged with the biggest on the left all the way down to the smallest on the right. A stuffed bear, taking its place in the size queue, had a brown vial on its lap. That windowsill, I knew, was the only orderly thing in the chaotic existence of some kid who would grow up to be either the same as the grownups who lived here or the district attorney. I could hear some movement inside, so people were there but they wouldn't answer the door.

The detail sergeant pulled up in a Humvee and asked me how far along we were. I showed him the map: two more blocks. He told me the rain was supposed to stop tomorrow morning and then we would see what we had to clean up.

When I was on active duty, I never felt that I would rather be anywhere else, mostly because there was nowhere else I could think of to be. But now I wanted only to be out of here with Max, going *somewhere else*. After our conversation this morning, I knew that the longer we were here, the harder it would be for him to break with his father. It's easy to overpower someone in an imaginary argument. I had won many arguments with my mother in the middle of the night in Afghanistan.

Max, as if reading my mind, called and said he was being relieved because the suburbs were dry and he was transferring to downtown to help us out. The water was still rising and sloshing into my boots. Jenna said the water was about a foot and a half in some places, already too deep for the plastic bags, and I should call in for rafts, and by the way, where was Sergeant Wolinsky?

"Duck?" Camacho was supposed to call me when we activated and I was to call Duck.

"Isn't he your—"

"Yes. Yes, he is, but I forgot." I snapped open my cell phone and dialed his home phone. No one answered, and his cell phone said he was out of range. "He's not answering."

"You're both going to get in trouble," Jenna said.

"I can't leave now," I said. Max was coming. I didn't *want* to leave.

"Camacho saw him driving out River Road."

To his father's hunting cabin, of course. I would have to go get him before we both got Article 15s.

"I'll get him," Jenna said. "If you know where he is, just tell me and I'll do you a favor and get him. You wait here for the rafts. You're in charge."

"He's probably at his father's hunting cabin. Here, I'll draw you a map."

"I could use a break," Jenna said. "I hate boats, anyway."

When I handed her the map, Jenna was smiling.

"Hey," I said. "You know they don't want us to help people with their bags and stuff because we'll get too tired. You shouldn't have helped those people carry their crap."

Jenna grabbed the map. "I live down here. What am I supposed to do, pretend I have a stick up my ass? You know that woman with the head scarf, the one all neat and tidy and ready to rock? For your information, that was my mother. So just back off."

TWENTY

DR. ASAD

Because of the flooding, Dr. Asad had closed Lucky Lady, and he and Houda were working out of their offices in St. Maron's, which overlooked the old downtown and the river from High Street. The flood would have to be twelve feet deep before they would need to evacuate St. Maron's. Thank goodness, Dr. Asad thought, because he had a hundred residents living there, all in various stages of incoherence. As it was, several staff members couldn't make it in, and some of the night shift had been asked to stay.

He and Houda had argued all morning about Max's wedding. "It's not *if*," he told her, "it's a question of *when*. Obviously, we will have to postpone if Max is still on duty."

Houda showed him the receipts. "We could get some money back on the catering if we canceled now, before Alfred Younis orders the food. But as soon as he orders the food, someone will have to pay for it, and you know it will be us, Papa."

After all the money Dr. Asad threw at Aladdin's, Alfred Younis should be hosting Max's wedding gratis. That Alfred didn't offer to host the wedding as a present was a bitter acknowledgment of the Asads' better fortune.

He was appalled at Houda's lack of faith in her brother, that Max wouldn't do the right thing for the family. He had spent the entire night awake, convincing himself that of course Max would marry Nadira. The entire Aloub clan was here, enjoying Dr. Asad's extended hospitality and understanding the fact that Max was unfortunately still on duty. Postpone, yes. Cancel, never. Max was raised to be his son and nothing else. He would wither and fade outside the embrace of his family, a fact Max understood. He could not support a wife on his own, and no matter how liberated American women imagined themselves to be, they, like women in Lebanon, wanted a man who could support them. His liaison with that girl would die a natural death if he didn't try to force them apart. He would postpone until Max came to the marriage with a clear head. He didn't care how much it cost. A ten-thousand-dollar catering bill was nothing compared to what he was going to be able to make downtown.

For a long time he'd had the idea of bringing a major casino to Warrenside, financed by him with Max as managing partner, but he had been reluctant to displace his tenants; two years ago he had commissioned an architect to come up with a plan that incorporated the deserted steel mill as the façade. The model was in his office and he looked at it every day, imagining the possibilities. This flood was a gift. Despite the insurance money, it would cost a fortune to clean up and refit the flooded homes, and even if he did he would have to raise the rents, which his government-subsidized tenants couldn't afford.

Frankly, no matter what the old guard said about the down-town "coming back," *no one* was coming back from the suburbs to live in row houses. The old guard had led the charge to the suburbs, into McMansions with five bathrooms apiece. The insurance money would be a substantial down payment on new construction. He felt a sense of excitement as he imagined the I-beam logo of Warren Steel, now stamped on every structure in town, replaced with the more soothing cedar tree of his native country. It was an opportunity that Max would not be able to resist.

Chris Schaeffer had slipped noiselessly into Dr. Asad's office and sat down. He stared stonily at Dr. Asad, who was still dreaming about his casino. It wasn't the first time he had seen the model, and Chris had spread the word to his neighbors downtown; the rag head, he said, had his eye on their homes. They should start looking for other places to live. From his own point of view, it would put Chris out of business, because all the businesses that he protected were within the red circle Dr. Asad had marked for extinction.

"Edward," he said.

Dr. Asad looked up, startled. "Yes, Chris."

"It's getting worse."

"Have all my houses been evacuated?"

"The ones that'll go."

"Who won't go?" He forced himself to the present. "Oh, of course."

The drug dealers wouldn't go. If they left, they would lose their turf. It wasn't only local addicts who depended on them. Warrenside was a distribution center for all of eastern Pennsylvania. Dealers from New York and New Jersey picked up their inventory in the downtown row houses on Third Street. The local drug barons paid their rent up front, a year in advance, in cash.

"That can't be helped," Dr. Asad said. "The National Guard will have to deal with them."

"There's some looting; you should know."

Probably the neighborhood bodegas. He was sorry about the looting, but it was not his concern. Anyway, the stuff would perish if someone didn't take it. He looked at the weather forecast on his computer. The rain was going to hold for one more day; then it would stop. It couldn't be more perfect. It would be enough to make the houses uninhabitable.

"Stay away from the downtown, Chris. I think it will be dangerous if there is looting and people get desperate." He was glad Max was working safely at the high school. Hopefully the worst would be over in a week; then Max and Nadira could get married and Max could begin thinking about how to convert the downtown from rows of unprofitable rentals into a high-yielding casino. The Oasis Corporation in Las Vegas was seemingly anxious to work with Dr. Asad and expand their empire to Warrenside. If the paradigm proved successful in Warrenside, he could partner with them in post-industrial cities in Ohio and New York.

Being from a desert culture, Dr. Asad was happy to be associated with a corporation called the Oasis. He felt the wind tickle his neck. Lady Luck was near. He could hear her approval in the breeze. "You have your phone, Chris?"

Chris got up. "I'll be in touch."

"Are you going home?"

"My block's been evacuated. I'll try to find a motel in Whitehall."

In the three years that Chris had worked for him, Dr. Asad had never thought about Chris's personal life. It certainly had never occurred to him that Chris was his tenant.

I spent the entire morning and most of the afternoon cleaning the cabin and shaking stuff out. Spiders crawled out of old bed linens, blankets, and kitchen cupboards. My grandfather's old aluminum coffeepot had become a dead mouse's coffin. And while I have a high regard for spiders and their seeming dichotomy of constant motion and willingness to sit for hours waiting for prey to enter their webs, I didn't want them sleeping or eating breakfast with me. And I didn't want to sip coffee with a mouse. So I washed everything with the bleach my mom had shoved in my duffel before I left her house.

I was supposed to be on flood detail. The rest of the unit was there, okay? But I was waiting for Kat, as my notifier, to officially notify me. If she didn't, it wasn't my fault if I didn't know to show up. And if she did—well, I needed to talk to her.

I was oiling my grandfather's Winchester when I heard a car pull up: Jenna Magee in a bright yellow Humvee. Despite my irritation that it was not Kat, I had to smile. It was actually good to see someone, even after only a day in isolation.

"Steal the Humvee, Jenna?" I asked.

"This isn't a social visit," she said. "You're supposed to get your ass downtown and help us." I followed her as she stomped around the cabin. "This place is kind of cool. You going to live here now?"

"Till I figure out what's next," I said.

She swung around suddenly, and I don't know how it happened but she was in my arms and we were all over each other. I couldn't help myself. Her body was like a drug I just couldn't get enough of, even if I was in love with Kat. I can't explain it to this day. At least not in a way that's flattering either to Jenna or myself.

"What are you thinking of right now?" she asked as we lay on the floor, naked. She flipped on top of me and looked me right in the face, forcing me to open my eyes. "I *knew* it. You're such a jerk. You're with *me*!"

"What? Why am I a jerk?" I asked.

We both started pulling on our clothes, because it was clear by the light that a couple of hours had gone by. I didn't bother locking up. The only thing to keep out were bears and golfers from the nearby country club.

By the time we got downtown it was raining harder than ever. The access roads were lined with people who looked like they were at a parade, rubbernecking and checking out the action. We parked the Humvee uphill from the flooding, and as soon as we got out I was almost knocked out by the combined smell of gasoline and sewage. The water was about three feet deep. Motorboats were getting their propellers jammed on the debris and pickup trucks were stalling out, trying to plow through the water. Several vehicles were abandoned. Garbage, gasoline cans, and a water cooler floated by. The wind was blowing fiercely and I knew that soon the electrical lines would be down. Warrenside created a plan a couple of years ago to put all the electrical lines underground, but the tax base had fled the city when Warren Steel closed, so that project was put on the "nice to have someday" list. What a disaster.

Our detail sergeant looked worn out. A flatbed with four canoes tied on it was parked in front of Colonel Duffy's Army Navy Surplus Store. Duffy was sitting in an open second-story window, smoking a cigar. Duffy conducted weekly bitch sessions—"salons," he called them—that attracted every conspiracy theorist, survivalist, battle reenactor, and generic nut within a fifty-mile radius; there are a lot of those in a town on the skids. He leaned out the window and said, "You can have the canoes for fifteen bucks an hour. Twenty-five for the whole day," and laughed.

The sergeant asked me if I could handle a canoe, then said, "Down on Second Street. There's a couple who won't budge. *Budge* 'em."

"Where's Bineki?" I asked.

Jenna shook her head. "You're hopeless." She started arguing with a hot-dog truck vendor trying to sell guardsmen dogs for five bucks apiece. Jenna got him to donate the whole lot to the rescuers.

"Bineki has one of the rafts," the sergeant said. "Looking for stragglers, I think. I haven't seen her in a while."

I got in the canoe. Other guys were out there, civilian guys who had rowboats and motorboats. That's the best thing about our country, I thought then, and still think now. We're *great* in an emergency. If our country was always in an emergency, we'd get a hell of a lot done without the bellyaching that normally goes on. We're not so good with time on our hands.

I paddled around Second and Front streets, closest to the canal. It must have been garbage day, because garbage was all over the place. Green cans were floating by and plastic trash bags were swaying in the water like ghosts. Porches were deserted. I looked up to see if anybody was hanging out of attics or bedrooms. The roar of the river sounded like a locomotive in the distance. An underground sewage line erupted with a periodic spurt.

And then I heard some splashing and panting. Two pit bulls, one brown and one white, were paddling madly for the back of a stalled pickup truck. I hate pit bulls. They look like dogs of hell to me. Pink-rimmed lashless eyes. I could put my entire head in their mouths. The Puerto Rican drug dealers own them to show how badass they are, and I'm scared of them because their owners fight them down by the canal after midnight. I don't know any white person who has actually seen a dogfight, but I know the fights occur, because I hear the PRs betting on them outside my shop.

The dogs were trying to jump from the water into the back of the truck, and they weren't making it. It went against my better instincts, but I paddled over to them and grabbed one by the collar, tipping my canoe enough so he could leap in, and he just about knocked me over when he did. He jumped from side to side, barking wildly, and I was trying to steady the canoe when the white one tried to jump in and missed. He knocked into the canoe and we swayed and I said, "Fuck no!" and we finally tipped. The dogs spilled out, me after them. They paddled away from me, but not before one buried his teeth in my shoulder. "Sonofabitch!" I said. "Get out of here!" The dogs were already going, carried away downstream to Race Street. I tilted the canoe, trying to right it and get the water out so I could get back in, but it was too heavy. The water had a swift undercurrent from the river, and every time I tried to stand up the current knocked me over. I thought I could stand by using the paddle, but the paddle had sunk into the muck. "Fuck it," I said, and stumbled through the water, hanging on to porch railings, to get to the slightly higher ground a block away. Finally I saw some of our guys in a deuce-and-a-half full of sandbags, trying to forge through the water to get to the river. "Hey, need some help?" I asked the sergeant in the passenger's seat.

"Hey, Wolinsky, is that you? Get up by the strip club. Can you make it? There's a bunch of gawkers over there. Try to get some order and clear out the nonemergency personnel. All the roads are choked with spectators. I don't know why the hell they don't stay home." And I said "Right away" or something, and "Hey, have you seen Bineki?" and he said, "She's at the high school, I think."

I slogged on, finally reaching a relatively dry street. At Lucky Lady, the door was open and I went in. It seemed odd that it was open for business. But it wasn't. The emergency lights cast a red glow on three guys behind the bar taking turns drinking beer with their mouths open under the taps. "Hey," I said. "You guys supposed to be here?"

A guy who was sitting on a barstool, smoking a cigarette, answered me. "Yeah. Why, who are you?"

"National Guard," I said. "Don't you guys know there's an emergency here? All businesses are to be closed and residents evacuated inside the three-square-mile downtown." I was starting to feel woozy and held on to the bar. It felt like someone had slipped me a drug. I thought it must be from wading through all that gunky water, a fast-acting bacteria, maybe where that dog bit me.

The guy who was at the bar smashed out his cigarette. "I work here. I'm Chris Schaeffer, Lucky Lady's protection."

"Protection?" I asked. "What the hell is that?"

One of the guys drinking beer looked up. "Hey, man, what's wrong with your arm?" he asked me.

The left sleeve of my fatigue shirt was brown. Blood was dripping out of the cuff of my shirt. All of a sudden, I felt like I was going to faint. And then I did.

TWENTY-TWO **WIND**

"Is it wrong to break a deathbed vow?" Wind asked Big Blue.

The question got lost in the wind. The rain was biting her face and she closed her eyes against it and the lush land below, which she was going to betray. She understood why Jimmy Bird wanted her to stay, like a place marker, for the Lenapes' return. But he seemed to be the only person who cared. She didn't see any other Lenape making a run from Oklahoma to Warrenside to change its name back to *que nahlach quamique*. She was, in fact, probably the only Lenape—no, the only *person*—who knew that Warrenside was not the original name of the city. If she left, would anyone even notice?

Wind always had to explain this to her clients: Indians don't analyze dreams. You already know what the problem is, so there's no point talking about it. To fix a problem you have to change your dreams.

To change her dream, Wind had to enter it, and, in her so-far agreeable dream, she was flying over the Catawissa on the blue heron's back. Hummingbirds escorted Big Blue, their sharp tiny beaks occasionally piercing her skin as they darted around her, but the race was over. Big Blue, slow and steady, had won, and the hummingbirds were sentenced to do his bidding, which consisted mostly of catching fish for him. But hummingbirds are horrible at catching fish—the ones they dove for were heavier than the hummingbirds themselves and they had to drag them on top of the water until Big Blue dove in to help them.

On Big Blue's back, Wind flew over her property, the thirty acres on the Catawissa where the Lenape had camped in the winter for centuries. Winter creatures were plentiful by the river, and naturally there was always water and fish. The Lenape named the river *catawissa*, "growing fat," because at that bend in its elongated neck, the river bulged like a pregnant mare. Wind often wondered why the Warrens and Cantwells kept the river's name even though they changed *que nahlach quamique*, "good bottomland far upstream," to Warrenside—after themselves.

The aboriginal people, whom the Lenape called the First People, found this bend in the river. It was a mythical sweet spot, the kind of place where at first look newcomers suddenly forget the strife that drove them there and picture their children having children. Home. There are only twenty-three sweet spots in the world. That was the myth that was still alive when Jimmy Bird had found his way here, and he'd told Wind that he'd felt its truth when he'd bought the thirty alluvial acres on the floodplain. This sweet spot had four-foot-deep topsoil, temperate climate, and a current powerful enough to move men and their things downstream in a hurry—and if you're living on one of only twenty-three sweet spots, you're always moving downstream in a hurry. Game swarmed the surrounding hills, and underground streams gushed from their sides and poured downhill to the great river below. It was sacred ground because it nourished their people for so many years. But more than that, it was also the place where human beings first became men.

According to the Lenape, the First People lived here in semi-darkness until one August the Catawissa caught fire at sunset. No one knew the reason for the spontaneous combustion, but the river burned for a month, mesmerizing the First People like a drug, and the flames shooting up into the sky illuminated the land and caused them to consider everything in a new light. It was then that the First People stepped out of the indistinct dusk and became men. Because isn't the ability to reflect, to name things other than food or foe, the thing that makes us human?

At the end of a month, the fire sputtered, sparked, hissed, and began to extinguish itself as inexplicably as it ignited. Several of the bolder First Men waded into the burning water, snatched bits of fire for their tents, and shut themselves off from the others. The desire to *own* such a phenomenon became their undoing. Perhaps they pursued mad dreams they saw crackling in the flames. More likely, they burned their camp down, scattered, and turned on one another. But they disappeared.

The Great Spirit, who told this story to the Lenape, didn't say what happened, and the Lenape, a wise people who knew that life means extinction, didn't ask. They lit torches every August along the Catawissa both to please the powerful spirit that performed that early miracle and to show the First Men the way home, and they repeated the story to Josiah Warren and Joseph Cantwell, who arrived from England with a dozen armed religious misfits on Christmas Day 1807.

Warren and Cantwell respected the power of mythic tales. They had plenty of their own, which were expert at squeezing the joy out of life and keeping their adherents in a sour state of industry. In their mouths, the story of the Burning River was transformed into a cautionary tale against the sin of slackness and a premonition of hell, which helped mythologize Warrenside's successful thrust into the industrial age.

"All people have myths," Jimmy told Wind, "to justify their desires."

The Lenape and the Europeans coexisted peaceably on the same land for the next hundred years because the Lenape, foolishly as it turned out, didn't think anyone could own land.

In 1907, Jeb Warren, the great-great-great grandson of Josiah Warren, had seized the Lenape land on the outskirts of Warrenside to build a second blast furnace. He had Cantwell, who had a more sympathetic relationship with the Lenape, present their chiefs with a deed stating that *tindey wachtsch*, "the fire mountain," owned it. Soon Warren Steel's furnaces were cooking orange-hot metal for a mile along the Catawissa and dumping molten waste into it. The story of the Burning River was reborn. And every school-kid in Warrenside knew who lit the fire.

"Go over there!" Wind commanded Big Blue, trying to steer him toward the country club by tugging on his feathers.

"Stop that!" he said, irritably, shifting his body, slender as a greyhound's. "You're heavy, and that tugging is ruining my balance."

"There, over there!" Wind said. "Something is there. It looks like . . . something."

As Big Blue dove toward the links and got closer to the ground, Wind tried to focus on the creature wandering around the green. It looked like a person, almost. Yes, it was a naked woman, big and white, like a whale. Was this an evil spirit? There was usually no doubt about an evil spirit's identity or purpose, but this time Wind couldn't tell for sure.

When an evil spirit appeared in a dream, Wind would expertly pluck it out with a scorpion stinger. When the evil spirit came out of the dreamer, it was in the form of black smoke blowing out of the dreamer's nose, or sometimes black liquid would pool around the dreamer's head. Only Wind could see it, but it was there. It was real. Wind could vanquish the evil spirit—and often dreamers would be appalled when they found out that she hadn't—but in Native medicine, balance was everything. Evil spirits, while troublesome, meddlesome, and sometimes deadly, were necessary for balance.

"Put me down!" she yelled, and Big Blue swooped over the trees, touched down lightly on the soggy fourteenth hole, and shook Wind off his back.

Wind walked up to the woman, who was digging in the ground with her bare hands. When she saw Wind she stopped scooping mud and shook her head, startled. Wind saw her weirdly chopped hair and the red paint smeared all over her face and breasts.

"What do you want?" the woman asked; then her eyes widened and she groaned. "Oh! It's *you*!"

"Do you know me?" asked Wind.

"I know you, all right. You're the one who is going to ruin everything. Everything!" She began crying.

"What are you looking for?" Wind asked. "Can I help?" She squatted down and began pulling up grass, which felt like silk in this dream.

"Stop! Don't pull it out! I'll have you arrested."

Wind peered into the woman's eyes. She was a crazy person, but Indians don't think crazy people are insane—they're seekers of truth, living on another plane of reality. "If you're looking for something, maybe it has something to do with me. I'm here for a reason."

The woman thought about that for a minute. "You *are* here, aren't you? But you're the last person I want to know what's in the ground."

"Are you going to find something that has something to do with me?" Wind's heart jumped as she realized the madwoman was Barbara Warren. She knelt on the ground and slid her fingers into the hole that Barbara had dug. She smelled it. Just mud. "Is something in here?"

Barbara sobbed loudly.

Wind said, "My people believe that the earth never forgets. That you can't bury secrets, because they rise in the rain. If you buried a secret here, it won't stay hidden."

Barbara stopped crying and looked at Wind. "You're the Love Shaman, aren't you?"

Wind didn't know that was what they called her. "Yes, I'm the Love Shaman. Did you bury something in here that has to do with love? Does it have something to do with Cantwell?"

"Cantwell?" Barbara said. "You think I'm in love with *Cantwell?"*

Her words became silver balls, flying out of her mouth and into the atmosphere; then they floated into Wind's mouth and she found herself saying them aloud too. "You think I'm in love with Cantwell? *Am* I in love with Cantwell? Yes, I *am* in love with Cantwell!"

Barbara started laughing. "You won't be in love with Cantwell when you see what he's done." She resumed her digging, and suddenly sludge began burbling up from the cup of the fourteenth hole, with vapors above it. It was an evil spirit if ever there was one.

"What is that?" Wind asked.

"I didn't do it," Barbara said. "It's important that people know the Warrens didn't do it. The *Cantwells* did." She opened her red alligator tote and pulled out a huge—five feet by six feet—yellow clothbound book, *The House Is Built!*. "It's all in here," Barbara said, tapping the book, then opening it and running her index finger over lines that detached from the book and ran away. "Come back here, you!" she yelled at the fleeing words. "Well, never mind. They'll be back. Where else are they going to go? It's all in this book, all of it. The earth doesn't forget, you say? That's right. The earth doesn't forget."

The gunk coming out of the fourteenth hole was mixing with the rain. Wind felt nauseated. The black sludge and its vapors were evil spirits and she wanted to set fire to them to destroy their power, burn them up before they could do harm. But she couldn't. Evil exists to create balance. At the most sacred moment in Indian ceremonies, clowns emerge from the sidelines to make fun of the elders, the shaman, and the ritual itself. You cannot take yourself seriously. Balance. Nothing, no one, no situation is completely good or evil. She watched the black stuff flow, hissing and steaming, poisoning her land and the mighty Catawissa.

"Stop! Please stop! Take me home," she cried to Big Blue. She felt as if she had been traveling for days. She was wet and exhausted. She willed her eyes open and woke up to the sound of Kat Warren-Bineki banging on her door.

I was counting cases of water in the back of a deuce-and-a-half when Max found me. *"Habibi,"* he whispered, climbing in the back. "You're okay." He kissed me hard. I felt for a minute that it was just us, and I wanted to ride that sensation as long as I could. "What are you doing? Did you get a break?" he asked.

I wanted to go away with him right then, to leave the flood and our families and betrotheds behind—we could e-mail from wherever we landed up—but there was a little problem, deserting the U.S. Army being a court-martialable offense.

"I thought about where we could go," I told him. My dad had said he was going to Buenos Aires, and I thought it was an opportunity to start over down there. "Have you?"

"I've been thinking about the *flood*, darling, and our responsibilities here."

His eyes had the hint of violence I had seen in them on the plane ride from Bagram. Apparently, when anyone pushed him, it would come out. Well, too bad. I wasn't just anybody. "I've been thinking about the flood, too, *darling*," I said. "While you've been translating for *nobody*, I've been putting plastic Baggies on old ladies' feet and escorting them through sewer backup. Pardon me for daydreaming about being somewhere else."

He was taken aback by my sarcasm and was obviously trying to control himself. "It's been a long day."

"Longer for some of us than others, apparently."

"You think I don't want to run away with you right now?" he asked. "That's all I've been thinking about. I just have so many more obstacles to overcome than you. But I will. You have to trust me. My life is complicated."

"Complicated by what?" I asked. "You just make the decision and walk away. There's nothing to it."

"It's easy for you. You have no obligations. You're a typical American who can go anywhere you want. I'm a very important part of my family. I'm expected to take over my father's business. The entire extended family and some of the Lebanese community here is depending on me to support them. Alfred Younis and his family would starve if it weren't for my father. All the families in the Burning Bush development couldn't have afforded the down payments on their houses if not for my family. I could go on and on. I can't allow myself the luxury of thinking only of myself."

That used to be the Warrens, I thought. Thirty years ago, we were the ones everyone depended on. We were the ones who gave out turkeys and hams at Thanksgiving and Christmas; the ones who everyone in Warrenside looked to, because without us there would be no Warrenside. The downside to that, of course, was that we made sure no one else was allowed in the inner circle. Yes, they could start their own businesses as long as we approved them and they would somehow benefit us. Those damned turkeys and hams were a cheap publicity stunt to make us appear magnanimous. The reality was, they cost us almost nothing because we owned the turkey farm.

And now my family was inconsequential—even to one another. I don't think my mother even realized I was gone for a whole year, she was so absorbed in her world and her problems.

"Without love, life is meaningless," I said.

"Without your family, you have no life."

My mother always talked about how her life was different before she married my dad. Every decision was made with her uncles' advice, with the idea that the Warrens were a clan whose history reached far back and gave meaning to present and future Warrens. They took care of her in a way that no one, certainly not Dad or me, could take care of her now. And yet Mom threw all that away for Dad. Now the three of us were superannuated and the Asads were the new game in town.

"My dad is going to Buenos Aires to start a new life," I said. "We could go with him. Start there. You're a great linguist; you could learn Spanish quickly."

The shadow of hatred would dog us if we stayed in Warrenside, and it would eventually shape us. But if we left, who would we be? We would have to define ourselves by who we no longer were. Plenty of people in the military and the contract companies—expats—do that, and they seem out of place no matter where they are.

So when I saw the sadness, the bewilderment, on his face, I recognized it for what it was and it broke my heart. "You think we're doomed!" I shouted. "Don't even think it! If you think it, then we are." I grabbed his shoulders and shook him, trying to dislodge the spell of family and the cloud of doom.

"No, *habibi*, we are not doomed." He took my face gently in his hands and kissed me and then went outside to find the detail sergeant.

It's funny how when you're desperate you stoop to thinking things that have no basis in logic or reality, convincing yourself that the supernatural will prevail when the natural has failed. I thought of Jenna Magee and her complete and utter belief in Jesus' taking charge. Jesus would help Jenna, tell her what to do. But Jesus didn't talk to me. I remembered girlfriends talking about Wind Storm, the Love Shaman, who lived in the woods next to the country club. I saw her once in town and asked someone who she was. But I'd dismissed the favorable results my girlfriends had reported after consulting her—a couple of engagements, a marriage, all of which would have happened anyway. I'd never needed voodoo to get a man's attention. But now I felt I had run out of earthly persuasions and needed some spiritual help to bring Max back.

I had been on duty since early in the morning and I was due a break. Jenna had come back with Duck. The Humvee was parked at the top of the street. The keys were in the ignition, and before long I was riding toward the country club and turning into the woods to Wind Storm's property.

It was hard to see the house. An ancient wisteria with a trunk about a foot thick wrapped around the porch and clawed its way to the roof, seemingly about to pull the house down. I yanked the brim on my cap and ran between craters filled with water to her front porch.

I pounded on the old farmhouse door, and finally the Love Shaman opened it. She motioned for me to wait and closed the door. I jumped around in the pouring rain, on one foot and then the other, until she reappeared.

"You don't have an appointment," she said.

She looked distressed herself, but I wasn't worried about her, just myself.

"It's an emergency."

I followed her through the kitchen to a sparsely furnished living room, so spare there was no place to sit down. "I'm losing my lover to his family. I think he might love them more than he loves me."

"Lie down on the floor, warrior girl," she commanded.

I did, although there was an awful chill on the floor and the fireplace was clean and cold. I felt like a fraud; the only warrior thing about me was my uniform.

"Do you dream?" she asked me, waving a sprig of some herb, sage, I think, under my nose and humming at the same time. It was so lulling and peaceful that soon I found myself near a field of lush green grass, and I immediately felt myself drifting toward it.

"Sometimes I dream," I said as I ran across the field. The sun was shining and I felt like dancing, so I did. "There's a bear," I said. "I'm not afraid of it." I could hear Wind's voice, even though I could no longer see her.

"Good," she said, and she began singing.

I don't believe I have ever heard such a beautiful song. "What is that song?" I asked her, and the question got incorporated into the song itself. I knew I had heard it before, though I couldn't place it. It was familiar and yet not. I sang along.

"It's your beloved," Wind sang, and I knew it was. The song was Max. I started laughing and the bear came up to me and put his paw out as if we were to dance a polonaise, something like in a fairy tale. I curtsied and placed my hand on his arm, and as we danced I looked into his eyes. He was someone I had never seen before, but someone I wanted to know very much, and knew I would, soon. Then the skies clouded over. The clouds were thick and dark and ominous and they, too, looked familiar, and then it seemed as if the clouds themselves were singing. Then it thundered and lightning flashed, and it started to rain and I started to cry. The bear picked me up and carried me across his back like a papoose and we ran across the field in the rain, both of us crying. If the bear hadn't been there, I would've died. "What do you see, what do you see?" I heard Wind ask through the thunder and lightning. "What do you see?"

I shook my head back and forth. It was painful, but I couldn't tell her why I found it so. It was only rain. "It's only rain," I said aloud, as full of anguish as if I were saying, I can't go on! Then suddenly I inhaled a sharp smell of vinegar and I opened my eyes.

Wind was kneeling over me. "Get up," she said.

When I rose to my feet, she was staring at my name tag, then me. "Are you a spy for her?"

"For who?" I asked, still upset from my dream. Jesus, it felt like someone had died.

She pointed to the WARREN-BINEKI stitched across my chest. "Maybe your mother doesn't know that this is Lenape land. I won't sell it to her."

I shook myself. My head ached. "My mother wants to buy this property?"

"For her golf club. So more people can play golf."

It sounded like Mom. She would want to buy more holes, even though the membership of the club had been declining for years. "I'm sorry, I don't know anything about it, and I'm not spying for her."

Wind crossed her arms over her chest and stared down at me.

"How much do I owe you?" I asked.

"I don't want anything to change hands between us," Wind said. "It could be construed as an agreement in court."

She had a pretty legalistic mind for a Love Shaman.

"Look, I'm sorry about my mother. I have nothing to do with that. But I need to know, is Max going to leave me? I *really* need to know."

She squinted at me. "He loves you more than life itself," she said. "Your love is green. New. It stays that way."

"That's good!" I said. "New love that stays that way is good. Isn't it?"

Wind nodded, but I don't think she was actually listening to me.

"Well, thank you, thank you so much," I said, relieved that Max wasn't going to leave me. "Do you have a stone or jewel or something that will, I don't know, keep him around?" My girlfriends said that sometimes she gave them stones to hold that supposedly held magic powers. I had laughed then, but I didn't feel above it now.

Someone was knocking on the door and Wind walked me out. Cantwell, the golf pro from the club, was there and, to my complete amazement, wearing my lapis lazuli. He saw me, but I didn't register on his scope; he only had eyes for Wind. He was clearly in love. A month ago I would have found it shocking.

I walked out the door, then turned around when I was halfway down the path. I could see them arguing and it made me cry, but I wasn't sure if I was sad for them, or for myself.

According to the weather report, the rain would abate early the next morning, after three more inches. The lowest parts of downtown, close to the river, were under four feet of water. Everyone who would go had been evacuated, and Dr. Asad felt comfortable that he had done everything required to be humane. But the residents weren't going back. The businesses—bodegas, check-cashing facilities, Western Union, dollar stores, storefront churches, pizzerias, the family planning center—wouldn't reopen. Dr. Asad didn't own a few of the more prosperous businesses: a tuxedo rental shop and a family house-painting business. They were owned by old Dutchies who shrewdly gambled on the fact that their property became more valuable the longer they held out. Dr. Asad was already discussing prices with Houda to hasten the deals. When downtown Warrenside reopened for business in three years, it would have a casino, a boxing arena, and a high-end shopping mall. Luxury condominiums, eventually, with a dock for boats. He was looking at the model of his dream emporium when Max came in.

Dr. Asad said, "This flood is a godsend. It is a sign that my plans have the blessing of fate."

"Fate?" Max asked. "I was just down there. Some of those people lost everything."

"Stuff. There were no deaths. They're losing stuff. That's what insurance is for."

"I don't think most of those people have insurance."

"Is that our fault?"

"No," Max said. "But do we want to build on others' misfortune?"

Dr. Asad thought that it might have been a mistake to send Max to the army to earn American bona fides for the Asads. The military—unlike Princeton, from which Max escaped unscathed intellectually—was a democratic institution and his letters were full of new thoughts about equality. But the truth is that *all* fortunes are built on others' misfortune. There was only so much room.

"This is all yours," he said. "I want you to be in on it from the beginning and you can shape it however you want. You will talk to the people from Oasis. They are anxious to begin construction. We have a beautiful design, but you are welcome to change it, of course. It is to be yours."

"What about the permits, the gambling license?"

"Oasis takes care of all that," Dr. Asad said. "But I don't see a problem when the state government sees the taxes and revenue we generate." He started fussing with the boxing arena. "I think there should be a boxing school to go with the arena, like a feeder system, don't you think? Perhaps it will channel some of that energy they put into dogfighting." Dr. Asad had nothing against dogfighting. It was typical of the lower classes in the Middle East to celebrate birthdays and holidays with dogfights. Max had written that it was a common pastime in Kandahar. But Americans looked down on it as a barbaric sport, and Dr. Asad wanted nothing to taint his son's reputation. If his son was to be the boss of downtown Warrenside, only activities with the wholehearted support of Americans, like casino gambling, would be sanctioned there.

Max looked at the model blankly.

"Who is luckier than you?" Dr. Asad said. "Generations of Asads have lived their lives to produce you. And now it is you who will fulfill our destiny. The Asads are conquering America. Sometimes I am in awe of how lucky we are. Why have we been chosen? It's humbling."

"I only have a little time," Max said. "I'm on break until they figure out what my next assignment is. Then I have to get back."

"Yes," Dr. Asad said. "Your assignment. You have to tell Houda when to make the arrangements for the wedding. I think as soon as the flood is cleaned up. There's no reason to wait. The Aloubs are very impressed with you and with what we are doing in the downtown. Very impressed. Joseph's brother is in the construction business, and I think it would suit everyone if we hired him to build our mall."

"Father, listen. I can't stay here."

"I know, I know. You must get back to your duties."

"No. I mean I am not staying in Warrenside."

Dr. Asad examined his son's face and saw a stranger. "It's that girl."

"Kat. Her name is Kat. We're in love and I want to start a new life with her. Away from here."

Dr. Asad began pacing. Although he was a scholar, he was not physically suited to scholarship, because he could not think sitting down. "I told you, you can have her on the side if you must. Here's something you don't know: *I* have a mistress."

"Yes, that dancer, Anika Lee. And before that, Sharon O'Neill. And before that, Marilyn something. It's convenient to have your harem on your payroll."

"Oh!" Dr. Asad didn't think anyone in his family knew about that. "Well, see? That doesn't disturb my home life or our business. You can satisfy your need for adventure easily. That's all it is, a need for adventure. You think it's love, but love is what you will have with Nadira."

"I have never even spoken to Nadira. And I don't have to, to know what she sounds like, what she thinks like. And she doesn't have to know me to know what I sound like and what I think. We're supposed to get married and we've never even spoken and that's not supposed to matter. We are part of a corporate merger: our real estate, the Aloubs' construction business. My brains, her beauty."

"The Warrens cannot do anything for you," Dr. Asad said. "Their fortune is minimal and their influence in this town, while mythological, is over. Over. I hear the mother is mad; that may be a rumor, but it doesn't bode well for children." Dr. Asad waited for Max to protest and when he didn't, he said, "Nadira is very beautiful."

"Yes, she is beautiful, but she is not surprising to me and I can tell you right now, in detail, all the conversations we will have for the next ten years, after which time we will stop talking to each other altogether because we will have had our children and she will get down to the business of raising them and I will get down to the business of building this cathedral to your ego, which will eventually turn into my ego, and I will sentence my sons to do the same."

"You can have it all, Max. You can have Nadira *and* that girl. And what you call the cathedral to my ego, you can make it into yours. I told you. You can do anything you want with it. I am not so current, so I don't know what the latest fads are. Maybe boxing isn't such a good idea. Maybe wrestling," he said, trying to distract Max. He was unused to being challenged by members of his family, by his employees, by anybody. "Chris Schaeffer is always talking about wrestling. Maybe something else altogether."

"Father, you're not listening. I want nothing to do with it. With this whole thing. With our family. With you."

"Ah." Dr. Asad felt the blow of his son's words. "You think that I, a scholar, someone who is more happy making sense out of the past than dealing with the mundane reality of the present, am happy to play landlord to people who can't pay their rent? You think I am happy babysitting businesses that I allow to stay open just because the same people who can't pay their rent need someplace to shop? You think this is the life I envisioned for myself when I was a boy in Beirut?"

"You lived through a war, Father. It's unfortunate but true. And you brought your family here, where things are done differently. Where people think differently. Where it is possible to make a good life for yourself in one generation. In your own generation! Not everything is done for your children, because in this country they can do it for themselves. And that's all I want to do. I want the opportunity to do it for myself. I want to make a life that surprises and delights me with a woman who delights and surprises me. Give it all to Houda. She wants it. In one stroke you can make everyone happy."

"Making people happy is not the object."

Max rose to leave. "I must get back to my unit."

Houda had been leaning on the doorjamb, listening. "You are going to let him call off the wedding?" she asked.

"Make me some tea, Houda," he said, trying to forestall a total mutiny.

"I am going downtown to Lucky Lady."

"Are you staying here tonight?" he asked her. "Or coming home?"

Houda kissed him on the forehead. "I'll try to come home, Papa."

I must have passed out, because in my dreams I was in heaven, Kat standing over me, waving a jar of mustard under my nose to rouse me. "Come on, Duck, wake up! If you don't wake up you're going to disappear." I wanted to tell Kat that it was okay, I understood why she didn't love me *that* way, she needed a man, not a soul mate. I had moved into my dad's cabin in the woods, and I was going to show her starting right now that I could change.

At the same time, it felt good to just let go, honest to God. I hadn't realized how *tired* I had become. "I'm going to show you something. Wait! Wait till you *see*," I said, and I struggled to sit up and show her, and when I opened my eyes I saw Jenna Magee. Camacho was leaning over me too. This was definitely not how I pictured heaven.

I was on the floor of Lucky Lady. I tried to remember how the hell I got there, and then I remembered. "Where are those guys?" I asked.

"You don't have to strain yourself or anything," Jenna said. "Just keep your eyes open. Camacho, dial the captain and tell him to get some medical help over here right away. You're bleeding like a stuck pig, Duck. And those guys who were here? They ran. What a bunch of assholes. They were scared you were going to die."

"You shouldn't have let them leave," I said. "They were trespassing and looting, drinking beer. They should be arrested."

"Big deal, some beer."

My arm really hurt from the tourniquet that Jenna had inexpertly but quite tightly tied. "I'm not going to bleed to death," I said. "Get this thing off."

"Lie back down," Jenna said. She put a seat cushion under my head. "You're going to be okay. You'll have to sit out the rest of the flood, though. You're lucky." She smiled and stroked my forehead.

"Hey," I said. "Have you seen Kat?"

Jenna yanked the cushion out from behind my head. "You're a world-class asshole, do you know that?"

"What are you talking about?"

"Kat, Kat, Kat! That's all you ever think about!" She threw the cushion at the bar, where it knocked over some glasses that smashed to the floor. "You love *me* and you're too stupid to know it."

"Kat and I are going to get *married*."

"If you think that, you're a thousand percent deluded."

I wasn't raised to be religious, so I didn't believe in any of the stuff that Jenna preached day and night. Actually, I don't believe in anything I can't see with my own two eyes, but I guess everyone has a need to believe in something bigger than themselves and what I believed in, the thing that kept me going ever since I heard that shot in my father's shop, was that Kat and I would always be together, getting old on the porch in matching rocking chairs together. The image was so familiar, it was as if it had already happened and I was just remembering it. "You don't know anything about it."

"Hey, man, you want a drink?" Camacho asked. He was opening a bottle of bourbon.

"You're not supposed to drink anything if you have a wound," Jenna said.

"I never heard that," I said.

"Apparently there's a lot you haven't heard," Jenna said. "Don't give him anything. The medics will be here soon."

It seemed like a lot of time had gone by already. I supposed they were concerned with people who needed help with the flood. "Don't you have to get back?" I asked her. "You don't have to hang with me. Either of you."

Camacho had poured himself a shot of bourbon. He held it up to me, said "Bottoms up" and drained it, and poured himself another.

"I *said* you don't have to hang with me."

"Maybe I want to," Camacho said. He went to the stripper pole and wrapped his legs around it like a fireman. "A hundred bucks says they're not going to tear this place down. Me and my mom got to leave, but the strippers get to stay. How come a fucking rag head gets to make the rules?"

"You were born unlucky," Jenna said. "Face it. You'd be better off going to Iraq with that contract you got from Charon Corp. It's not going to get any better for you here."

"Fuck that!" Camacho said. "Why should I fight a white man's war? What did the white man ever do for me?" He shook his hips.

The thing about Camacho is, he's so pretty, he'd actually make a stunning stripper—a Chippendale I guess, better than a lot of the dogs that Asad booked. But if you told him that, he'd cut your heart out and make you eat it.

"I'm done killing people," he said.

"You didn't kill anyone over there," I said.

"I was ready to. Fuck you, don't say I wasn't ready." He punched his fist into his palm and the medics came in, flashlights searching the three of us, and decided that I was the one who needed help. They went out to get the gurney.

"Nothing's going to happen for you here," Jenna said. "What are you going to do, deal crack, then go to jail? What a career! Meanwhile, your landlord is ejecting you. What are you going to do with your ma?"

Camacho lived with his mother in a beat-up row house a couple of blocks from Lucky Lady, a couple of doors down from Jenna and her mother.

"You, too." Jenna, who was sitting on my feet to keep me from getting up, suddenly turned on me. "What are you going to do here? Wait for the South Side to come to life, meanwhile following Kat Bineki around with your tongue hanging out until she finally trips over it and notices you?"

I didn't actually have an answer to that, because that's probably what I would have done if things had gone the way I wanted.

Chris Schaeffer and his three henchmen swaggered back in.

"Hey." I tried to get up from the floor. "You guys got to get out of here."

Chris said, "I'm responsible for this joint. Actually, I have to ask the rest of you to leave."

He sat down at the bar while the medics hoisted me on the gurney and rolled me outside. I felt foolish. But the rain felt nice on my face and soon I was riding in the ambulance to Warren Hospital, the paramedics asking me my name and the date and who was president of the United States to make sure I still had all my marbles.

The South Side was coming down, there was no question about it. I had heard the rumors for a couple of years too, that

Asad wanted to knock down the row houses by the river and make way for some big mall or something. I felt sorry for Jenna and Camacho and all the other poor suckers who were going to have to move and try to make a life somewhere else because they were going to be displaced by new people, people who in some instances were stashed illegally in the homes of relatives and friends and who, like the soldiers in the Trojan Horse, would come out when you weren't looking and take your job and work for a couple of bucks an hour and no benefits. It was a different kind of warfare, and I don't think any of us downtown realized that we were under siege. Once we realized that we were in combat, it would take us a long time to see that this war wasn't being fought with bullets, it was being fought with money. And when you're up against the almighty dollar, there isn't much you can do about it.

The medic said he hoped I didn't lose my arm because the damned tourniquet was so tight. "That's what I thought," I said, cursing Jenna's attention but understanding her reflex to squeeze tightly whatever she loved, even if she squeezed it to death, thinking she could keep it close.

TWENTY-SIX

WIND

Wind could hear the sirens wailing off in the city all night long: fire engines, police cars. The sounds of emergency echoed the sounds in her own spirit. She wished that Cantwell hadn't left, because she felt lonelier than she had since her father died and would have liked someone to talk to.

Somewhere during the night—between the police sirens and the ambulance wails—she'd decided to sell her property to Dr. Asad. She was in a fugue state, listening to the sound of the over-flowed creek rushing past on its way to somewhere else and the complete silence of the night animals, who knew better than to bring attention to themselves during a disruption of nature. She lay there for hours, feeling like a soldier in camp, knowing the next day was the big battle, knowing she might die in that battle.

She slipped off her mattress and went to make coffee in the hoary dawn. Something about the light made her think that the rain would stop, but when she stepped outside, it was still pouring. It unnerved her that Kat Warren had come to her, obviously spying for her mother, so she decided this was it. She wasn't a full-blood Indian, but she was enough of a warrior strategist to know when she was surrounded.

She had put the aluminum coffeepot on the stove and fired up the gas burner when Cantwell knocked on the door. Although she had yearned for him all night, in the dawn's light she knew what she had to do. He was just another lying, spying, thieving white man.

Wind pulled open the door.

"Let me in!" he said, laughing. "You promised me turkey."

She couldn't look in his eyes or she would be lost. "You must leave. *I'm* leaving," she said. "And I never want to see you again."

"Are you crazy?" he asked. "When did this happen?"

Wind couldn't tell him it happened when she was going through her father's few possessions, a thing she couldn't bring herself to do before last night. She found an uncashed check from the United States Government to compensate him for his exposure to Agent Orange in Vietnam. She could never be sure if Jimmy's odd quirks of speech and memory lapses were caused by Agent Orange—as some lawyers claimed they were—or if her older brother was stillborn because of it—as her mother bitterly claimed—but there was no doubt that the lung cancer that finally killed him was caused by his repeated exposure to the defoliant. And the federal government finally, grudgingly, admitted that this poison—which killed all plant life that even *whiffed* it—might have altered the man who was Jimmy Bird and then did what it always did to fix collateral human damage. It wrote him a check.

"I'm selling the property, so tell your boss the fight is over, okay? But I'm not selling to *her*." She knew from her dream that

Barbara Warren was trying to hide something bad on the land and that selling it to her would guarantee that the land was poisoned forever.

"I don't care if you sell to her or not, I'm leaving too," Cantwell said.

"You can't leave," Wind said. "*I'm* leaving. I said I was leaving first."

"We can both leave. There's no law against that."

"Well, we can't go to the same place."

"Can I come in? I'm soaking wet."

"I can't understand how someone who can kill and gut a turkey without flinching is so pathetic about a little rain."

"Why don't you come out here and see how it feels? I'm cold and damp and you probably don't even have a fire going in there."

She didn't. And the turkey was uncooked in the sink, cold and raw. "There's absolutely no point to your coming in here. I'm leaving. I'm tired of being the goddamned freaky Indian in the woods who can help you with your love life."

"No one thinks you're the freaky Indian in the woods."

"Well, maybe *I'm* starting to think I'm the freaky Indian in the woods."

"And you certainly haven't helped me with *my* love life."

"You're her flunky," Wind said. "How can I trust you if you're her flunky?"

"I *was* her flunky, but I'm not now. I swear. I quit!"

"I don't believe you. You're not authentic. If you were authentic you wouldn't have worked for her in the first place."

"What are you talking about? Our ancestors came over on the same boat from England, hers and mine. I would say I'm being perfectly authentic working for her. I may not have been completely honorable; that's a different issue. But authentic, I am. I would say, as a matter of fact, that you're the one who isn't being authentic. You can't pretend you're still living in 1700. It's 2004. You're an Indian living in 2004 and you have to figure out how to be authentic in the time you find yourself in, not some romantic past that probably never existed the way everyone wants to remember it."

"You have no idea what it's like to be part of a culture that no longer exists."

"Are you kidding? You think the Cantwells and the Warrens mean *anything* anymore? They're just names. The culture my family thinks so highly of is over, too, Wind. You're half Swedish. Where's that? You can't just acknowledge the part you want. How authentic are you if you don't acknowledge the rest of you?"

"I didn't even know my mother. She left because she thought I was deformed or retarded or something." The Agent Orange chemical that oozed out of those orange barrels in Vietnam and into Jimmy Bird's veins had drowned the entire Storm clan.

"Well, you're certainly acting retarded now. She was probably right."

She was still living her father's life, living out his dream of what a real Indian should be. The only problem was, there was no guide for what that should look like. Jimmy Bird may have thought he was a purebred, but he wasn't only an Indian. He was a pothead Vietnam vet killed by Agent Orange. How much was he Jimmy Bird the Indian and how much was he a fucked-up stoner Vietnam vet?

The check that he never cashed was for twenty-five thousand dollars. Enough to clean up the mess he left and buy passage to someplace new. It would be up to Asad to clean up whatever the hell was lurking underground.

"Look," Cantwell said. "Can I make an appointment and hire you for an hour? You can dream and see if your animal spirit says we should give it a try."

Wind had asked Big Blue if Cantwell loved her, and he said to ask him herself. So she did. "Do you love me?" she asked.

"If you let me in, I'll tell you."

"But why should I trust you? You're a white lying thief."

"You're white too. And I trust you."

She moved away from the door so he could walk in. He shook himself like a wet dog.

"God, it's freezing in here. How can you stand it?"

"I'm waiting."

"Look, Wind, how can I tell you I love you? If I believed in love at first sight, I would have to say yes, I love you madly. But I don't think that's what you're looking for."

She stared at him.

"Is it?"

"I don't know."

"Let me light a fire at least. And how's that turkey coming along?"

"It's in the sink."

Cantwell built a fire with wood that had been stacked outside for months. Jimmy had stacked it until he was too weak to do it anymore, saying that Wind would have to learn how once he was gone. But she hadn't learned. And she didn't want to learn. Then Cantwell plucked the turkey and put it in an old enamel spatter-ware roasting pan, after scraping the crust off it. It was one of the artifacts her mother had left behind. Neither Wind nor Jimmy ever used it. Jimmy would just make a fire outside when he wanted to cook something, put a skewer through it, and rest it on two forked branches over a fire. She assumed that's how Indians did things and thought it would have been inauthentic to cook something in the oven. That she didn't want to cook like a white person was her excuse for not cooking at all.

"We got a couple of hours to go on that turkey," Cantwell said. He took her face in his hands and kissed her. She allowed herself to be led to her mattress, where they made love, and Wind wondered afterward if it was love she was feeling. She certainly felt peaceful, like the weight of her past had been lifted off her shoulders.

While Cantwell slept, Wind rubbed some sage on her upper lip to induce a dream, and it came immediately. She was in a field—no, it was the golf course. And it was sunny; the rain had finally stopped.

"Finally!" she said aloud. Big Blue was there, standing on one foot. "What are you doing on the *golf course*?" she asked.

"I can't see the distinctions you do, because you are a human being. You build all this stuff on the earth and say this is a road and that is a golf course, and you expect the rest of us to understand that we aren't wanted there and you expect us to stay away. Why do you think animals always get killed in the road? How are they supposed to know it's a road?"

"Still, a *golf* course."

"See?" Big Blue said. "I don't see a golf course. I see hilly green fields and lovely ponds with carp in them."

"They're water traps," Wind said.

"Whatever you want to call them. They are carp traps." He laughed. "They don't know who's eating the carp because I fish when it's dark. I think they're after a bear. They set a trap down by your property line, by that row of juniper trees."

Wind lay down on the green field and a tree started growing from her navel and it was suddenly as big as a circus tent; then it got bigger and bigger until it shaded the entire world. She tried to get up and couldn't. "Help me! I can't move. I'm stuck."

"You can get up," Big Blue said.

"I'd like to see you get up with a giant tree growing out of your navel."

"What kind of tree is it?" Big Blue asked.

"What does it matter? It's a tree. It's big. And I can't move."

"Well, I can!" And he took off, leaving Wind on the ground with the tree still growing bigger, its roots probing ever deeper into the earth beneath her. Big Blue circled overhead. "It's only a tree because you call it a tree. Try calling it something else."

Finally, she thought, some good advice. But all she could think of was *tree*, and so a tree it remained. It had red flowers on it, unlike any tree she had ever seen, and soon hundreds of hummingbirds were swarming the blossoms, bumping one another to get to the nectar.

"What are you doing here?" she asked the birds.

"Follow us," one of them said. "We're on our way to someplace amazingly cool."

"I can't fly," Wind said. "I can't even get up."

"Then you can't," the bird said, and zoomed off.

She had to rename the tree or it would stay a tree and she would be bound to this dream, stuck in a weird shaman no-man's-land, and so she shouted the only name she could think of— "Cantwell!"—and woke from her dream to see Cantwell leaning over her.

"Wind! Hey, Wind," he said, shaking her. "Wake up. You're having a bad dream."

"It wasn't a bad dream," she said. "It's just . . . I have to follow those hummingbirds."

"Hummingbirds?" Cantwell laughed. "When you knock out—"

"Cantwell." Wind interrupted him. "You said you were leaving Warrenside. Do you know where you're going? What you're going to do?"

"I haven't thought that far ahead. I want to start somewhere where no one has ever heard of a Cantwell. My family would be very surprised to know that isn't so very far from here."

"Take me with you."

TWENTY-SEVEN

BARBARA

She looked left and right, then charged down the garden walkway to the street and turned right. At first, she had the street to herself, except for her car and driver, which followed her at a respectful distance, taking care not to splash her with the windshield wipers. She asked the driver what he thought he was doing, and he smiled and said, *"Plena mujer."* Of course, she thought. He doesn't speak English.

Six o'clock was dinnertime, and even though it was still raining, as she marched on she was joined by an entourage of fathers and their progeny who had jumped up from the dinner table to follow her. A little girl ran ahead, got a good look at Barbara's chopped-off hair and the red lipstick smeared all over her body, and screamed. Someone tried to slip a raincoat over her shoulders. She shrugged it off. How ridiculous was that, a raincoat when she wasn't wearing any clothes?

Emboldened with each step, she walked on until she reached the Harlan Gardiner Bridge, where she stopped to reach into her fake alligator tote to retrieve her wallet and driver's license. She tossed them over the guardrail into the river. She watched them hit the water and wash away. "Good!" she said. It was important that the Warren name be tossed into the river, to find a good hiding place beneath a rock or a log. Then she proceeded across the bridge into the old downtown.

Most of her entourage turned back at the bridge. Her driver got out of the car to look at the swelling water. He tried to call Mike, who didn't pick up. A truck was waiting at the stoplight at the bottom. The driver honked his horn. "Hey, babe, need a lift?" Barbara clasped her tote tighter under her arm and kept walking.

On Sixth Street, she turned left into unfamiliar territory, Warrenside's downtown. She was immediately up to her ankles in dirty water, engulfed in a not unfriendly but not respectful sea of brown, tan, black, and yellow faces. Some were in cars, watching the flood rescue efforts. The men had their pants legs rolled up and were wearing black garbage bags with their heads poking through holes. It was a picnic atmosphere, with people chatting and sometimes shouting directions or greeting friends. There were so many people looking at her that she was glad and proud of her perfect skin. The men swarming around her wore baseball hats twisted sideward. She tried to figure out who they were supposed to be and to see where the hell she was. The only landmark she could make out was the façade of the old Warrenside Plaza Hotel on the hill above her. It had been turned into senior apartments. Lights were on in the building and several old men were watching her from the windows.

"Excuse me," she said, pushing her way through the crowd. Not one person she recognized. When she was a little girl, her family knew everyone in Warrenside. Everyone either worked for the Warrens, delivered things to their houses, or attended their parties. They all asked about her and were concerned with her welfare. The indifference of these strangers with their foreign faces alarmed her.

A man grabbed her breast and showed everyone that lipstick had come off on his hand, then said something she didn't understand. She slapped him away.

He pursed his lips and made a vulgar kissing noise.

"Stop it," she said. "You don't even exist for me."

Exhausted and confused, she plopped down on the steps of an old stone church that had recently been purchased by a Puerto Rican congregation. A carving on the lintel proclaimed ST. PAUL'S EPISCOPAL in Fraktur. A tatty banner beneath the lintel said IGLESIA PENTECOSTAL DE DIOS VIVENTE. How could this be allowed? she wondered.

"She's loco," someone said. "Crazy in the head."

The words worked like sanctuary. The disrespecting stopped.

"*Aquí*. Over here," someone called to a paramedic in a Humvee.

She started to walk away from the paramedic and two policemen who were coming at her with a gurney, but as she trundled down the street the water got deeper, swirling around her knees. She couldn't remember why she had come downtown and she walked farther and farther; then suddenly she recognized the spires of Warren Steel's cold blast furnaces and knew where she was. The stacks were black against the gray sky. She sobbed, remembering how their fire used to light up the night, orange and hellish, raining soot on Warrenside, yes, but also raining prosperity. Everyone was rich then: the owners, the management, and even the unions—after the workers locked horns with Pinkerton guards, spilling some blood and thereby proving themselves. No one was fighting over using old stuffed sofas as porch furniture because everyone could afford to buy new. And it was because of the Warrens. And now no one even knew who she was.

Barbara peered at the faces that had followed her into the roiling waters and saw one face that looked familiar. He was wearing an army uniform and coming after her, striding through the water. She was trying to place him when he said, "Come with me, Mrs. Warren," and placed his arm out for her to hang on to, and her heart sang that he recognized her; of course he knew her, knew who she was in this nightmare scene where everything was topsy-turvy—of course someone would rescue her!—and her white knight motioned to the cops to back off—"I know this lady"—and they treated him with a deference she recognized as belonging to *her* family. Then he led her into a windowless building where it was dry but dark, and Barbara tried to make sense of the people who were at the bar drinking beer, a couple of soldiers, a female soldier, and one who looked familiar, and then she remembered he was eating a sandwich at her home earlier that day, asking for Kat. Now he looked away. Her rescuer led her out of the barroom—it was Asad's strip club, she realized now, and thought she should protest, although the irony of being naked in a strip club did seep into her consciousness and make her snort—and up a flight of steps to an apartment where a tall Asian woman with sleek black hair, wearing a bathrobe and smoking a cigarette, let her in. "This is Mrs. Warren," the soldier said, and, to Barbara, "This is Anika Lee. She will take care of you until we can get you home." Anika wrapped a kimono around her while the soldier whispered something in Anika's ear. "I'll take care of her, Mr. Asad," Anika said.

Barbara looked at the soldier questioningly.

"She's a good person," he said. "You'll be okay."

Barbara touched her knight's arm and said, "Thank you." And he smiled and Barbara saw he was beautiful and then she recognized him as the man Kat had brought to the house. It was Kat's lover.

Barbara sank into the sofa. Candles lit the apartment because the electricity was out downtown, and in the candlelight Barbara could see that the apartment was sumptuous. Rich tapestries hung on the wall. Beautiful brass and ceramic bowls and pitchers decorated a shelf. A giant hookah was on the coffee table. The couch she was sitting on was very comfortable. Most unlike the Louis XV, she couldn't help thinking. The place was so sexy, it made her blush.

The soldier left and Anika lit another cigarette—"I hope you don't mind. It kills my appetite"—and Barbara nodded.

"I'd like one," Barbara said.

Anika laughed. "You don't need to kill your appetite. My looks are my ticket."

"Are you a . . ." Barbara didn't know a polite word for stripper. "Dancer?"

"I'm trying to retire. But I don't know what I would retire to. I'm sorry we don't have television. The electric's out. We should eat stuff out of the fridge before it goes bad."

Anika went into another room and came back with a little girl, about four years old, who said, "How do you do," like she'd learned English in a prep school, and Anika said, "This is Allie." And Allie joined Barbara on the couch while Anika prepared a meal with the defrosting food. Barbara felt so comfortable that she dozed, waking when Allie tapped her knee. There was a tray of cheese and crackers and cold cuts and a bottle of white wine on the coffee table. Anika held out a glass to Barbara, who thought that alcohol didn't mix with *any* of her chemicals, natural or supplemental, and was going to explain to this sophisticated woman what she knew about *that* before she took the glass and drank deeply. Allie took a sip out of her mother's glass when suddenly the sound of breaking glass broke Barbara's euphoria.

Anika opened the apartment door, and the sounds of shouting and cursing burst through. She nodded calmly to Barbara, sat down on the sofa between her and her daughter, stroked Allie's hair, and, reaching behind her with her free hand, retrieved a red velvet pouch containing a small pink revolver from beneath the cushion. Deliberately, she went into the kitchen and got six rounds from a sugar bowl, loaded her revolver, and put it in her bathrobe pocket. The yelling grew louder, then subsided to a few voices; then a woman screamed; then there was a tiny pop, like a champagne cork, then a second pop, and everything became eerily still.

I think the most beautiful things in the world are things in flux: fireworks, water rushing over rocks, the ocean sparkling under a bowl-like sky, plants growing and dying. I find snapshots to be unsatisfactory, as they only catch an object in one place, frozen en route to becoming, then decaying, then dying. Born, becoming, decaying, and dying. I don't mean to sound maudlin. I'm not sad. The decaying and dying are part of life in a weird way because something always comes up to take another's place; sometimes *the very thing that died* comes back with a few alterations for the better. Water is cleaner for having tumbled over rocks. Plants have seeds and always find ways to rebroadcast themselves, through birds or bees, et cetera. I guess it's sad if it's you who is dying or if it's someone you love. But at some point you know you are part of a continuum, and the beauty of life and love is knowing it won't stay the same.

Max came wading through the filthy water, tied my raft to a porch railing, and led me without a word to the old Warrenside Plaza Hotel, which was now his father's, and up the back steps to an empty room with a made bed. He locked the door. The flood rescue and evacuation were such chaos, no one would miss us. I was still flying from my session with the Love Shaman, convinced that the bear I saw in my dream was the Max I didn't know yet. There was so much to know about him, and somehow it felt imperative that I find out everything *immediately*. I wonder now, is it like that with all new lovers?

After we made love, Max said, "I told him, *habibi*. We will leave as soon as we are released from duty."

His voice was so introspective that for a minute I thought he wasn't happy, but he smiled to reassure me and I was filled with the endless possibility of our lives. "I have some money," I said, "so you don't have to ask your father."

Max leaned over me, resting his head on his elbow. "Are you worried about money?"

"Of course I'm not worried about money. I was just saying, in case *you* were worried, you shouldn't be."

"Are you taking that away from me? My ability to take care of you?"

"Max!" I said, laughing. "We're so beyond that male/female thing of who has the money and who takes care of who. I'm just saying I have money, so you can walk away from your father without that hanging over your head."

He ran the back of his index finger down my arm and over my breast. "In Arabic myth there is a djinn, Nasnas, who is half human, with half a head and half a body, one arm and one leg. He is the son of the demon Shikk and a human being. Now you love me because I am a full man with the power of my family behind me, but I wonder what you will feel when I am like Nasnas."

"You don't need your family to be whole. Anyway, I love you, not your family."

"I am part of my family. Without them, I will have no context. I wonder what I will be like without my father and uncles and the weight of my family's past holding me up. Even my sister, Houda—she is shrewd and cunning, but in our culture she is just a woman."

"You think she's happy with that?" I asked.

"She is not like you, *habibi*." He laughed. "She accepts her limitations."

"Limitations put on her by a bunch of tent-culture patriarchs."

He smiled. "Whatever. Yes. A bunch of tent-culture patriarchs. Which is what I am. I think it would be impossible for me to really love a woman from my own culture like I love you. I think of them differently. Do you hate me for that?"

I couldn't help thinking of the mythological and beautiful Nadira. It would be impossible for a man not to love someone as perfect as Nadira was reputed to be. "Next you're going to tell me that you love me because I'm a Warren."

He surprised me by saying, "It helps. Even if your family is no longer relevant to Warrenside, you know what it is like to be part of a family that people revere; that they look to for leadership. It's important that we have that in common."

I grabbed a pillow and hit him with it. "I've spent my whole life disowning the Warrens and now the man I was meant to be with is telling me *that's* what he's in love with?" I wasn't sure what I was angrier at: the fact that he'd said a truth that our family had long suppressed, which is that the Warrens could just go away and no one would even notice, or that for the first time in my life the idea that I was part of a family that no longer mattered made me feel obsolete, like last year's model.

"You'll be the same person when you leave your family. Women are very adaptable. They're stronger in a lot of ways because of this. Men become weak without their history. It's like taking away their oxygen."

"Are you chickening out on me?"

"Really, it's different for a man, *habibi*. When I was a little boy and my father took me to New York City, sometimes we would talk to taxi drivers, some of whom were quite articulate, *amazingly* articulate, and my father would ask them where they came from and what their story was. My father knows many languages and he is curious about other cultures and he knows how to draw strangers out. Anyway, sometimes they were doctors in their own country, or engineers, or important leaders even, who were driven out of power and influence by their opponents. Most countries don't deal with defeated politicians like Americans do, which is to give them a lot of money to write books about why they should still be in power." He laughed softly. "When they talked to my father, for a moment they became whole men again, talking about their professions and the culture in which they mattered. They made decisions; their families depended on them. They don't matter here. They are chauffeurs for other people who *do* matter. They are like Nasnas, Kat. Half-men, raging for the beast that killed their other half."

"What are you trying to tell me? This is America, Max, and you are an American." I got up from the bed and started pulling on my uniform. "That's what America is all about, reinventing yourself. You come here, your family comes here, and you reinvent yourself." Just yesterday I'd thought that we, Max and I, would have to hurt people because of our love. Now he was making it sound like I was the one doing the hurting, and one of the people I was hurting was him.

Max and I left his father's assisted living facility and walked in silence down to where our temporary headquarters was: the back of a deuce-and-a-half.

"Don't be angry with me, *habibi*. I have to say the worst possible thing out loud so it loses its power over me." Max kissed me, then continued downhill to the flooded part of town. "I'll find you," he called over his shoulder.

I nodded and began loading cases of water from a forklift onto the truck. No one else was around and it felt like the rain was stopping. A weak sun had forced its way through the thick gray clouds, creating a muted, pearly light. I was pretty sure everyone who wanted to be evacuated had been and I was thinking that we were looking at another week or so of cleanup when one of the privates in our unit came jogging up to the truck. "You wouldn't believe it," he said, out of breath. "There's a big fat naked woman walking around down there. Just walking around like she has an appointment or something. I gotta find the captain."

He grinned, and I felt my mouth go dry. "Maybe she's lost and needs help. Did you try to help her?"

The private shook his head. "There's only one way I can help a naked lady," he said.

"Shut up!" I said. "Just shut up!" Since the first time my mother took off her clothes and took a walk, I'd learned that it wasn't as uncommon an occurrence as I'd believed. But something—maybe that I had upset her by bringing Max home—told me it was Barbara. "Where exactly did you see her?"

The private pointed toward the river. "She was walking

toward the old steel mill. Some cops were after her, but a soldier intervened and walked her to the strip club on Sixth Street. I didn't recognize him."

"Lucky Lady?"

"Yeh."

The Asads' club. I don't know why, but I had the feeling it was Max who was taking her there. I had told Max about Mom, how she was unstable and how, when she stopped taking her medication—which she did a lot—she would become agitated, take her clothes off, and go for a walk. Her clothes oppressed her, she told me. I thought this new medication she was on, Abilify, was better because she hadn't taken a nude walk in a couple of months, according to Dad. I shoved a carton of water at the soldier. "Take over here, private," I said.

I jumped off the back of the truck and began running toward Lucky Lady. I'd made Duck take me to the club's opening eight years ago. I was seventeen, but I'd gotten a fake ID from Josh Mulvey, who, like Camacho, was a thwarted artist and could fake anything. Duck wanted to hang by the door but I insisted we sit right up front, and soon he was transfixed by the gyrations of the beautiful Korean dancer in front of us. I was so used to his having eyes only for me that I got up and walked away and sat down between two guys in UPS uniforms who made room for me and bought me drinks while they stuffed dollar bills into a blond stripper's G-string until Duck yanked me off the stool and out the door. That's how I remembered Lucky Lady.

Tonight the place was lit by exit signs and emergency lights, which glowed a bloody red, and it took me a minute to see that there were a lot of people behind the bar, helping themselves to drinks, and several others sitting at the bar, among them Jenna and Camacho. "What's going on?" I asked.

"Where were you?" Jenna shot back.

"What do you mean, where was I? At the truck, loading up water, where you were supposed to be."

"Bullshit," Jenna said. "I saw you go into the old hotel with Max Asad. You think you can just sneak around and no one sees what you're doing? I saw you. I'm turning your ass in, Bineki."

"You know, I'm really getting tired of your spying on me."

"I wasn't *spying* on you. Who *cares* where you are. No one cares where you are except Duck. Aren't you engaged to him? How come you're not asking where *he* is?"

I hadn't given Duck a thought. He always turned up eventually. "Why should I ask where he is? And no, we're not engaged."

"He thinks you are."

"I'm looking for Max Asad. Have you seen him?"

"Max Asad? You mean your boyfriend, whose father is going to bulldoze our homes and kick us out into the street like a bunch of dogs? *That* Max Asad?"

"Where do you get these ideas? No one is bulldozing anything. Jesus, you're so *ignorant*."

The guys behind the bar had stopped drinking and were looking at me.

Camacho, who used to be scared of me in Kandahar, mostly because I outranked him, said, "You *fucking* that asshole?"

"None of your business, private."

"What're you doing fucking an Arab asshole?"

I felt like my magical protective armor had been removed from me. Whatever I had that had made people respect me was gone because of my alliance with Max. I turned to Jenna. "Is Max here? Is he?" I tried to be calm, but I could feel the menace in the room.

A guy sitting on the bar slid off. "Don't upset the pretty soldier. Chris Schaeffer," he said, holding out his hand. "I'm the manager of this joint. Why don't you step into my office—it's downstairs—so you don't have to listen to this trash talk." Everyone laughed.

"No one is supposed to be downtown," I said.

"That's damned convenient, isn't it?" Jenna said. "Evacuate everyone, condemn the property so folks can't come back, and then—presto!—you got yourself some nice real estate without the inconvenience of deadbeats actually living in it."

Max had said his father had plans for the downtown, but I honestly didn't know what they were. I shook my head.

"You're the rag head's bitch. Stop pretending you don't know what she's talking about," Camacho said. "What are we supposed to do, huh? Where the hell does he think we're going to go? We don't all have rich daddies who'll bail us out when we're thrown out of our houses. And it's our fucking town. It's *our* town. We pay our rent. I don't know what the motherfucker wants."

"We're Christian Americans. We have rights," Jenna said. "It's our country."

"Yeah," said Camacho. "Us Christians have rights."

Camacho was drinking straight from a bottle and was dangerously drunk. I say dangerous because he wasn't drunk enough to pass out. I'd watched scenes like this in Kandahar, where there was plenty of bootleg hooch and plenty of anger and a wrong word was all it took to ignite a shoving match or cause a punch to be thrown. But this was different, scarier, because beneath Camacho's anger he looked like he'd been crying. Jenna and the men watching from behind the bar were all in despair because they'd already been beaten and they knew it.

Now I just wanted to find my mother and make sure she was okay, and I guess I looked desperate because Jenna said, "She's up there." She pointed to a stairway. "Your ma. Him, too."

"Thanks, Jenna," I said.

Just then the front door opened and a woman wearing a yellow slicker with matching high yellow boots and a rain hat entered. "You, behind the bar, what are you doing? *Drinking?* Chris, what the hell is going on here?" she said.

"Well, well," Chris said. He'd taken ahold of my arm when he'd made his gallant offer. Now, in two bounds, he was in the woman's face. "Let me introduce you to everyone here. Houda Asad! The scumbag's daughter."

I stood frozen halfway to the stairs and suddenly Max was coming down them. I remember hoping he'd heard how much these people hated his family so he'd be glad to go to a place where no one knew him. He saw me and nodded and I knew my mother was all right, and I smiled at him. He was carrying a green money pouch with a little padlock on it. He held it out to show his sister as he crossed the room toward her.

"Great," she said.

Camacho grabbed Max's arm and it looked like he was going to punch him, but Max was faster. Max put his leg behind Camacho's and flipped him backward to the floor; then he bent, grabbed his collar, said something in the prone man's ear, and stood up. It might have ended then, but Jenna jumped off her stool and, her carrot-red hair sticking out like she'd put her finger in a light socket, tossed her beer in Max's face. She backed away, laughing. "Now you look like us. Like a drowned rat!"

Max started after her, then stopped.

"Aren't you going to do something about that?" Camacho asked, taunting him. "Mr. *Maricón* Asad. Or are you scared of Jenna Magee? Come on. Let's finish this. You and me, *pato.*"

"I've seen you fight, Camacho," Max said. Calmly, he wiped the beer from his face with his sleeve and turned away from him.

It was clear to me in that one moment that what everyone

hated about Max was exactly what I loved. That he could overcome the brute instinct to pound people who insulted him; walk away from a fight that he could clearly win, then recite Rumi to me later and make sense of the whole thing. That he was more interested in showing me the beauty in life rather than showing me how he could destroy life with his bare fists. I think that's all I ever wanted: a man strong enough to see poetry in life and who knew how to make me hear my own. A man who looked at life and didn't see a series of dogfights with the meanest dog winning, but who saw life as an endless dance through time and knew the only important thing was to find a partner who heard the same music.

I knew then that despite everything, we were going to make it. I smiled at him, and he pointed to the stairs.

"Go," he said, and smiled. "Take care of your mother."

Before Max could turn around, Camacho grabbed a barstool and brought it down on Max's head. Max fell to his knees, kind of knelt really, rubbing his head as if he were deciding if he was hurt. Camacho tore a leg off the stool and struck Max in the back of the head with it three, four, five times, spittle flying from his mouth with each blow. It happened so quickly and was so unbelievable, but my adrenaline was pumping so hard I saw everything. I could feel tears running down my cheeks, and I wanted to scream but couldn't. No one moved or spoke. It was as if a switch had turned us all off, then come back on, because suddenly Chris Schaeffer bolted out the door and Jenna was shouting for help and Camacho was poking at Max with the stool leg frantically, saying, "Get up! Get up! Goddammit, get up!" when it was pretty clear he wasn't going to.

Houda walked up behind Camacho, reached into her pocketbook, and calmly put a Berretta to the back of his head. She pulled the trigger once, then moved it behind his ear and shot again, and blood spurted out his mouth and pooled on the floor as he fell forward slowly. She knelt beside Max, put her ear over his heart, listened, then pulled the money pouch out of his hand and looked up at me curiously, because I was the only one who hadn't run. "Call someone," she said coolly.

What looks like randomness is merely unawareness of the time it takes for the wheel to turn a click.

Lady Luck is usually pictured on a wheel with the four figures representing stages of life: *I shall reign* on the left; *I reign* on the top; *I have reigned* on the right; and, on the bottom, *I have no kingdom*. Sometimes she is dressed like a tart to show her willingness— her eagerness!—to throw her help to the highest bidder. Medieval pictures and statues of Lady Luck depict her with half her face painted white and the other half black because of her duplicity and fickleness. She's blindfolded, as the goddess Justice would eventually be, to show her blindness to the unfairness of life.

But of course, Dr. Asad thought, if Luck were fair no one would be slipped a death sentence alongside the slap on the ass at birth. If Luck gave any thought at all to fairness, his beloved Max would not have been beaten to death by a drunken comrade in his own establishment, which he'd named for his Benefactress out of gratitude.

He had been home watching pay-per-view television with the Aloub men, waiting for Max to come home with news about his release from duty so his life could resume. Bernice was upstairs with the women when the doorbell rang. Bernice ran down the stairs; she had been laughing with the women and was still smiling as she moved the curtain above the sofa in the living room aside and saw a man in an army uniform standing in the portico.

Dr. Asad glanced back at her and said, "*Habibi*, open the door!" but Bernice said, "Oh, no! No! No! No! Don't let him in!" and fell into a chair with her face in her hands. Puzzled as to what had upset his wife, he opened the door to Major Ted Wayland, an army chaplain, who asked if he could come in, removed his hat, and told him without preamble, as he was trained to do, that Max had been killed in the line of duty.

As the chaplain explained the curious circumstances of Max's death, *in the line of duty*, Dr. Asad made himself think of other things. He remembered how he had seen people murdered in the streets of Beirut as he walked to work. How his wife and daughter had died in a cross fire, running to meet him from the other side of the street, running to him for protection. He remembered a scene in a Kurosawa film he had seen in Paris of a hara-kiri disemboweling. He had left the movie theater delicately probing his belly but had gone on to eat a huge Parisian dinner, thinking how lucky he was to still have a gullet to enjoy French cooking. His mind was firing like a pistol without aim. When the chaplain started to recite the "Your boy has gone to a better place" boilerplate, Dr. Asad gestured for him to stop. "Please," he said, putting a hand on Bernice's shoulder and motioning for him to leave, before he remembered his manners and accompanied him to the door.

The Aloub men called their women downstairs and ushered them out the door without explanation, Nadira between her brothers. At the sight of Bernice, an old aunt began keening. Dr. Asad escorted her out the door and suddenly the house was still.

He dabbed at his eyes with his handkerchief as he remembered the house he planned to build Max and Nadira as a wedding present. His fickle goddess had decided to crush him. "I will not allow it!" he said angrily. He was a powerful man and was unwilling to concede that, like the figure at the bottom of the wheel of fortune, *he had no kingdom.* This would not be the ending to his story.

The phone rang. It was Houda, calling from the county prison where she'd turned herself in.

When they found out what happened, everyone in the unit said it was Jenna's fault that Max got killed. If she hadn't been spouting off about the Asads wanting to turn the downtown into a fancy cash cow, Max would still be alive and so would Camacho. He survived for a while but died on a gurney in an EMS van because the Warren Hospital emergency room was overflowing with people injured in the flood. They didn't arrest Jenna, but she needed a lawyer and she didn't have any cash, so I was pretty sure she was going to get squashed by a legal system that was blind to shades of blame as explained by the heart and its fears and only understood subtleties of guilt when expensive lawyers presented them.

Jenna herself told me this. She came to the hospital where they were keeping me for observation or some such bullshit, there being nothing much to observe except a sore shoulder where a crazed dog bit me. She was still in her uniform and crawled into the hospital bed with me, crying. "I don't know what I'm going to tell them," she said. She had run out of Lucky Lady before the cops got there, but Kat had seen her and Houda too, and Chris Schaeffer and all the guys who worked for Dr. Asad would be more than glad to deflect the spotlight. They looked guilty just for being alive and had no real story to justify what they were doing in the club, getting drunk while the town was drowning.

I told Jenna I would take out a mortgage on my father's shop to pay her legal bills, and she laughed. "Fat fucking chance. They wrecked it. It's wrecked, Duck. I saw it when I was looking for evacuees. They broke in and stole your tools and trashed the shop. There was a crack pipe on your desk. The whole downtown is wrecked." I said she could come live with me in the cabin. "Your mom, too, until you get set up somewhere else." She just shook her head. "You don't want that," she said and bolted away, probably one step ahead of the police. I guess she was thinking that if anyone brought up what happened with Barzai Marwat in Kandahar, they would try to make her an accessory. The story would be that she was a fucked-up poor girl who was always causing trouble, which of course was one way to look at it.

A nurse came in and adjusted a saline drip in my arm and I asked her how much longer I had to stay here, and she said, "You're dehydrated. We're going to keep you overnight," so as soon as she left I ripped the needle out of my arm and walked out of there and went to find Kat. Whatever she thought she had going with Asad, unofficially she was engaged to *me*. I know it sounds egocentric, but things happen for a reason and I was telling myself that Max was killed so Kat would come to her senses about *me*. She had just been attracted to the fact that Max was unattainable, because I don't know what bullshit Max was telling her, but there was *no way* he was going to cross his father and not marry the girl his dad had picked out for him. And give up an empire? No way.

I walked to her house and no one answered the door, so I just went in. I had been doing that since I was a kid. I hollered "Hello?" and "Anyone home?" and went down to the basement where Mr. Bineki had his office. His office was partitioned off with unpainted drywall and a cheap hollow door from Home Depot with a big padlock on it, but the door was open and I could see him in front of his computer, wearing a dingy white tee and looking like he hadn't showered in a month. He heard me and got up right away.

"Not here. No one's here," he said, clearing his throat and trying to close the door on me.

I stuck my foot in. "Where is she?" I asked. I realize now that the year in Afghanistan had made me kind of belligerent, but honestly I didn't know that's how I was coming across.

"Hey, hey, no need to get violent," Bineki said. "I just said she isn't here. You okay?" He pointed to my arm where the tape from the IV was dangling. I hadn't bothered to pull my sleeve down.

"Where's Kat?"

When I look back on it now, I have to say, he looked insane. His eyes were glassy and he stank. Empty pizza boxes were piled up next to his desk.

"I thought she was with her unit. With you," he said.

I ran up the stairs and out of the house, thinking she had to be with his body, which was a sickening thought, and by the time I got all the way downtown, cop cars with their bubble lights flashing were in front of Lucky Lady, which was cordoned off. I pushed my way in. "U.S. Military, U.S. Military," I kept saying as if that granted me special access, and magically it did. Everyone respects the military.

A couple of detectives were making notes. On the floor were two chalk outlines where Max and Camacho had died. I thought

I was going to throw up. Chalk outlines were for people I didn't know, not for people who had said good morning to me about a thousand times in the past year.

I saw the back stairs and hoped maybe Kat would be up there. When I knocked on the door at the top of the steps, for the first time in my life I imagined the black world I would live in without Kat. When she answered the door, all I felt was relief, as if death were catching and Kat might have been in the way of it.

"My mom's here," she said, letting me in.

Anika Lee and her kid, Allie, were sitting on the sofa, playing checkers with Mrs. Bineki, who was oblivious, as usual, to what was happening around her. I wondered how the hell she found her way downtown—until I saw she was wrapped in a too-small kimono, and then I knew.

Anika Lee offered me a drink, which I took. Everyone knew that Dr. Asad kept a mistress, one of his dancers. It was an erotic fantasy that a lot of guys in town got off on—a beautiful Asian living upstairs at your beck and call—and I was trying to will Kat to see that this is what she would have been to Max, a mistress kept out of sight, but suddenly she was in my arms, sobbing. "They killed him, Duck, they killed him! For nothing! He died for nothing."

I stroked her hair and let her cry. I would have liked to tell her that he died for something, but in the bitter end we all die for nothing no matter what kind of awards they give you for doing it or for whatever cause people think your dying furthered. Although it's the bullshit they fed us in Afghanistan, it's the biggest lie in the world to say, someone died for this or that cause.

And I would have liked to say that I was sorry Max was dead, seeing how he died for nothing, but in all honesty I wasn't sorry. I wanted Kat. I needed Kat. And once Max was out of the way, it would be the way it was between me and Kat before that plane ride home. I had given Kat a lot of line, but now she was tired and I was going to reel her back in where she belonged. Did either of us need proof that this was the way it was supposed to be? If Max had to die for it to happen, so be it.

I asked Anika Lee for a blanket and put it around Mrs. Bineki's shoulders—she was going to be part of my official family now—swung an arm around Kat, and said, "Let's go. I'm taking you home."

Wind and Cantwell moved to the second floor of her house while the water seeped in through the kitchen door below. Cantwell helped her bring up a few things and they stayed in her mother's room playing backgammon "for blood," Cantwell screamed, "not money!" When Wind asked him why for blood, he said, "That's how you know you mean business, you're for real."

It was her father's backgammon set. Jimmy was very good at it and he and Wind played on those nights when he wasn't stoned. Sometimes then, too.

The board lay between Wind and Cantwell on an ancient turtle shell, a wedding gift from her father to her mother. Jimmy Bird told his wife that the dreams of women created the world. What they dreamed became real. Women revered the turtle because it carried its house on its back, and Jimmy had had his own dreams, Wind thought, of a warm hearth and home. Dreams that hadn't come true.

Wind easily won the first game, and halfway through the second game they lost interest in backgammon and made love on her mother's bed, which was made up with the same linens as on the day she left. Wind washed them meticulously every month, at first in anticipation of her mother's return, then out of habit, then finally in a superstitious ritual. If she didn't wash the linens, her mother would never return; she wouldn't find her way back.

By four o'clock in the morning, they were lying on the bed, touching each other for reassurance in their sleep, when Wind was awakened by a sliver of light coming in through the curtains. She opened the window and stuck her head out. It had stopped raining. She tiptoed down the stairs so as not to disturb Cantwell. The water in the kitchen had receded, although the floor was muddy. It was normal for a river to flood, and the Lenape understood it was life renewing itself. In one of their earliest myths, a flood got rid of the first humans, who were irredeemably flawed: total flops.

Total flops. She wrapped her blanket tightly around herself and pulled off a few stems of sweetgrass from the pot on the windowsill, closing her eyes to inhale their aroma, and when she didn't instantly slip into a dream state, she shoved the stems up her nose, trying to force them to produce a dream. Still nothing. She grabbed her small drum and began thrumming with her thumbs. Faster, faster, faster. Nothing happened.

Cantwell heard her drumming and came down the stairs wrapped in her mother's sheet, smiling. "What are you doing?" He let the sheet drop open, and Wind saw again how beautiful he was. He was slim and taller than she was. The lapis lazuli hung in the hollow of his throat, glowing. It was a love stone and she thought it might be the only reason that Cantwell loved her, because she knew now he did love her, but she didn't know anymore *what* he loved. If she'd lost her ability to dream, she was no longer a shaman. If she was no longer a shaman, who was she?

She opened her mouth to tell him she had lost her powers when he said, "My God, look! It's stopped raining. The moon is out." He drew her to him and kissed her passionately. "We are each other's lucky star."

PART THREE

The 501st was released from active duty two weeks after Max and Camacho were killed. Everyone was exhausted, riding a tide of anti-Max reflux. He'd been an anomaly in Afghanistan, a cultured head among tattooed dropouts, and now key details of his difference surfaced from the murky reef of "they said." They said he kept a silver-framed photograph of his grandfather in his locker, they said he read books without the mandatory porno pictures, and, worse, that some of those books were in Arabic. They said he thought he was better than everyone else. Well, he did. Did he deserve to die for that?

In the courtyard of the Asads' assisted living facility, Max's father created a memorial to his son: a fenced-in little park with a pair of bronzed boots and a bronze M-16 upright in the boots, topped with a bronze helmet on a marble pedestal. It was a replica of the ad hoc memorial that soldiers in the field construct for their fallen buddies, and it implied that Max had died in combat.

The soldiers were furious that Dr. Asad assumed Max was entitled to a war memorial when, as Chris Schaeffer insisted, Max was killed in a barroom brawl that got out of hand. Of course, it was in Chris Schaeffer's interest to deflect attention away from his participation in what was essentially a hate crime, as if renaming it would lessen the horror. And of course, if anyone in the unit was *entitled* to a war memorial, it was Max. He'd spent the bulk of his enlistment in the Hindu Kush patrolling with the Special Ops while the rest of us unloaded boxes. But it was just one more reminder of how totally fucked they knew they were after Dr. Asad sprang his gigantic surprise on them.

There was talk at first that the Army Corps of Engineers would be called in to mop up after the flood. Then a rumor spread that deactivated soldiers would be hired to start reconstruction. But the trucks and heavy equipment that poured into the city were all marked with the logo of the private contractor from Kandahar, Charon Corp. None of the Charon men were from Warrenside or even Pennsylvania, and in some cases they were from other countries. Looking back on it, I can see the business reason Dr. Asad decided to use them for what he was about to do. They had no sentimental attachment to the downtown or anybody in it. But I think there was more to his decision than ruthless pragmatism. Employing an outside organization for work in a town teeming with unemployed men was the first dose of his unforgiving medicine for the murder of his son.

The Charon mercenaries routinely used physical force to pry residents—who slipped back downtown to pick up their belongings—out of their homes. At first these confrontations were covered by Channel 3; then all of a sudden it stopped—the coverage, not the confrontations—because Dr. Asad *bought* Channel 3 and nixed all reporting on the flood, the cleanup, and Max's and Camacho's deaths. The only way to find out anything was through the grapevine. You had to go downtown to the Toad Bar and Former Grill, where Chris Schaeffer held court. He knew everything that was going on. But even that became impossible after two months, because most of the downtown was razed. Wrecking balls knocked it down: steam shovels, backhoes, and dump trucks hauled out the remains of the structures that used to be riverfront Warrenside until the bend of the Catawissa that had been the South Side looked like it had been swallowed by an earthquake.

The grapevine at the Toad Bar and Former Grill buzzed with the unfairness of money and how—more than guns or anything else—money controls whose history will be remembered, which was true, because after a month our last link to information on Warrenside—the grapevine—was silenced when Dr. Asad condemned, then razed, the Toad Bar and Former Grill, which he could do because, naturally, he owned the property.

Even Duck, who always went out of his way to be fair and see all sides of a situation, forgot himself one night and said the Asads had ruined "his city." His cabinet shop had been demolished. The Asads paid him off, but it was "the principle of the thing," Duck insisted. "Can they just come in and take *everything*? Things that don't belong to them?" He was talking primarily about me, of course, and how Max had just taken me. But the workshop, too. Once the workshop was flattened, there was no reason for anyone to remember anything about Duck's dad and say, "That's Eugene Wolinsky's cabinet shop. Duck Wolinsky's father, remember him? He built the forty-foot mahogany bar at the Franklin Hotel on Front Street, the most gorgeous bar in the northeast United States." No one would remember that that was where Eugene Junior got his nickname, ducking to the fatal report of his dad's shotgun, then ducking to every loud noise until he was *grown*, practically. So it was a memorial too. But without a plaque to mark it or people hanging around there who *remembered*, it was just five hundred square feet of dirt, about to be the floor of a slot parlor, if the grapevine was to be believed.

My reaction to Max's death matched the violence Dr. Asad was wreaking. I cut up all my army uniforms, desert fatigues jacket and hat, combat boots. I cut off my long auburn hair because Max had said it made me so exotic. I couldn't bear to look at any of it. I couldn't bear to look at myself. I had heard of death, of course, but I had never been a guest in its house, which I now lived in day and night. It was a jail. Even being awake was no escape. Grief was a shoal in an underground cavern where shimmers of light came in through the cracks overhead, where murmurs echoed off the water and walls, and I looked for my beloved among those shimmers and murmurs, running ecstatically after a shadow I thought was Max only to have the figure turn into a grotesque stranger. I knew that life lay on the other side of the grotto, but I had neither the energy nor the desire to search for it.

My mother, to her credit, waded into the shoal and sat on the edge of my bed while I sobbed and she lulled me to sleep, saying, "I'm so sorry, so, so sorry," and at the time I didn't think to ask her if she was sorry because Max went into his father's club only to rescue her or if she was sorry that I was living in this dark world and she might never see me again. And when I thought to ask her, I couldn't, because two months after Max was killed, she and my father and her chauffeur flew away to Argentina, leaving me alone in the house.

The army conducted a 15-6 JAG investigation to determine the official who-did-what-when of the double murder. It dragged on for months until finally the army determined that there were no army personnel to try. Houda Asad pulled the trigger that killed Camacho, and as a civilian she would be tried in a civilian court. At the time the 15-6 was conducted, news of Max's death didn't get any specific national media play except as part of the trend of returning warriors going berserk. Jenna and I were subpoenaed as witnesses for Houda's trial, and that looked like it would drag on for years, as Houda's army of attorneys filed motions for postponement, change of venue, et cetera, at Dr. Asad's behest. It was as if he wanted to prolong the trial to keep Max alive. If no one could agree on the exact circumstances of his death, maybe it hadn't happened. If his name was shouted out in court, Max wasn't relegated to the past.

As soon as Dr. Asad erected Max's memorial, it was regularly defaced with graffiti—scrubbed off every day—until Dr. Asad hired a detail from Charon to guard it. When I go by there now, I am met by a guard—usually the same one—who unshoulders his weapon and regards me suspiciously until he recognizes me. Even then, he doesn't acknowledge me, and I am left with the feeling that he knows me, knows my story, and doesn't approve *at all*. The violence of Max's death sticks to me.

Duck came to the house. Naturally. All the time. Waiting for me to snap out of it. Waiting for me to ask him, "How long did it take you to get over your father, Duck?" which I didn't, because it wasn't the same thing at all. I didn't think I would *ever* get over Max. Duck made sure the grass was cut, the garbage put on the curb, et cetera, still trying to show me what a great husband he would be. I was too depressed to put up a big fight, but I put him off. I had known real love and I knew what it was like to be alive, because that's what being in love *is*. How could I go back to being *not* alive?

I wanted to distract myself from my grief in the traditional way by numbing myself with television, but the only television in our house was downstairs in my dad's office, which was cordoned off with yellow police tape. The FBI took away Dad's computer and his files a week after he left for Buenos Aires. Dad was wrong about the new IT department in Jakarta. They caught on to him right away and did the right thing, reporting their findings to Titan. But the federal marshals won't find anything, because Dad wrote a self-destruct program to destroy his files as well as the database linked into Titan when someone tried to access either of them from his machine. "Who do they think they're dealing with?" he kept shouting at me as he explained the intricacies of what he had done to embezzle more than three million dollars. "Chump change," he said. "They won't even miss it. Members of the club get bonuses bigger than that!" Criminals, I've read, need witnesses to their brilliance, but Dad's shenanigans weren't brilliant. Titan's computer security was almost nonexistent. The executives couldn't imagine a member of their old boys' club doing the company harm, and they were probably right about that, but at the end of the day Dad *wasn't* one of them, which fact they never let him forget. So he didn't.

Since compulsive television-watching wasn't an option, I started to plow through the books in my mother's library. Most of the books were old, like her Harvard Classics series, which might have been used as more than décor at one point. It's funny, the things and ideas that endure and those that, while highly touted in their day, are out of date almost immediately. There was a whole bottom shelf of paperback romances and old women's magazines, and I felt a tug of sympathy for my mother, retreating into a fantasy life while she ignored her real life in our basement. But I guessed that was over now. She was with my dad, and she was almost giddy when she made the announcement—in Spanish, I almost fainted when I heard *that*—that she was going to Buenos Aires with him. Dad left me a twenty-thousand-dollar stash in hundred–dollar bills whose hiding place he informed me about from the airport before the phone was tapped.

The big surprise on the bookshelf was my grandfather's book, *The House Is Built!* It was a joke between me and Dad when I was growing up that Mom was getting secret instructions from it. She certainly was obsessed with it, reading it propped up on the table while we were eating, and probably in bed, although I don't know that for a fact. My dad said she read all one thousand pages all the way through at least six times, underlining passages that struck her, like some people read the Bible. So is it any wonder that I wanted nothing to do with it? Two copies, spines intact, perched on the shelf. Neither of them had passages underlined, so I guessed that Mom had taken her copy with her. Both of these copies were signed *Best Wishes, Malcolm Warren.* Reading that impersonal inscription, which sounded so much like Mom with its propriety, was the first time I'd laughed in months.

And there was Duck. There was no magazine in my mother's stack that contained advice on how to deal with Duck. No relationship advice on how to mute the insult "You don't make me come alive."

Duck came every night after my parents left. We talked about everything—except Max. The Asads were knocking down Warrenside and he was waiting for me to get over some mystery ailment so we could get on with our lives. He didn't have to stick around Warrenside for Houda's trial because he'd been in the hospital when Max was murdered, and I knew he was getting ready to make a move. I *knew* him. One night when he came, he talked briefly about what he would do with the money he got from the Asads' plowing down his cabinet shop.

"Fifty grand isn't a lot of money, but it's something," he said. "It could give us the down payment on a house. A pretty big house. Or we could live here. Your dad told me the roof never stops leaking. I'd probably replace the whole roof. "

"He never said anything to me about the roof leaking," I said.

"Well, it's guy stuff, roofs. We had the hoses out a couple of times, trying to find out where it was coming from."

I was startled to hear they had conversations that didn't include me, one way or another. "I didn't know you were that chummy with Dad."

"We have a lot in common."

"Are you, like, *friends*?"

And I didn't have to tell him how Dad got the money to suddenly retire to Argentina. He knew. There was probably a lot I didn't actually know about Duck. One thing I did know, though. Since Max, Duck had grown a protective shield around himself. He never let his guard down. And I know it sounds contradictory, but sometimes I wanted the old Duck back.

"You're going away, aren't you?" I asked him.

"Depends on you," he said. "We've been talking about getting married forever and I guess I would like an answer, yeah."

"I have a lot of baggage," I said.

"We all do."

When we were kids, Duck's mother drove him to our house and from there we would walk to summer day camp, where we made lanyards and pot holders and popsicle-stick picture frames with everyone else until the day we came home and my mother was naked on the sofa, fanning herself and begging me for a foot rub while Duck and I giggled upstairs, scared to come down until we heard the front door bang and I knew the worst possible thing was happening. Duck followed me out of the house as I trailed my mother into town, yelling at me, "Kat, Kat, come back. *It's not you*." And I didn't know why he was saying, "It's not you," because of *course* it was me, how could it not be? And we ran after the crowd that trotted in her wake like she was the Pied Fucking Piper and we were all going to follow her right into the river and drown, and Duck kept saying, *"It's not you!"* and I remembered that over the years and wondered sometimes, "How did he know to say that?" and then, when his father killed himself, I knew. When the police finally caught up with her in town, in the middle of a crowd, Duck pulled me away and walked me home and he never said a word about it, and when I insisted that we get our own table at summer camp after that, he didn't protest, he just helped weave the cocoon around me, around us. And that's the cocoon I'd finally cut open, to let whatever creature had grown in there out for air, to live if it could or die.

On the bus home from Fort Dix, I saw a sign on the lawn of a church that said:

I KNOW EVERYTHING ABOUT YOU, BUT I STILL LOVE YOU ANYWAY. SIGNED, GOD.

I was deeply in love with Max at that point and trying to avoid comparisons between him and Duck, but the message on that sign struck me as the reason Duck's love didn't count somehow. Because what kind of love is it that doesn't see your flaws and hold you accountable? What exactly is it that such an indiscriminate lover *loves*? How jealous is he that he wouldn't want you to be the best possible thing you could be?

"We probably know each other better than any two people on the planet," Duck said.

And while that was the line we had been feeding each other since I could remember, it no longer seemed true. "We know certain things about each other, Duck. But in a way we don't know anything." We knew the particulars of each other's lives— some of them admittedly pretty awful—but that was it.

"When I say I have baggage, Duck, I really mean it." I tittered because I was nervous.

"It's okay, Kat." He was suddenly less wooden. "I told you a million times, it's okay. But we got to start making plans. Start living our lives."

He looked at me with such love in his face that I stared for a minute and smiled back, knowing he would never feel the same way about me after I told him what I had to tell him, knowing I would never see that look again.

I reached out and touched his hand. "I'm pregnant, Duck."

In chapter one of *The House Is Built!* my grandfather Malcolm Warren finds out his wife, Marion, is pregnant with my mother. He writes about fixing up a room in their old Tudor mansion for the baby. "But," he writes, "the time is past for fixing up the past. It's time to build something new." It was 1961 and Malcolm, alone among his contemporaries apparently, understood that Warren Steel's time was running out. He wanted to modernize the plant to prepare it for the changing economy, but he was voted down by the board of directors, who wanted things exactly as they always had been, who thought their time of ascendancy would last forever.

And *that*, Max had told me in our brief time together, was what his father called the fatal flaw of man. Man could not accept that the wheel turns and then it's someone else's time to ride up to the top, and that was why he makes such a noisy mess of things when he begins the inevitable slide down the chute. After my grandmother got pregnant with my mom, Malcolm started plans to build the modernist house I'm living in now. It was to be a showcase of steel I beams in residential construction and an upgrading of construction materials. Malcolm wanted to take Warren

Steel in a new direction, but he was voted down and then—which was big news to me—he was voted out. I didn't know that by the time he finished his showcase house and plunged into the sea from a Costa Brava cliff, his office door at Warren Steel had been overwritten with someone else's name.

Barbara found out that her driver's name was Pablo.

She'd had a long rest after her downtown walkabout and, this morning, a double dose of Abilify, probably unnecessary and certainly not recommended, and this time Mike watched as she swallowed, as if she were a child, she thought, and waited until the chemical veil covered her eyes, and after Mike exhaled and went down to his basement office, Barbara finally decided to go about her own business as well, which was seeing what the flood had done to the club.

At first, and as usual, she didn't pay attention to Pablo. He drove her to the club, opened the door, and followed her respectfully, carrying a tote bag she had for the receipts, which she had only a faint hope of retrieving. She'd seen the looters carrying things out of the stores downtown. There was no reason that that particular disease—the disease of theft and lack of honor—hadn't spread to the club.

The grounds were soggy and the floor of the clubhouse, although slightly higher than the grounds, was coated in mud. She went immediately to the Nineteenth Hole, the club's restaurant. The manager had emptied the drawer. Credit card receipts clipped to coupons and cash were in the money bag in the false front compartment behind the single-malt scotch. She took out *The House Is Built!*, which she carried everywhere in her tote, to make room for the money bag and, feeling buoyant with this evidence that Western Civilization had not yet breathed its last, she asked Pablo to please check the men's locker room for her, and he came out holding a blue stone hanging on a piece of leather. It was the lapis lazuli that Cantwell had been wearing. He must have dropped it when he cleaned out his locker.

"Oh!" she exclaimed. "Bring that here!" She ran into the women's locker room, washed the mud off the leather strap, and wiped the stone dry. The stone was pulsing and her cheeks and breast felt hot as she stared at herself in the mirror for what must have been a very long time, because Pablo opened the door a little and said, *"Señora. ¿Hay dificultad?"*

"Come in here, *please*," she said, leaning over the sink. "I need your help." She held out the lapis lazuli to him and asked him to please tie it around her neck, *please*, and when his fingers brushed the fine hairs on her neck, her mouth started to water, her salivary glands began pumping out phenylethylamine, which caused an addictive reaction in her, like she wanted to touch him, which she did, brushing her hand over his as he knotted the leather, which caused neural transmitters in her pituitary gland to start chugging out oxytocin, which caused her palms to sweat, her knees to shake, and a general restlessness to overtake her, which could only be assuaged by kissing him fully on the mouth, which caused the substantia nigra and the ventral tegmental areas of the brain to produce dopamine receptors, which made Barbara feel just plain good, like she wanted more, more, *more*, until her adrenal glands kicked in with norepinephrine and she learned after an exhausting—exhilarating!—hour on the women's locker-room floor that Pablo, in his native Chile, had been a lawyer who had emigrated to America after becoming obsolete in 1981 when Pinochet took power and began a systematic abuse of laws and human rights. "I am now," said Pablo, who had only pretended not to speak English, "a man out of place and time." He rolled over and propped himself up on his elbow. He traced the voluptuous curve of her belly, *"plena mujer,"* down to her ripe thighs, *"luna caliente,"* and up to her breasts, *"manzana carnal."* "You are like a Botero nude, Señora Barbara."

Pablo continued: *"¿Espeso aroma de algas, lodo y luz machacados, qué oscura claridad se abre entre tus columnas? ¿Qué antigua noche el hombre toca con sus sentidos?"*

"It sounds dirty," Barbara said. "Did you write that?"

"It *is* dirty," Pablo said, laughing. "Pablo Neruda is our most erotic poet."

"I want to read *everything* he has ever written," Barbara said.

"He is different in Spanish. You must read him in Spanish," Pablo said. "Let me teach you."

Barbara got up slowly, amazed at her grace and beauty. She hadn't felt this way since she was very young. She smiled at Pablo's nude body. She hadn't realized how a mature potbelly covered with a lawn of hair could be so sensuous.

"Don't dress right now," he said. "You are so beautiful. Let's stay just a little longer."

Mike came up from the basement to make a speech to Barbara. The speech was that he was going to Buenos Aires and he was only going to ask her once: Did she want to come with him?

Barbara was sitting on the Louis XV settee, her face a pretty pink, pretending to read a magazine, although she couldn't seem to find anything interesting in them anymore.

"To Buenos Aires?" she asked. "For how long?"

"Forever. You're my wife and I know we've had our problems, but I want to give you the chance to say yes or no."

"Well, I say yes."

"If you don't want to, I completely understand."

"I said yes, Mike."

"You're coming?"

"When are you leaving?"

"I got to be out of here in two weeks. You can't take much with you. I figure we can buy what we need down there. You can only take what you can't buy there."

"I'm ready now."

"Aren't you going to ask me why we're going? What we're going to do down there?"

"Why are we going, Mike?"

"Because I embezzled three million dollars from Titan Insurance, and I'll go to jail if I stay here. Titan has moved statistical tracking functions to overseas facilities in Indonesia. A normal audit switch would take six months to complete, but I don't trust those gooks. Some crafty little hacker will smell the giant hole in Titan's books and instead of reporting it to Titan or the FBI like an *honest* citizen, he'll try to blackmail me. And that's not going to happen! I worked too hard for this money to just hand it over to some Javanese asshole trying to game me."

Barbara often thought that there was no difference between her ancestors who founded Warren Steel and pirates who sailed the seas, taking what they wanted when they wanted it. The elder Warrens took the land around the Catawissa, named it after themselves, skimped on their laborers, and did whatever they had to do to destroy competitors. So she had nothing against pirates. Isn't that what Mike did when he married her? He took something that didn't belong to him. Isn't that what Pablo was doing now?

"What are you taking?" he asked.

Barbara stood up and stretched. "Just Pablo."

"Who's Pablo?"

"The chauffeur."

"I'm surprised you know his name," Mike said, going back down to the basement.

THIRTY-FOUR

DR. ASAD

One old man, Stu Karol, was a casualty of the flood. He wouldn't leave his house despite repeated attempts by guardsmen to force him to do so, and a Charon Corp cleanup crew found him sitting stiffened in a mud-caked La-Z-Boy recliner with the remote control clutched in his hand, waiting for the electricity to come back on so he could watch his favorite show, *Oprah*, which neighbors and bystanders, trying to be helpful, trying to figure out why the old man wouldn't just evacuate like all the other lemmings, told the police he watched every day. He loved *Oprah*, loved *Dr. Phil*, loved the luxury of thinking about the nuances of life instead of just living it like a brute, as he had done for his entire working life. The water didn't seem deep enough for Stu to drown in so the cause of death was up to a coroner to decide and the coroner determined that a combination of respiratory and kidney failure did the deed. Stu Karol was a widower and a retired employee of Warren Steel, an annealer, the guy who heated, cooled, then pickled steel I beams in a chemical bath before they went on their journey into the world, the very same chemicals that seeped into his body and probably helped him out in the end by killing him before he had to endure the indignity of life on someone else's terms. Channel 3 had done a piece a year before about how Stu was the last employee of Warren Steel—the employee who had turned out the lights, as it were—and Channel 3 ran a feature of him reenacting that live. He had one son, Teddy, a not very successful motivational speaker turned game-show contestant who put aside his personal grief upon hearing of his father's death to try to wring some money out of it.

Dr. Asad had received the summons from Teddy Karol's lawyer that morning. He put it in the pile of summonses on his desk to give to his attorney later in the week. He marveled again at the American idea that someone should pay for your losses: how life and property were part of a cosmic inventory and when yours went bad someone *somehow* owed you. Why couldn't they see that life was a series of losses, and entering supposed blessings in the credit column was cooking the books? These musings only stoked his rage at the death of his son.

He'd quieted Anika Lee's restlessness by relocating her and Allie to their own house, not far from his own in Rambling Rose, where the other Arab women in the neighborhood would be glad to report any indiscretions on her part. Then he had mounted the cab of the first wrecker, moved the wrecking ball into position, and taken the first swing into Lucky Lady himself, initiating the demolition of downtown Warrenside. Houda had warned him that former residents might picket the destruction but, as he suspected, none came. They were scrambling to make new lives for themselves elsewhere.

Houda, who was out on bail wearing an ankle tracking bracelet so the authorities would know her whereabouts, had slowly taken over the day-to-day operations of the Asad empire. She showed Dr. Asad a tax map of the downtown properties they didn't own. There were six of them that stood out like cankers on his plans, stuck in the middle of his holdings. Houda, following her own business instincts, had bribed their owners with more money than their properties were worth, although significantly less than they would be worth as the Asads' development plan materialized. One of them was a woodworking shop owned by a Eugene "Duck" Wolinsky. Months earlier, Dr. Asad had received a private detective's report that said Wolinsky had been in Lucky Lady when Max was killed, and he assumed he was part of the mob that beat Max. He authorized the razing of the shop before Wolinsky was even contacted, then claimed it was a mistake because he owned all the abutting properties. He'd told Houda to offer Wolinsky ten thousand dollars' compensation. Houda offered fifty thousand, if Wolinsky signed a document forfeiting the right to sue. Dr. Asad was surprised at how easily Wolinsky had capitulated, and would have liked to see him suffer more for his part in Max's death.

He'd had Houda describe to him, over and over, how it felt to kill Camacho. He would have given anything to have been the one to pull the trigger, and his dreams were filled with Camacho's death. The enormity that this *nothing* was the one to kill Max tormented him. If his Max was denied a heroic death, he would have liked the murderer to be something more than an insect. The coroner's report said that Camacho had a contract in his pocket from an organization called Charon Corp. He'd had research done on Charon. It was a brand-new entity in the American business landscape: a pyramid of ex-military mercenaries posing as an S corporation. It had been in Kandahar when Max was there.

Dr. Asad had started the rumor that the deactivated men of the 501st would be used to reconstruct the downtown for one reason only: to make sure they were still in town to witness Charon rolling into the downtown on a Sunday morning, honking the horns of their flatbed trucks where the men brandished chain saws, pounding shovels on the floor of the trucks, and singing uncouth songs like Saladin's army entering Samaria. He had orchestrated the last flourish by paying each crew foreman five thousand dollars.

It sounds cold, but something clicked off inside me when Kat told me about the baby. Right in the middle of talking marriage, she casually drops that bomb, which basically shattered my life as I knew it. We were sitting in the kitchen. I'll never forget it. I was thinking, She's going to finally say yes, let's get married, and then she tells me this. I got up, excused myself, and left. I told her everything was okay, but I felt like I was going to throw up. After all we'd been through, Kat's having someone else's baby was the ultimate betrayal. It was like the world we built for ourselves, our home, was ripped open and hey, everyone, come on in! I didn't think I would ever be able to even look at her again.

Of course, not seeing Kat again posed an even bigger problem for me, because I had spent most of my life waiting for Kat in one way or another, and when I wasn't doing that I didn't know what to do. I drove around for a couple of hours, and then I found Jenna at the church she hangs out at.

The JAG had cleared Jenna of any direct wrongdoing, so she didn't have to wear an ankle bracelet or anything, but she was to make herself available for Houda's trial, and who knew when the hell that was going to be. The Asads kept buying legal roadblocks to a fair and honest proceeding, and you don't have to be a genius to know that Houda was going to walk away from killing Camacho, even though she pulled the trigger twice. If she were smarter, she would have fired once and she could have claimed passion, heat of the moment, but that second shot—aimed precisely behind Camacho's ear as if she were a freakin' anatomy scholar—reeks of premeditated murder, if you ask me.

Everybody talks about Houda's second shot—"It was cold-blooded, dude"—on Sunday mornings after the ten o'clock service at Reverend Bob's City of Grace Church at Sixth and Hill streets—one of the few English-speaking churches remaining in what used to be a city of Anglo church spires. That's why we used to say we were lucky in Warrenside—we built nice places for God to visit, so when He came to town He sprinkled luck and a lot of heavy metal on us. City of Grace sits right on the edge of the Asad path of vengeance. Reverend Bob welcomes everyone, especially those who need a quick fix of acceptance: souls on the run and souls who have forgotten who they are, like Camacho's ex-girlfriend, who acquired a new boyfriend while Camacho was in Afghanistan. The new boyfriend is a Crip enforcer who was going to snuff Camacho, so Camacho would have gotten killed one way or another. His luck had just plain run out.

Reverend Bob's specialty is lost souls like the unlucky Reuber, who'd walked away from deadbeat-dad work release a month after the sheriff picked him up at the Armory, only to find that his house had been bulldozed. Other rootless soldiers from the 501st found their way to Reverend Bob's, thanks to Jenna's pestering and their reluctant acknowledgment that no, they really didn't have anything better to do on a Sunday morning, and yes, a little singing and praising the Lord might lift their spirits. A lot of us were having a hard time living up to the returning-warrior mythology the hometown culture required of us.

After Reverend Bob preached his message of unequivocal love from a tit-for-tat Jesus, Jenna manned the sixty-cup coffee-urn-and-doughnut reception in the basement of the church. Since she didn't have any place to go, Reverend Bob let her stay in the nursery in the basement until she got her act together, in exchange for cleaning the place and making the coffee on Sunday mornings.

The central message in Reverend Bob's theology was, you got a clean slate when you accepted Jesus. No guilt over past sins, but no remembering past glories either. You had to give up who you were, but if the person you had been wasn't much of anything, it doesn't seem like much of a sacrifice, does it? Most people give it up without a fight. Even I could see where it might be kind of a relief to wipe Kat and my life in Warrenside from my soul and start again. I told Jenna that. We spent quite a few nights staying up and talking—after some incredible sex, of course—in that tiny little nursery.

She told me how she got her tattoo. In high school she went to a biker artist with her babysitting money and the biker, Sean Roper, fell in love with her. She said she became intoxicated with the sex, the bourbon, and the pot that Sean gave her before each session. Jenna wasn't a beautiful girl, not like Kat is beautiful, so I guess she was intoxicated with his attention too. After he finished the tattoos she had money for, he continued writing on her for free. He said he was making her a goddess, a queen, Persephone! Then he rode out of town on his beautifully painted Harley.

Her mother became suspicious of her cranky hangovers and failing grades and began watching her. She barged in while Jenna was showering and saw that her daughter's body had become a mural for someone's pagan fantasies. Not only her skin but her womb as well: Jenna was four months pregnant. Her mother told her the fetus was like a bad appendix that had to come out, so "don't go naming it," and when the social worker scooped her baby away almost as soon as it was born, Jenna, who is a lot stronger than people give her credit for, said she turned her face to the wall, determined not to see it so she wouldn't bond. She found Jesus a couple of months later at City of Grace, where Reverend Bob introduced her to the army recruiter who was there looking for low fruit or fallen fruit, and who told Jenna she looked "just like a peach." Her tattoos were a secret she managed to keep the whole time she was in Afghanistan—from everyone but me—by sleeping with her clothes on and showering at odd hours. The only friend she had there was Barzai Marwat, who she thought had a crush on her until he asked her in his faltering English about the beautiful Kat Bineki. "Is she not interested in Arab man?" He lusted after Kat Bineki, and for that he had to pay.

When she confessed that to me, she cried, and when I tried to comfort her, she brushed me off. "Are you feeling *sorry* for me, Duck? Don't you *dare* feel sorry for me. I was a *queen*, Duck! And when I'm in heaven, I'll be a queen again." We told each other everything, and I was undoubtedly in love with her then. I would have stayed in love if she had said she was a queen *at that very moment*, because I needed something to hold on to right then.

Ordinarily, I would have never hung out with a bunch of desperadoes at the City of Grace, but Jenna was there and no one seemed surprised to see me after Sunday morning services pouring coffee into Styrofoam cups with her. Reuber came every Sunday, looking for action.

"There are a lot of fine-looking *chicas* here," Reuber said, appreciating the young Latinas who had been shimmying and shaking and praising the Lord during the service and who drank coffee with lots of milk and sugar and eyeballed him back.

"I would have thought you'd have had enough of that," Jenna said.

"You can never have enough of that," Reuber said.

"Well, they're not interested in you," Jenna said. "They're looking for rich guys. Someone who will take care of them and their babies. You can't even take care of yourself."

"Bitches are always trying to scam us."

"Yeah," Jenna said. "Like you aren't trying to scam them."

"I'm just doing what comes naturally," Reuber said. He hitched up his pants—desert fatigues—which he wore because women responded to them, thought he was tough and macho.

Most of the women had babies in carriages or in their arms or holding on to their legs. Jenna had never *ever* laid eyes on her daughter, yet when we took walks together through what used to be her neighborhood, she looked for her everywhere as if she were hiding under an old hubcap or something. She would be three years old now. She was horrified when Asad plowed over the downtown, thinking her daughter was dispersed into the greater world where the chances of ever meeting her were smaller. It wasn't fair. They couldn't afford their kids any more than she could afford hers, yet they got to stroke their hair and their soft arms, hold them, dress them, laugh with them *every day*! And look at Kat Bineki. I had told Jenna that Kat was pregnant with *his* baby and was probably going to keep it. I think that pissed her off more than anything.

"I got a big secret to tell you," Jenna said one Sunday.

The last time Jenna told me a secret, it was about Max Asad's memorial and she had goaded me and Reuber into writing graffiti on it "just so they understand that we know who he *really* was, not some big war hero." Even though we'd run before anyone got a good look at us, I was ashamed I'd done it. Jenna was always harping on the fact that Dr. Asad could hire everybody in the 501st if he wanted to. Why didn't he do *that* to honor his son's memory instead of building a memorial that made the rest of us feel like we weren't important? He was just another rich foreigner, Jenna said, who didn't give a damn about Americans and sent all his money back to whatever weird country he came from. She was always harping on *something*.

"What's up, Jenna?" I asked.

She leaned in, beckoning me and Reuber to come closer, then whispered excitedly, "Dr. Asad isn't going to let anyone who had anything to do with the 501st work for him. As a matter of fact, he's hired those Charon pigs to do everything."

"He can't do that!" Reuber shouted.

Jenna smiled a Buddha smile, as if to say, *I told you he was a soulless body*, which she had actually said a million times. "Well he can, and he is. So fuck us."

I wanted to get Kat and the whole Asad mess behind me. The only problem was, there seemed to be no way to go forward and nowhere to go. I felt like I was in one of those dreams where you're trying to run but your feet weigh like a thousand pounds apiece and you can't pick them up, even though something horrible is gaining on you.

After the river subsided, Cantwell cleaned out his locker at the Lenape Country Club and moved in with Wind, who had begun looking at the world through the eyes of someone who had no shamanic gifts, because those gifts had fled her spirit. And if the earthly physical world seemed a little gray—nothing spoke that couldn't speak, nothing flew that couldn't fly—she was at first dismayed but then accepted that the nether world of visions and spirits belonged to those with no attachments to the physical world. They belonged to those who could fly from the physical world without regret. And now she was *moored* to the physical by her love of Cantwell. It seemed like a curse from the gods to her, that she couldn't be herself and in love with Cantwell at the same time.

What she told Cantwell, however, was that it was her land that tethered her, the land that was cluttered with the lives of all her ancestors and, more importantly, the life of her father. Jimmy Bird saturated the property. Dr. Asad had withdrawn his offer to buy and Barbara Warren had disappeared.

"Let's just burn this crap down," Cantwell said. "This entire collection of your dad's. Then you can start over again."

Since she'd lost her shamanic powers, Wind had been doing a lot of reading about ancestors. She found out, for example, that her Swedish ancestors used the same slash-and-burn method of farming that her Lenape ancestors did. Both prepared fields by clear-cutting all the trees in an area in early spring, then letting the slashed woody material dry out until the rainy season was about to begin, when they burned it in a celebration. The burned material added nutrients to the soil and got rid of bugs and weeds. They would plant and grow for five years, but inevitably the weeds and pests took over again, at which time they moved on and let the field go fallow for twenty years to recover before burning it again.

She would slash and burn, too. Together, she and Cantwell dismantled the outbuildings that her father had collected over the years. Twenty outhouses, ten sheds, piles of shutters and barn siding and beams. In a month they had torn down all his buildings and laid a gigantic bonfire with the wood. When the material dried sufficiently in the sun, they would torch it. All the city zoning and code officials were so busy monitoring the much more interesting dismantling of downtown Warrenside that they hadn't followed up on Barbara Warren's eyesore complaint in a month, and Wind thought she was home free. She would burn everything, and she and Cantwell would walk away and let the land go fallow. Maybe in twenty years their children would find their way home and be able to use the land again. Maybe.

Cantwell had found the thick yellow book *The House Is Built!* by the cash register in the snack bar at the club. When he saw it was written by Malcolm Warren, he took it with him. It was a book about the building of Warrenside and was fully indexed with pictures. Wind thought it peculiar that the Cantwells got little mention, considering they were co-founders of the city, but there was one unflattering chapter devoted to them.

"It says in Chapter Eight," Wind said, "that Noah Cantwell started burying contaminants in trenches under the country club. Did you know that?"

"Is this a deal breaker?" he asked.

"I'm just asking." When Cantwell delivered the book to her, she flipped through it eagerly until she found the part that Barbara alluded to in her vision: the Cantwells had something to do with polluting her land. It seemed now that they had *everything* to do with polluting it.

"The Cantwells were joint owners of Warren Steel when it was founded. They sold out to the Warrens before I was born. If they had anything to do with disposing of their garbage, how would I know? Does it matter? It wasn't me, it was my grandfather. Are you responsible for the Indian massacre of the farmers after the Lenape were cheated in the Walking Purchase?"

"Sometimes I do feel responsible for that."

"Well, you're not. Malcolm Warren wrote that damned book, anyway. Of course he's not going to say that the *Warrens* were responsible when he could easily deflect the blame. The Cantwells aren't speaking to the Warrens anymore."

They argued like this for a month, waiting for the wormy wood to dry out enough to burn, designing a new house they would build on the property. Cantwell was all for saving the old farmhouse and adding an extension with a modern kitchen, but Wind wanted a clean sweep. Everything would be torched.

"We need five children's rooms," Cantwell said.

"No one has five children anymore."

"Don't you wish you had lots of brothers and sisters?"

Wind was scared to plan as far ahead as children, thinking it would jinx this new happiness she was feeling. She didn't feel entitled to it. "You're right, though. If you have two, you might as well have ten."

"I didn't say ten."

"I could do ten. Don't you think I could do ten? Maybe you can't."

They were in the middle of this argument when a black Hummer came up the car track. Two men with HOMELAND SECURITY stenciled across the back of their T-shirts climbed out.

"Is there something I can help you with?" Cantwell asked.

"We're looking for Ms. Wind Storm."

"What for?"

One of the men flashed an ID. "Is she here?"

"I'd like to know what you want with her first."

The man looked behind Cantwell to Wind, who was leaning on the open door.

"Is there a problem?" Wind asked.

"The director of Homeland Security, Warrenside, would like to see you downtown."

"Am I being charged with something?"

"Under the Patriot Act all we need are suspicions, which we have. Homeland Security doesn't charge, we just question."

"Well, what's the question?"

He produced a photograph of Wind picketing the returning troops of the 501st with a placard that read 3,000,000 AFGHANI REFUGEES.

"Is that you, ma'am?" the officer asked Wind. She had been picketing with Jimmy Bird for so many years with no blowback, she didn't think there would ever be any. Of course, times were changing. Lately, she could feel the earth trying to shake her off.

"Will this take long?" Wind asked. "Because I have things to do."

"Well, of course, *everyone* has things to do," the agent said.

"I'm right behind you," Cantwell yelled as they shoved her in the back of their Hummer. He trotted down to his Jeep and jumped in.

Big Blue had said the best part of a relationship was the beginning, before you thought of reasons it wasn't going to work. Her relationship with Cantwell could work if she could find a path between being the keeper of the flame for her ancestors—being a professional Indian, as she saw it—and being a woman in love with a scion of her archenemies. As they drove her to town, she began to steel herself against the reality that when she got out of this she could no longer ignore the fact that being authentic didn't mean cooking a turkey the right way or preparing your fields in a time-honored way. Being authentic meant starting fresh and creating yourself. And that meant getting rid of everything.

Dr. Asad was aware that Houda hadn't come into their shared office at St. Maron's for several days, but he was too involved in his new writing project to protest or inquire, and he'd almost forgotten about her when she reappeared, her eyes black-and-blue, wearing bandages over her nose.

"Houda, what happened?" he asked.

"It's nothing to worry about." Houda flung her purse onto her desk. Since her arrest, she was no longer allowed to carry a handgun. Her purse didn't have the satisfying heft it used to have, so she picked it up and slammed it down again. She began to go through a stack of mail, ignoring her father's stare. "I had rhinoplasty," she said, not looking up.

Dr. Asad nodded before he comprehended. "You had nose surgery?"

"Yes, Papa. Warren Hospital is outside my permit zone. I had to get a permit from the court to change the GPS setting on my ankle monitor."

"I didn't know," he said.

"You know now." She ran her fingers over the bandages self-consciously and breathed noisily.

"You won't look like my Houda," he said.

"Your Houda no longer exists," she said. "I am not an Arab-American. I am just an American. This is not the old country, Papa. Americans don't have big hooked noses."

"Houda! You had a magnificent nose. It was fierce and beautiful."

"No," Houda said, "*I* am fierce and beautiful. No one could see me because of my nose. The bandages will come off in a week. Then you will see the real me."

She was wearing a houndstooth miniskirt with black stockings and stiletto heels, which made her ankle tracking device look like a style statement. Dr. Asad was unsure whether to admire his daughter's brazenness or to chide her for thumbing her nose at the old guard his natural reserve made him wary of.

She gathered up a file. Sheldon Simon, owner of the Oasis Corporation, was waiting for them downtown in her trailer office. "We have to go downtown. Let's go. We can walk."

"You can't walk like that." He was embarrassed by her nose bandages and ankle bracelet. "Your heels are too high."

"I'm fine."

The Oasis people seemed more impressed with Dr. Asad's use of Charon Corp than his casino plans, but in the end they came to a tentative agreement to have their attorneys draw up contracts and begin the licensing process for slots. Licensing live gaming would take longer. Warrenside's white old guard still controlled the county power structure and they would drag the process through a battery of objections, which the state would eventually override because of the tax revenues gambling would generate.

As they left the trailer, Sheldon put a hand on Dr. Asad's shoulder. "Did the Charon personnel give you any trouble?"

When Dr. Asad answered "None," Sheldon said he was thinking of using them to contract out the building for him. "That way we don't get into a tangle with the unions. Using unions, you can figure on tacking on another thirty percent to the costs. Pickets at the drop of a hat. We don't need that bad publicity."

Dr. Asad took a pad out of his jacket pocket. Houda assumed he was making notes for the contracts, but he was making a note for the new book he was writing. He felt as if he'd grown old in the last three months. Because, he thought, what is old age but the diminishment of hope? Without Max, he had no hope because there was no future for him. If only Max had married Nadira before he left for Afghanistan, he would have had a son waiting for him when he returned. Dr. Asad would have had a grandson. He recognized the insanity of creating a reality out of what might have been, but he could not stop himself from going there. He saw Anika's daughter Allie occasionally, but, while pretty, she gave him no pleasure. A girl, anyway. When the bandages came off Houda's face, he would no longer recognize her. She might marry someday, but it was increasingly unlikely—she was picky—and she wouldn't marry an Arab man. She was frightened, she told him once, of Arab men—even if they were Christian—going crazy in middle age and making their women put on the veil. It was true; he saw it himself, even in the Lebanese-American men in Warrenside. There was Stephan Atiyeh, for example, covering up his beautiful wife, Durrah, which pained Dr. Asad very much, as one of his private joys was gazing upon Durrah. But as a man he recognized the need to develop a system, a grid through which you passed all the facts of life and made sense of it, slotting your emotions and wayward feelings into boxes where they could do no harm. Sometimes, veiling your women was a way to mute their irresistible force and the random lust of the men they came in contact with, thereby simplifying your life. And theirs as well. Why could they not see the protection, only the oppression?

He saw himself dying alone in a foreign country, surrounded by a bizarre version of family: Allie, Anika, Bernice, Houda. All women. It confirmed his belief that there was no God, for what god would deprive a man of his son? What was the point of a man accumulating knowledge and wisdom and a worldly empire without a son to inherit it? He thought of the story of King Solomon, whom the Old Testament God had gifted with a magic carpet, sixty miles long and sixty miles wide, which transported the king and his men. One day Solomon was riding on it with his men, thinking with pride that he was greater than other men, wiser. For this arrogance, God made the wind blow with such fury that it shook the carpet and all forty thousand men were thrown off. Solomon reprimanded the wind for its mischief, for its impertinence, but the wind answered that Solomon would be more fortunate if he turned again to God and banished his pride.

But Dr. Asad could never turn to the God that Solomon worshiped, because what kind of god would punish you for possessing the hubris you needed to prevail and reward you for a humility that kept you small?

This was what he was making notes about while Houda and Sheldon talked about Charon Corp and the pluses and minuses of union labor.

"My daughter just did that," Sheldon said to Houda, gesturing to his own nose.

Houda smiled.

It was all to be in Dr. Asad's book, the final one he would write. He would give it to Anika to give her daughter, who would hopefully bear sons one day. There was nothing left for him but to live out his life on earth and hope that one day Allie's sons would be curious, open the book, and find out what Dr. Asad had done for Warrenside.

In the last chapter of *The House Is Built!* Malcolm Warren writes of his plan to move to Spain and restart his life—*their* life—as the Warrens of Catalonia. He knew there were only so many clicks of the wheel before he would be catapulted into the airless void of the obscurity that precedes death, and he intended to fight it the only way he knew how—by rolling his dice on a table whose surface wasn't grooved with his familiar moves.

Malcolm had fallen in love with Luis Buñuel's *Tristana*, which he and Marion had seen at the Cannes Film Festival in 1970, and, in the manner of everyone who falls in love, decided to move to Spain to be closer to the object of his love, in this case the aura—the possibilities—created by a convoluted love story, which he analyzed in *The House Is Built!* by saying that love stories reminded him of corporate politics, both in the seeming randomness of their beginnings and the viciousness of their endings. He also thought he could work with Franco, because in a dictatorship there are no committees or electorates to get in the way of progress, and what is a chairman of the board if not a dictator? Malcolm met Franco and wrote that they were *muy simpatico*. He and Marion were scouting locations for a villa from which to stage their new lives, in the mountains north of Barcelona, when they hit a patch of oil on a car track a thousand feet above the Mediterranean, leaving it to their orphaned daughter back in Warrenside to navigate the journey of the Warrens into the future.

Which Barbara was doing by dancing the *milonga porteña* every night in the tango halls of the Flores neighborhood of Buenos Aires. At first she went with Mike, who never got out on the dance floor, saying it "looked pretty faggy," before going out onto the street to have a cigarette, then wandering home to their four-bedroom luxury apartment in the Manzana de las Luces. After that she took Pablo, who was a wonderfully sensuous dancer, until she realized that *all* the Porteños were wonderfully sensuous dancers, and soon she was dancing all night, every night, and spending her days shopping in the Avenida Alvear boutiques for dresses in which to show off her own sensuous grace and beauty. The dance floor was her natural habitat. She moved as elegantly there as a seal moves elegantly in the water.

"You are like Isis, the mother of all goddesses," a Greek shipping magnate told her as he whipped her into a state of bliss on the dance floor. "I worship at your feet."

He told her this in Greek first, then in fractured English, and he followed up with dozens of roses because she told him the only thing she missed about Warrenside was her rose garden.

She found a dress designer, Juarez, who brought out bolt after bolt of satins and silks and draped them around her body, which was going through a realignment because of all the unaccustomed exercise but was still roundular and womanly and grander than those of all the fashionistas who stalked across the dance floor "like storks," as her latest admirer, a fifty-five-year-old Dutchman named Willem with a handlebar mustachio, told her. "All women should look like you! You are the prototype of classical femininity!" and their legs moved in tandem, the heat building between their contiguous hips and rising up to their flushed faces. "This is how Helen conquered Troy," Willem told her before dropping her at home in his Bentley. He buried his hands in her rich auburn hair. "You have the locks of a seductress," he said. "I am helpless in your presence. I surrender my will to conquer, but want only to be conquered."

Pablo left their ménage. He found a position teaching Spanish to foreigners, which Barbara said was probably more dignified than driving her and Mike around all day, seeing how he got to pick his own suit, one whose pants closed over his growing waist, but they remained friends and sometimes dance partners in the tango halls, which Barbara was frequenting less because of her new occupation as a muse for Juarez, who had begun to manufacture a line of lingerie—called Erato, his name for Barbara—for large-sized women.

Mike was smoking more. It seemed as if his profession was smoking and buying the English-language *Buenos Aires Herald*, looking for some hint that his plot to bring down Titan Insurance was activated by the FBI's opening his files. But there was nothing in the *Herald* about it. Either it wasn't big enough news or his worm had failed. He even e-mailed Kat about it from a cybercafé, and she answered that all she knew was that his basement office was still cordoned off. He became depressed because no one in Warrenside had witnessed his trick of extracting three million dollars from an outdated insurance company. He wanted someone to recognize his greatness. He wanted acknowledgment that he'd more than evened the score; that he'd bettered the boys on

Titan's top floor who thought he wasn't in their class. But no one would ever know about his hocus-pocus except Kat—and Barbara, of course, who was looking smashing, he had to admit. He'd forgotten how sexy she was, and soon he began accompanying her to the tango halls and lining up with her other admirers for a dance, and he was grateful for her hand on his as he forced the wheel to turn.

Jenna and I tried to stay in love, but once Kat was out of the picture we lost interest. Jenna was turned on by the idea of taking something that belonged to Kat. She talked endlessly about how she, Jenna, was sexier, smarter, *better* than Kat. That's what our relationship turned into, bitch sessions about Kat. And the sex simmered *way* down, which extinguished any feelings I had for her. I wanted to think that I was fucking irresistible, I guess; that Jenna had succumbed to our illicit attraction in spite of her religious beliefs and despite the fact that I was taken. But it was just jealousy fueling her passion. I wanted to show Kat that the other half of her equation, me, could ignite someone else. Well, Kat was doing all the igniting, directly or by proxy. Once she was out of the picture, I saw me and Jenna for what we'd always be: two losers who would never get that fillip you need to succeed in life, in the form of either an inheritance or a dollop of talent or brains.

We would be forever grousing about how the game was rigged. The only way to win was to change games.

So I gave Jenna twenty-five grand, half of what Asad gave me for my workshop downtown, figuring it was a clean slate between us, hoping she wouldn't see it like I was paying her for something. I just wanted to give her a fighting chance. She was friendless and broke and accepted it without a word.

I went to see Kat a week after she told me about her baby. She was all cozy in the living room. A great big fire in the fireplace. I never saw that before. It was a cool autumn day and it looked inviting.

"Hear from your dad?" I asked her.

"He can't believe he didn't bring down Titan," she said. She'd just gotten an e-mail asking if there was anything on TV yet about Titan's demise. "He's like stalking them on the Internet, trying to see what they're saying about him. It seems as if they're saying *nothing*. Poor Dad. I think he just wanted them to see him."

Back when we went hunting together, Mike had told me he knew they would fuck him in the end. But he wouldn't go down without bringing the whole place down. "We're just a couple of dumb Polacks," he used to tell me, "who don't have the sense to know their place." I pretended to agree, but I didn't believe it. I thought I was going to marry Kat and my place would be right up there with the Warrens. I don't know why it didn't occur to me that he must've felt that way once too.

Anyway, Kat and I really had nothing else to say. My being concerned about her was a habit. I would like to think that Kat was sad because we were over, but honestly I don't think that was even on her mind. I wondered if she ever loved me, but you can make yourself crazy thinking of lost opportunities and wasted emotions, and I'd already decided that I would have to make my own life without her and, more important, without the Warrenside that had raised me, because *that* Warrenside sure as hell was gone. Asad was going to build some kind of sports mall—there was going to be boxing, basketball, cineplexes, and so on—all topped by a giant slots casino, but I honestly didn't give a damn. Dr. Asad had blackballed everyone in the 501st, so I couldn't exactly see a world of possibilities opening up for me. A few of the guys had grown beards and dyed their hair and bought forged IDs at a thousand bucks a pop, but none of them made it through the grid Houda had set up with fingerprinting and lie detectors.

I was living in my cabin, doing a little hunting and trying to figure which direction I should aim my feet in, when the recruiter from Charon Corp, Jim Benson, found me. It seemed like an accident that I bumped into him in the woods, but he told me later he was hunting for me.

"Ruffed grouse!" Benson enthused as he appeared out of nowhere, near to where I was stalking a deer. "Pennsylvania is a great state, isn't it?"

Benson was bow-hunting like me. Most people think it's more authentic or something to hunt with a bow and arrow, like the animal has a fighting chance, but it's romantic bull to think that. A bow and arrow are just as deadly as a rifle and can do as much harm. If the hunter isn't any good, the wounded prey runs off into the woods to die slowly or else lives on with an infected wound. I've seen animals in the woods with bullets *and* broken arrows in them. My dad taught me to kill the walking wounded if I saw them, to put them out of their misery. After a while you get used to it—committing violence to end suffering—and stop thinking about the fucking philosophy behind it. Anyway, Benson was fitted out with brand-new Orvis gear, like he was a great white hunter, when he was just some city guy pretending to be regular.

"Yeah, there's a lot of game here." I was looking for a buck, even though I wasn't sure I would be around long enough to eat the whole thing if I bagged one. I could give it to Mom and Gus.

"You been doing this a long time?" Benson asked.

"Since I could walk, practically."

"You still interested in that Bineki girl?" he asked.

I was surprised that he knew anything about me and Kat. And I was doubly surprised at how protective I still felt about her. "It's over," I said.

"Good."

We walked through the woods to a spot where I had seen a young buck my last time out. I was hoping Benson would go away, when he said, "There's nothing here for you, Wolinsky."

I saw the buck then. He'd frozen, having heard us. I put my finger to my lips. But it was too late. Deer don't see as well in daylight as at night, and if you're perfectly still you can fool them, but Benson didn't know that and he crouched to get leverage to pull back his bowstring, and the buck saw us and leaped away in that graceful arc with his white tail flashing, which always makes me shake my head in admiration and wonder, Why in hell would I amputate such beauty from the world?

"Why didn't you shoot?" Benson asked. "That's the one you were looking for, isn't it?"

"It wasn't a clean shot. Only amateurs shoot at everything."

I was trying to chastise him, but he laughed. "You're right, Wolinsky. Look, let's get right to the point. I got a contract in my pocket and we can fill it out in your cabin and you can be on your way to training camp next week, or I can let you have it to mull over and wait for the perfect moment to sign it. Whatever works for you. There's noise that the 501st is being reactivated to go to Iraq, and if you join Charon they won't call you up. You can be doing the same thing you did in the army except you'll be paid ten times as much for your expertise. Plus a signing bonus. I need a communications guy and you're more than qualified. We value expertise, Wolinsky. We value your integrity, and we value your commitment."

It had been a long time since somebody valued anything about me, and I liked the way it felt: being seen for what I was. "My commitment?"

"What do you mean?" he asked.

"You said you value my commitment. What commitment?"

"Your commitment to whatever you decide to commit to. You know how rare that is?"

We went to my cabin and I filled out the paperwork. I would be doing communications and security work, probably in Iraq, perhaps Afghanistan. I had to pay for my training, which cost twenty thousand dollars—most of the assignments Charon landed was for stuff I'd never thought of—but it was more than offset by my signing bonus, which was thirty thousand dollars. I gave it to my mom, who joked that I should keep it as a dowry for when I get married, which will be a long time from now, if ever. If I could be so wrong about Kat and even Jenna, for Pete's sake, if I could be so wrong about my place in Warrenside, something big will have to happen before I can trust myself to try to imagine my place in the world again.

Reuber is coming with me. When his ex-wife, Linda Pasko, found out the kind of money he would be making as a mechanic in Charon Corp, she called off the sheriff and submitted paperwork to get more money for child support. Reuber is another guy who can't be trusted with his own life.

When I was in Kandahar, guys from Charon were training the Afghani police force and army and I used to wonder what kind of man would take a job that thrust him far from home, from "the world." What kind of man swears allegiance to the highest bidder? Now I know.

Benson and I agreed to wait until bear season was over to start my training. Bear hunting is back because the bear population has exploded in Pennsylvania to the point where they're becoming pests, so they're letting hunters thin them out a bit. Bear season in Pennsylvania is three days, right after Thanksgiving. Although Benson decided I was his new best bud and went hunting with me all the time, I shook him off for my bear hunt. It might be the last time I ever saw my dad's cabin, and I wanted to experience it alone—without Benson's constant yammering about what I could do on leave in Bangkok. Even if I make it home from whatever exotic locale I'll be working in, the way things are going, my home might be paved over for a shopping mall and everyone will be speaking a language I'm too old to learn.

Nothing is prettier than the Pennsylvania woods in late November. The air is clean. The water that finds its way through ancient grooves in the forest floor is cold and pure. Vegetation has died down, revealing the skeletons of trees and bushes, making it easier to see where animals have been. I'd seen tracks by a creek near that crazy Indian's house. The tracks were deep, so I knew the bear weighed at least three hundred pounds and had been there a lot. Bears return to the same place repeatedly. Like people, they prefer to walk on cleared trails. They only go into the brush to get berries or to sit in a pool of water on a hot day. He would be easy to track.

That morning there was a glaze of frost on the crunchy ground, making it easier for me to see and hear the bear, but making it easier for him to see and hear me. I was counting on him being groggy in anticipation of going into hibernation in one of the caves above the river, where the sow probably already was. I tied a bag of jelly doughnuts so it hung off a tree at a height I thought he could reach, then went into the bushes about fifty yards away and sat on my poncho. It was a clear morning and the rising sun made prisms out of the ice on the branches. In between the sparkling of the icicles and the glittering frost, a huge black bear moved down the path on all fours. I stood up and prepared my bow while the bear, who was easily three hundred and fifty pounds, reared up and swatted the bag of sweets. He was ravaging the bag with his needlelike claws when he became aware of me. I had pulled back the arrow in the string of my compound bow, already visualizing the arrow piercing the top of his shoulder. But the big guy turned and was looking at me. I had seen that look in animals I had harvested before and it never stopped me. At some level all creatures are aware of their place on the food chain. It's your turn to eat or it's your turn to be eaten. But I hesitated, thinking about the fucking philosophy of it all, as my dad would say, and in that moment's hesitation the bear lowered himself onto all fours and ran into the thick brush.

I was still holding the bowstring back, poised. It was as if my arm was frozen, and I was shaking and crying. I told myself it was a stupid reaction to having missed my chance. But it wasn't that. It was me. Kat had often dismissed me for being ordinary, and in that moment I knew what she meant, realized what an indictment *ordinary* was. Alone in the woods with an unspent arrow in my bow, and the biggest black bear I ever saw escaping when I had a clean shot at him, I saw myself for what I was, and I guess that moment is traumatic and the same for every ordinary guy. I saw I wasn't the kind of man who acted decisively and damned the consequences. I would never start a war and I would never end one. I saw I would never think great thoughts that would change the way we see the world. I would never do *anything* other than try to live my life causing as little collateral damage as possible and in a way so I could sleep at night. But that only meant I wasn't a big enough person to cause bigger damage, not that I was so great or wise or sensitive. I certainly couldn't stop the losses that seemed to be life itself. I was twenty-five years old, and I had already lost the great love of my life. I had lost my father and was losing my home. I was twenty-five and I was brimming with passion and intensity, and this may not seem original, but I knew those were not commodities to be squandered. It's in your youth that you find the passions that fuel the rest of your life, and I had a long road to travel. I wanted to live, not be one of those people who take an early hit and limp their way through life, licking their wounds. If the things I had loved were lost to me, so be it. I would find other things to be passionate about. I still had time.

I aimed my arrow at the sky, the rising sun almost blinding me; pulled back the bowstring even farther until my arm couldn't take the pain anymore; and opened my hand and released the arrow with all my passions and all my desires flying with it into the sky, farther and higher, until they pierced the sun itself. Then I left Warrenside to find my destiny.

FORTY **WIND**

The last time Wind saw Cantwell was Thanksgiving Day when they were firing up the bonfire they had laid the day Homeland Security picked her up. The wood had dried out, and the air was clear and blue. There had been no rain since the flood, and the leaves on the ground were crackling and sparking with electricity.

Cantwell had packed up all his things in preparation for leaving. He was going to Alaska to be a wilderness guide. Pennsylvania, he said, was getting too overdeveloped. Of course he meant Warrenside, where a cinder-block, aluminum-sided, flakeboard building boom was choking the downtown like a big-box convention and accreting around the edges of the Historic District he'd grown up in. There'd been a spate of backyard coyote sightings, with the resulting hysteria that they mauled children and ate pets. Deer were browsing on West End development lawns, and everyone with a gun—that is, everyone in Warrenside—was getting trigger-happy. There had been reports of wild packs of dogs by the river, probably dogs deserted in the flood. A black bear had been seen ravaging a Dumpster behind Dunkin' Donuts. As for Asad's casino emporium, every job was filled with Charon Corp personnel or experts from New York and London. A world-class operation required world-class skills, which, Asad claimed, couldn't be found locally. In the neighborhoods around the site of the future casino and out in the burbs, crime rose, and unemployed guys with blue lights on their vehicles and shotguns behind the seats patrolled the streets looking for varmints of either the four-legged or the two-legged variety.

"It's like the Wild West out there," Cantwell said. "Do you want to live in the Wild West?"

No, Wind did not want to live in the Wild West.

Cantwell cooked a turkey he had downed the previous day. "You want to throw it out," he asked, "or eat it?" And Wind had to admit that it was really a stupid gesture to throw away a cooked turkey, especially if no one knew about it. What kind of symbolism was that? She felt foolish about almost everything she'd once believed. But if her beliefs were jettisoned, she would be left with nothing. There's little comfort in knowing what you're not until you find out what you *are*.

"You could come with me for a while, till you figure out what you want to do," Cantwell said.

If she went with him, she would be Cantwell's woman and nothing else. Was that such a bad thing? Millions of women had lived their lives contentedly as someone's woman. Some women managed to have both their own identity and be totally with their man, but Wind felt her spirit was empty now and would attract things at random. She had to choose what she kept close.

She had been flabbergasted that the director of the newly opened branch of Homeland Security in Warrenside was Krista Heffelfinger. When Wind was brought in, Krista, who was clearly pregnant, came out of her office to greet her. "Omigod, thank you for coming!" She put her hands on her belly. "You were right! The bear in my dream? I found him and he gave me my baby!" Then Krista, who was adroit at pigeonholing her emotions, said, "We've got serious problems here, Wind. You can help us."

"Am I under arrest?" Wind asked.

"God, *no*! But I didn't think you would come voluntarily if we just asked you. Would you have? You're such a *wild thang*." She laughed as if they were intimates.

Wind felt like slapping her.

Krista wanted her to psychically spy on Edward Asad and his daughter. Every door, Krista said, was blocked. "We think they're funneling money to terrorist organizations," she said. "Laundering a portion of the gigantic monies that flow in through the Oasis organization and all the other corporations they work with, then sending it over there. We've been monitoring Asad's personal bank accounts. He wires fifty thousand dollars a month to a numbered account in Beirut. We just don't know what happens to it after that. What his intentions are."

"He probably has family there. Lots of immigrants send money back to wherever. Anyway, they're Christians, aren't they?"

"That's what they *say*," Krista said, "but they're Arabs. At the end of the day, you're loyal to your kind."

"So you don't really know anything for sure about the Asads. You don't know that they're doing anything wrong."

"Oh, they're doing *something* wrong, all right. Unfortunately we have to have a few more specifics to shut them down. That's why we need you. To look into their hearts, like you did mine.

See what they're thinking. We need some leads; then we can nail them. In times like these, you understand, it's a giant inconvenience to have to go through due process to prosecute someone. I don't know why people don't understand that we're just trying to protect them."

Wind had a sickening feeling of déjà vu: the powers-that-be taking what they want and demonizing those who owned it to justify their crime. The Heffelfingers were the biggest construction company in Warrenside, and you didn't have to go into a trance to figure out that Krista's father-in-law wanted to get something on Dr. Asad because he'd been blocked out of the shower of construction contracts by Charon Corp, with their no-bid policy. Charon Corp had their own boys.

From her few meetings with Edward Asad when he wanted to buy her property, Wind knew he wasn't a terrorist, so she agreed to work for Homeland Security because their witch-hunt infuriated her. She would become a fifth column, feeding them misleading information, which was all the information she could get, because Wind had lost her powers.

Wind gave Krista weekly reports, but they were confusing and garbled. "I don't understand all these weird animals in your reports," Krista said. "Can't you just separate them into good spirits and evil spirits and tell us what they mean?"

"I can't do that," Wind lied, "or I will lose my powers."

"But if I don't know if the animals are good or evil, the reports are worthless."

"I can't help that. All I can do is provide you with the spiritual data. It's for you to interpret."

Wind hoped they would stop asking her for reports, but it seemed like once you were in the clutches of Homeland Security, you couldn't be released. Her request for reports came weekly with her paycheck. Wind felt the net of worldly attachments closing in around her.

After they ate their Thanksgiving turkey, Cantwell dipped rags in gasoline and stuffed them under the bonfire. He struck a match and threw it into the woodpile, and within seconds the pile was blazing.

"Do you want me to wait?" Cantwell asked.

"Just go," Wind said. "Before I change my mind."

They had agreed that Cantwell would get settled in Alaska and then send for her, and she would join him when she was ready. And no, she said, she didn't know when that would be.

He intended to drive the four thousand miles to Juneau, camping in the Rockies, taking his time until he felt he'd shed his old skin. He picked up his duffel bag and walked down the road to where he'd parked his Jeep. He looked back over his shoulder. "Don't let that thing get out of control."

"Who do you think you're talking to?" Wind asked. "I'm an Indian."

They'd said goodbye the night before, so Cantwell put his Jeep in gear and let it roll down the trail, looking back at Wind in his rearview mirror. She watched him until he was out of sight, then walked back to the house thinking she was probably the biggest fool in the world for letting Cantwell go off by himself while she waited for some sign from her ancestors that it was okay to leave, that they could find their way home without her. Now that she no longer had visions, she doubted that she had *ever* had them. Even Big Blue, whose bony body she could still feel under her as they flew over the Catawissa, was probably just her way of keeping her father alive, of talking to him when she was lonely. She had put on her ceremonial buckskin shirt and pants and moccasins that morning. Ceremonial fires were solemn, and she wanted to honor the occasion. Her little drum was tied around her waist, and she beat it now and then with her thumbs, hoping to be transported into a dream world.

The fire burned for the whole afternoon and into the evening, Wind throwing planks into it from Jimmy's outhouses, his shutters, his barn siding. Slash and burn, she thought. When it got dark, Wind went into the house to make coffee, and when she was done she soaked the pink bathroom towels with gasoline from a five-gallon galvanized can and stuffed them under the shag carpet in her father's bedroom. She spent an hour improvising wicks out of towels, clothing, carpet runners, and rags on both floors and under the wooden back porch of the two-story house. She took out a box of blue-tips, thinking a proper Indian would start a fire using the two-stick method, brushed a match against the sandpaper on the box, and threw it onto the towels. She went from room to room upstairs and down, tossing match after match onto the gas-soaked wicks.

She paused in the living room near the front door. Thick smoke curled off a curtain behind the sofa and danced across the ceiling, igniting the other curtains, which dropped onto the round coffee table Jimmy had built out of an old machine pattern. A bead of fire sped toward her across the geometrically patterned carpet Jimmy had bought at auction because the auctioneer swore Navajos made it.

Wind ran out of the house, tripping on the porch, sweating and out of breath, the light of the fire already showing through the windows on both floors as if there were a celebration going on inside. It crackled and hissed, sounding as if people and animals were inside, laughing, and Wind laughed too. Suddenly, the house convulsed and emitted a giant belch; then the upstairs windows exploded out.

The flames reached higher and higher into the sky. An acrid

smell filled the air as ceiling tiles, fiberglass insulation, asbestos shingles, electric wiring, twenty years of bank receipts, forty years of tax returns, bounced checks, plastic computer parts for a computer that never got assembled, a black-and-white television that received only the local Philly channels, the polyurethaned dining room set, the overstuffed sofa in the family room with forgotten photos under its cushions, Jimmy's army uniforms, her mother's wedding dress, Wind's Girl Scout uniform, CD cases, DVDs, vinyl records, comic books, ceremonial headdresses from powwows, oatmeal boxes, Cheerios and Hamburger Helper boxes, coupons for McDonald's, video games, winter coats, Tupperware, John Deere baseball hats, sweatshirts, checkered underwear, toothpaste, deodorant, Pepto-Bismol, Alka-Seltzer, dental floss, hemorrhoid ointment, Band-Aids, knee supports, electric fans, letters from dead relatives, birthday cards to and from Wind, souvenirs of mostly unhappy vacations, Wind's high school diploma, her mother's tortoiseshell wedding present from Jimmy—all of it crackled in the holocaust, begging her to notice.

"You are not me," she said.

As Wind staggered backward, driven by the intensity of the heat, Big Blue landed on the one remaining pile of wood. She smiled up at the heron as she struck a match. The heron dropped gracefully to the ground, so close to her that its wings brushed her face.

"All done, then?" it asked.

Wind smiled, happy with the blaze. She could feel her spirit soar as all the things that weighed her down rose up in flames into the sky. She was free. Then suddenly the wind shifted and a pinwheel of cinders ignited a pile of dry leaves and a path of flames sped through the tree line toward the golf course.

"No!" Wind shouted. She grabbed a shovel that Cantwell had decided against packing and beat at the flames, but, like beads of oil, they wouldn't be captured and divided into new paths as she struck at them. She ran ahead and dug a trench in their path and shoveled dirt on them, but the fire was like a dragon, spewing sparks and traveling faster than she could dig. It was going right into the golf course, which was curious, because there were no leaves there. She pulled out the cell phone Cantwell gave her as a present and was explaining to the dispatcher at the fire department how to get to her property when she saw a mushroom cloud of smoke and ash and flames rise up over the fourteenth hole, which was closest to her property, and then explode, pieces of debris rocketing into the air like fireworks. She dropped the phone and ran to the golf course. A giant crater was where the green had been, and black sludge was gurgling up, feeding a single, weirdly colored plume: purple and green and a hellish pink. It was a chemical fire. She couldn't breathe; the fumes were suffocating and metallic. She could hear the fire trucks in the distance, then closer; then they were driving across the golf course, red lights flashing. She ran toward the river, which looked like it was glowing; its surface was covered in an oily burning skin. The Catawissa was on fire.

Wind watched the conflagration helplessly. The line of pines along the riverbank was scorched naked, the needles afire and writhing in the oily water. A large fallen log was causing debris to back up behind it. Wind grabbed onto a charred branch and swung out to free the log, but the branch snapped and she fell into the water. She clung to the log; then, with a mighty heave, swung herself up on it and sat down on it like a jockey. The log tried to spin in the current and it took all her strength to keep it righted. Her buckskins were waterlogged and weighed her down, so she stripped off first her ceremonial vest, then her pants, and finally her moccasins and stood up, naked, running on the log like a lumberjack to keep from falling in. Big Blue appeared above her.

"Help me!" Wind yelled.

"You don't need me," Big Blue said.

The spinning log rolled into sight of Warrenside. The wind was blowing orange cinders toward the few buildings along the river's bank. An old wooden grain mill caught fire and reached a flash point in minutes. Mesmerized by the sight of the burning river, Wind lost her footing and slipped off the log. As she went under, her drum eased up her waist, off her neck, floated for seconds by her head, and then sank out of sight, looking for a place in the silt where it wouldn't be discovered for millennia. Finding a glacial boulder on the river bottom, it burrowed under.

Wind pulled herself back up on the log, gasping for air, holding on to the nub of a broken branch like a pommel. Getting her bearings, she stood up again. Big Blue buzzed her, his wings brushing her forehead.

"Help me! I can't hold on much longer!" Wind yelled to him.

"You can fly! Can't you feel it?"

"No."

"If you say you can, then you *can*, damn it! Fly!"

Wind began running on the spinning log again, faster and faster, until finally she felt air beneath her feet. She rode the warm draft higher and higher into the sky, her feet still moving like she was pedaling a bicycle, and she saw what the First People must have seen: the universe, wide and grand with stars and suns, and plenty of room for her to create her own story. The burning river illuminated her path.

She began to chant, her arms keeping a beat against her thighs, moving to an ancient rhythm, then faster. A fire engine siren wailed somewhere far below her, then another. Their wailing mixed with her chant until she couldn't tell anymore which was which, and she chanted louder and louder, and she followed the flames reaching into the sky until the entire night was ablaze and she could see everything, because suddenly everything shone with the ancient light of her ancestors and she was sailing through the cold night air and dancing with the stars.

Considering the way life turns out *completely* the opposite of the way you hope it will, and random events you do not initiate intrude all the time—considering all *that*, I guess I shouldn't have been surprised when Jenna Magee showed up at my house. And I guess I shouldn't have been surprised that I let her in, because having only *The House Is Built!* for company, I was lonely.

"Nice place," Jenna said, with her usual aggrieved air, marching from room to room. "I figured it would be nice." She arrived on a windy October evening. No one except delivery people ever came to the house, and at first I didn't recognize her in civilian clothes: tight jeans, a Christian rock group T-shirt, and flip-flops. She tossed her duffel bag on the sofa, as if she intended to stay for a while. Her mother had moved in with her boyfriend in Whitehall when her house was razed, but Jenna wouldn't leave Warrenside, because she was convinced her three-year-old daughter was still somewhere within the city limits and she wanted me to help find her.

"I know she's still here. I can feel her," she said. "You have connections and I don't. I'm sure you know someone who can help me."

She was hostile to me, as if I'd *personally* made her give up her kid for adoption. She'd been one of the instigators in the fight that killed the love of my life, the father of my child, and I should have thrown her out on her ass. But her appeal to my ego swayed me, and I did try to help her, and for a while we settled into a weirdly familiar living arrangement. She harangued me with Scripture every evening, and the noise of that, oddly enough, took my mind off Max and made me long for the release of sleep.

During the afternoons, I would drive downtown and walk around, watching the demolition of the old wooden and brick structures, hoping to bump into Dr. Asad. I wanted to talk about Max, like any lover wants to talk about her beloved, and Max had told me that his father was the only person who really knew him. The conversation I would have with him changed each time I imagined it. I was brimming with tortured emotions, and thankfully I never saw Dr. Asad, because he would have thought I was *insane*.

But I did see Houda. She was everywhere in town, wearing a hard hat, clipboard in one hand, BlackBerry in the other, ankle tracker blinking red when she was on the outer reaches of her allowed territory. I felt invisible, like a cat sneaking around the ruins of a war zone, so I was surprised to receive an e-mail invitation to Houda's office, sent from her BlackBerry, of course. I called her assistant to accept and suddenly I was downtown, stepping in tracks in the dirt left by giant earthmoving vehicles and giving my driver's license to a security guard from Charon Corp. He ran it through a quick check apparatus and asked me to put my index finger into a slot in the same machine, which produced a pass I was not to lose; then he motioned to a trailer. I knocked and a good-looking guy in a rumpled suit let me in.

"Jonah," he said.

"I'm—"

"Marketing," he said. "And a little PR. Whatever they need."

"Great," I said.

The inside was fitted out with stainless steel and black. Houda was sitting behind a polished stainless slab mounted on sawhorses. Everything about her looked pointy. Her *absolutely* straight black hair cut at a beveled angle, thick eyeliner applied as precisely as Cleopatra's. Her legs were crossed and I could see her ankle tracker beneath her black trousers.

She stood up right away when I came in, moving from behind the desk and making me sit down in a visitor's chair after pumping my hand. I remembered she'd killed Camacho with that hand, and I pulled back.

"I haven't seen you since . . . that day," she said. There isn't a socially accepted vocabulary for referring to the day you murdered someone.

"I've been busy."

"We all have." She looked really happy, and I saw Max had been all wrong about his sister. She wasn't a passive Eastern woman at *all*. She was in charge of everything and seemed pleased about it.

"How are things going?" I asked.

"Tre*men*dously!" She put a hand on my arm, and then she really looked at me and her gaze settled on my baby bump. "How far are you?"

"Four months."

She nodded her head, her eyes unfocused as if she were calculating. "It doesn't matter."

I put my hand protectively over my baby. "It doesn't matter for what?"

"You must be wondering why I wanted to meet you and asked you to come down through all this awful dirt and noisy construction."

"I like it, actually," I said. "The activity."

"Me too," she said excitedly. "Well, I'll get right to the point. We're doing an ad campaign for the complex, and *naturally* it's near the site of the old Warren Steel mill and everyone associates Warrenside with the Warrens, naturally, and our ad exec"—she pointed to Jonah—"he said we needed something, an icon, to give the complex a connection with the old. At first he said, like Indians or whatever aboriginal people were here, but the Warrens sort of co-opted that image with the Lenape thing they had going. The country club. The restaurant on the other side of town." She was referring to the Lenape Luncheonette, which had served breakfast all day to steelworkers when they got off work from second and third shifts. It hadn't been in business for years, since the steel mill closed. "We want a *complete* break with the past—physically, that is. Spiritually, however, we know in this day and age the only thing that distinguishes one place from another is its history. So we're trying to give the project some *romance*, and you get that with history. Having said that, everything in this complex will be amazingly and stunningly new."

"They tore that down," I said.

"They tore what down?"

"The Lenape Luncheonette."

"Oh, did they? I didn't know. I just knew it existed. Well, anyway, it seems pointless to go back that far, because I don't even think there is one Indian *left* in the whole of Warrenside, is there? Anyway, are Indians romantic? I don't think so. Maybe once they were."

Everybody had heard about the Love Guru's—as the cable station called her—arson and her nude ride down the Catawissa on a log. There were rumors that she had been working for Homeland Security, which I found laughable. But she disappeared after that, and who knows anything about the human heart after all? "And so?"

"So!" Houda smiled and gestured toward Jonah and said, "Tell her!"

"Well," Jonah said, sitting up and looking like he was shaking himself awake. "We want you, the *last* of the Warrens, to be the face of the complex: Warren Fields."

I'd read the previous week in *The House Is Built!* that several generations of Cantwells had been intimate with the Lenape chiefs. They'd assembled an extraordinary collection of Algonquin, Iroquois, and Delaware artifacts—all lost now, probably sold to pay debts—and had built the Eastern Indian Museum on the site of the first Joseph Cantwell's summer hunting cabin. Their philanthropic motives didn't help the Lenape, the last of whom had left the Catawissa Valley by 1920, and the museum had closed for lack of local interest in 1958 and was remade into the clubhouse for the Lenape Country Club. I knew enough about the Lenape to know that the logo the country club fobbed off as authentic wasn't actually Lenape: it was Sioux. Just like the new face—me— of this latest venture wouldn't be a Warren but a Bineki carrying an Asad. How do things get so convoluted and symbols imbued with such cockeyed meanings?

"You want me to be your *spokesperson*?"

Houda nodded enthusiastically, then laughed. "Isn't it great!" She kept staring at my baby bump.

Having a job would be better than sitting around reading in the family manse, waiting for my passenger to disembark. That's what I felt like, being pregnant: I was an ocean liner carrying a passenger across the sea until he found the land that was his. All that was important was that I reach my destination with the passenger intact so he could go ashore and start walking toward where he was meant to be.

"That's all for now, Jonah," Houda said. She waited while he slowly picked up his hard hat and left the trailer before turning to me. "It's Max's, isn't it?" she asked.

Here's the deal: I was carrying a boy, and I knew how much joy that fact would bring to Dr. Asad. But I wanted to deny him that joy, to punish him for denying my right to be with Max. He would never know about him. "It's his son," I said.

She looked like I'd stabbed her. "Bastards—excuse me, but that's what your baby is in our culture—are not accepted. There is no reason to tell my father. Don't upset him with this."

I knew Dr. Asad would give anything to know Max had a son.

"We can give you something—money, of course—if you need it."

But, of course, I didn't need anything.

Jonah told me it wasn't his idea *at all* to use me, it was Houda's. "I thought you might be a little too pregnant," he said. "No offense. I'm totally sold now." Houda had seen me skulking around the demolition site and asked him if he thought I looked pregnant. When he said yes, she cooked up the idea of using me for their icon. Clearly, she didn't want me out of her sight.

Since I *was* pregnant, I was a little insecure about my looks, but Jonah assured me that I was *quite distinctive*, and here's the thing about men who find you pretty or sexy or distinctive—you start to think *they're* kind of sexy and distinctive. Jonah was always in the room, directing the photographer and making astute observations about my best angles et cetera, and being the center of that kind of attention is a sexy thing, and soon I saw the glimmer of a *possibility* that one day I would get over Max. Not for a long time, but someday.

The thing I was concentrating on then was my passenger. The toughest thing was to try to think what I was going to tell him about his father, because in some ways I knew nothing about Max at all. I mean, you don't need details to know you love someone. I knew his favorite poets and his favorite fables. If someone asked me to describe him, that's what I'd think of. He read me a poem from Rumi on our second night together, and this line stopped me: "The minute I heard my first love story, I went looking for you." It seemed to confirm what I felt from the moment I saw him, that Max and I were destined to find each other and become lovers.

But other poets say that love is over as soon as it begins, and I cried that night because I saw the ending had been written into our story. *"Habibi,"* Max had said that night, consoling me, "it's true for all love. It's over as soon as it starts. That doesn't mean we shouldn't enjoy what comes in between."

Jenna got two letters from Duck in the month she stayed with me. It shocked me, because I didn't know they were good friends. I didn't even know where he was. He was supposed to have been my best friend, but after he left Warrenside I hadn't heard from him once. The first letter came about two weeks after she arrived at my house, and she squirreled it away immediately, before I had a chance to ask her about him. The second letter she picked up from the table in the foyer with a great deal of fanfare. She looked at me slyly, then opened and read it in front of me.

"What's he say?" I asked, picking up supermarket circulars as if I was mightily interested in the price of canned soup. "That's from Duck, right?"

"He's coming home in April. He'll be done with his training and is coming home to see his mama and some *friends* before going to his station."

I missed Duck. He was the only real friend I ever had. So who wouldn't miss that? "Are you going to see him?" I asked.

"If I'm here. He told me I should ask for your help. He said you were a good person, despite my personal opinion."

It turns out one of my family's lawyers, Jumbo Knight, knew someone who knew someone in the county courthouse, and the sealed adoption papers for Jenna's baby mysteriously peeled open for a quick peek before they shut again. Money that I slipped Jumbo was the solvent for that glue. Afterward, I was kind of sorry I did, because Jenna started getting paranoid, speculating on what kind of a palatial home these people provided for her kid and how she would always be the loser biological parent, and I was scared she was going to stalk her kid's adoptive parents in Akron, Ohio. From Warrenside to Akron. Her kid was clearly destined to travel roads with no outlets. It made me think of Camacho.

"What makes you think they're going to let you see her?" I asked.

"It was a Christian adoption agency. These people are good Christians. They'll let me see Sarah."

"Her name is Matilda. It said so on the papers."

"I always called her Sarah."

"You're going to need some money." I was prepared to give her a stash to start her life over in Akron, but she surprised me by saying she had some.

"Duck," she said.

I guess it was the first time I really saw her.

She got a bus ticket to Pittsburgh, a transfer from there to Akron. Before she left, she had me down on my knees again, although this time she wasn't trying to save my soul. She held my hand, crying and begging my forgiveness. The thought of seeing her baby released a delayed flood of maternal hormones in her, I think. She'd been loopy since we found the kid's coordinates. So she was crying and asking me to forgive her and I kept interrupting her: "There's nothing to forgive. It's all over. In the past."

"You *have* to forgive me," she said, "or I can't do this thing. I want to start over again and I *can't* if I have this stuff hanging over me. Say you forgive me, *dammit!* Just say it."

I had the feeling it wasn't me she was asking; she needed to hear a human voice say the magic words to spring open the bars of her guilt. God knows, I thought she had quite a bit to be guilty about, starting with Barzai Marwat. But it's a funny thing about forgiveness: as soon as I said the words, *I* felt tremendously relieved, as if I had been incarcerated with her. And when I said the words I thought of my mother, too, with the first kind thoughts I remember having of her in a long, long time. I will never know what demons drove my mother any more than I know what demons drove Jenna—or even Camacho or Dr. Asad, for that matter—and it wasn't maliciousness on their parts if they hurt me—or me them—it was just random circumstance that put us on colliding courses, so when I said the words—"It's okay, Jenna, I forgive you, I forgive you, I forgive you, I *forgive* you, I forgive you"—it was like shouting a magical chant into the heavens, and the light shone on the path out of the prison I hadn't even known I was in until that very moment, and I was able to walk through the door and finally, finally, *finally* move on.

I had my baby in March, and I named him Max Timothy Asad Warren-Bineki. The Timothy is after an uncle I didn't know I had until I finished reading *The House Is Built!* Timothy was my mother's older brother, who was killed when he was two years old when a mountain lion escaped from our family's private zoo—which I also didn't know we had—and mauled him. Some working-class boys were spying on the Warrens for sport and opened the gate to its cage. His mention in the book is the first I had heard of this dead baby, Uncle Timothy. It's also the first I heard that women in my family don't inherit as much as sons do. That's why my mom isn't as rich as her male cousins. I thought she was cut off because she married my dad, but it was because she was a woman. Is that antediluvian or what? Anyway, after I read about Uncle Timothy, I said his name aloud so often, trying to conjure up the spoiled little prince with his zoo, that when my baby pulled into port, the name was there to meet him. So Max Timothy Asad Warren-Bineki he is.

The groundbreaking ceremony for the casino at Warren Fields was the following month and I was a VIP guest, *naturally*, considering that I am its face. It had taken them months longer than normal to get permits et cetera, mostly because what was left of the old guard in Warrenside put up every obstacle possible to keep Warren Fields from happening, and they used Asad's aspirations as leverage to get him to set up an irrevocable trust to clean up the Catawissa, which will be dead for the next fifty years at least, thanks to the sludge seeping from the landfill under the country club.

It was a clear April day and about eight hundred people lined up in the dirt where the casino was to be built, next to a huge white heated tent where the reception would be held afterward.

I brought little Max in a baby carriage. About thirty Charon Corp security guards lined the perimeter in the special uniform that Houda designed for them on this project: olive-green berets, bloused khaki slacks over brown jump boots, and long-sleeved khaki shirts with the Cedar of Lebanon embroidered on the right chest pocket. Charon Corp is the perfect chameleon. Houda introduced the mayor of Warrenside and county officials to the crowd as if they were her old friends instead of people who had spent the last few months strewing sticky red tape in her path, and they spent their time at the dais bragging about their enormous helpfulness in getting this project—which would generate millions of tax dollars—off the ground.

I saw Duck then. He was in the crowd, dressed in a Charon Corp uniform with a lightning bolt embroidered on his pocket and a navy-blue tam. The beautiful Eurasian woman by his side was dressed identically. Duck's mother was on the other side of the woman, chatting with her as if they were intimates. Laughing. Jenna had written to me that Duck was being assigned to a project in Nigeria and was in Warrenside to see his mother before he left. He waved to me and pointed to his woman, like he wanted to introduce me, and I knew then that the Duck I knew no longer existed.

Dr. Asad was in the crowd, speaking to someone, and he turned around and caught my eye—probably because he felt my stare boring into his neck—and he looked as if he were trying to remember where he knew me from, and then suddenly his eyes widened in recognition and he was at my side.

"I haven't met you yet."

I put out my hand and said, "I'm—"

"You're Ms. Warren, the face of Warren Fields. Accept my apologies. I look at your picture every day, on proofs for magazine ads and billboards, on videos for television promos." He shook my hand and I couldn't believe he didn't know who I was. "Excuse me for not making a point of meeting you sooner, but I've been extremely busy on a personal project. I'm an academic by training, and we academics can get lost forever in our books."

I saw a flash of Max in Dr. Asad's face—that same amused expression Max got when he searched for the words of great men, looking for a reference to describe what he was feeling. Max told me it was important to learn the stories of other cultures because nothing ever changes, just the names. Random good luck—the missing ingredient in most people's endeavors—is perceived as a favor from the gods, but stories from every people on earth prove the opposite. Just because history is written by the winners doesn't mean that the names of the winners stay the same. A strong wind will always blow dust over both victory and defeat.

"This is a great thing you've done here," I said. "Reinventing Warrenside. I never thought it would happen."

"It was a distraction from many personal sorrows. I wonder sometimes how much achievement in life is just that. Is this your child?" he asked politely.

"He's one month old."

"Your family must be very happy. What's this?" he asked, touching the lapis lazuli that I'd tied to the handle of Max's carriage. My mom had sent it to me when she found out I was pregnant and told me to give it to Max when he was older.

"It's from Afghanistan."

"Ah. For good luck, then. What's his name?"

I felt a gentle breeze on my neck and turned to see who was there. Little Max had started to fuss; he felt it too. "His name is . . . Timothy," I said.

Houda frantically motioned to her father, who bowed politely and said, "It is time for my part in all this. Excuse me."

Max had told me lots of stories during our short time together, and I'm trying to remember them to tell little Max. My favorite was a Sufi tale that tells of forty birds—all different kinds—who long to know their god, Simorgh, a beautiful ancient bird who lives in a land also called Simorgh, situated on a beautiful lake. The journey is arduous: the birds must travel over seven valleys in which they encounter physical dangers and spiritual challenges requiring knowledge of self, an experience of love, and a spirit of detachment and selflessness. Some of the birds cannot meet the test—only thirty birds reach Simorgh—but when they arrive, the birds see only the reflection of themselves in the lake and a flash of breathtaking colors and fiery light. Together they *are* Simorgh.

It's the first story I'll tell little Max when he's older, and together we will try to untangle his knotty roots and see what they mean.

Dr. Asad bowed to the crowd and accepted their applause. Houda handed her father a beribboned silver-plated shovel with a cedar tree embossed on it. He took the first ceremonial scoop of earth out of the ground and turned it over.

ACKNOWLEDGMENTS

A couple of years ago I got an e-mail from Morton Miller, who claimed to be the basis for a character in my first book. After a quick consult with my lawyer, I admitted it was possible, and he and his wife, Judith Farmer Miller, became my great friends, as well as a constant reminder to better cover my tracks. I thank them for that.

I would like to thank Martin Kohn, who insisted that my writing needed more jokes and sent me as many as he could—none of which made the cut, but they kept me in excellent humor.

I would also like to thank my friends, who politely refrained from asking the obvious question, which is: What's taking you so long? For their tact, thanks and love to Carol Ellis, Jimmy Ellis, David Schwartz, Karle Maurer, Fanny Barry, Pam Boyer, and fashion-and-style writer G. Bruce Boyer, who won bonus points for telling me, "I read fiction to learn how to live my life."

I am thrilled for the opportunity to thank my agent, David Kuhn, for his savvy, patience, and tireless work on my behalf.

And thanks to the brilliant Billy Kingsland of Kuhn Projects, who is the keenest reader and parser of fiction in the world; and to Jessi Cimafonte, for keeping it all together.

Many thanks to Liz Beirise at Art Services International for obtaining Fernando Botero's permission to use his painting *The Bath* as an image on the cover of *Nude Walker*.

Special thanks to *Baba* Mike Hoffman, Pamela Varkony, and Houda Atiyeh.

Namaste to Jeff Pezzella, my marketing guru. If you're reading this, he did something right.

I would like to express my gratitude to the folks at Sarah Crichton Books / Farrar, Straus and Giroux for publishing *Nude Walker* in such a grand style: Susan Mitchell for the extraordinary cover; Abby Kagan for the book design; Maureen Bishop in the art department; Janet Baker, copy editor; Susan Goldfarb, production editor; Debra Helfand, managing editor; Erin Pursell, who should get a promotion; Jeff Seroy for his marketing expertise and enthusiasm for this project; Sarita Varma, publicist extraordinaire; Daniel Piepenbring for saving me from humiliation at the hands of freshmen college students; and, of course, my editor and publisher, the incomparable Sarah Crichton.

Behind every writer there is a thankless nag who pushes them out of bed at five in the morning, and that job belongs to Einstein, my cat, and his assistant, coincidentally my husband, Paul Fuhrman, who compensates for the rude awakening by brewing me a splendid cup of coffee and switching on the sun.

BATHSHEBA MONK is the author of *Now You See It . . . Stories from Cokesville, PA*. She lives in Pennsylvania, where she is writing her next novel and developing a musical. She writes radio essays and interviews other artists on National Public Radio's Lehigh Valley affiliate, WDIY. Visit her online at www.bathshebamonk.com.